BLEEDING HART

ALSO BY CONOR METZ

The Edgewood Nightmare
The Thing in the Lake
Castillo Cove

BLEEDING HART

CONOR METZ

Shining
Fright
Books

Published by Shining Fright Books, Bellevue, WA

First Edition: July 2024

Library of Congress Control Number: 2024903238

ISBN 979-8-9895822-2-8 (hardcover)
ISBN 979-8-9895822-0-4 (paperback)
ISBN 979-8-9895822-1-1 (ebook)

For Wyatt

WAITING FOR A GIRL LIKE YOU

1

Fans of comic books, movies, and television had all gathered outside the convention center that Saturday morning, eagerly awaiting the time the doors would finally open. As they inched closer and closer to that moment, anticipation had built to a breaking point. Like the timer on a bomb reaching zero, it was ready to blow. With only a few minutes before the crowd was unleashed inside, Chris worried what might happen to the clumsier fans. If any were to trip and fall, they could easily become squashed grapes under the mob swarming the show floor. But at San Diego Comic-Con, nobody cared when it meant the difference between experiencing their favorite event—or missing out entirely.

For Chris Hart, it was his third time at Comic-Con in three years and he was starting to feel like a seasoned pro. Yet with all this experience, he still felt foolish rushing to get inside when the doors opened. However, this year there was a method to his madness. And that madness was completely centered around the film adaptation of the popular comic book *Black Berenice*.

While never as popular as most of the superheroes from the Big Two, *Black Berenice* had its share of fans. The comic book was consistently written and drawn by the same team over its two decades of existence and the quality had only improved with time. Which probably explained why it was the most beloved comic series in Chris' collection. So, when a big-budget movie was announced, he was beyond excited. Then rising star Marie LeBeau was cast as the titular character and he found himself on the verge of nerd ecstasy.

Ever since she exploded on the scene five years ago, the French-Canadian actress Marie LeBeau seemed an unstoppable force in Hollywood. Every film she touched proved dynamite at the box office and *Black Berenice* was her most ambitious project to date. It was also Marie's first producing credit alongside the one and only Milton Humphreys. Which wasn't entirely surprising considering Milton had given the actress her first big break. That role had even earned her an Oscar nomination. Marie had none of those lofty aspirations with Berenice, but the character was one she professed to have admired and was honored to have the chance to bring to the big screen.

The film was due out in theaters in less than two weeks, but as the studio wanted to build excitement and word of mouth, supposedly there would be an advance screening in San Diego that evening. Things were kicking off with a signing in the morning, then a panel in Hall H, and hopefully soon details would be revealed where and when the screening was happening.

Unfortunately for Chris, as was common with Comic-Con, fans had to choose their battles wisely. It was unlikely that anyone would be able to visit Hall H, get an autograph, and get into that screening. There were lines to consider, distance, time, and other events that might get in the way. As much as Chris wanted to attend that panel taking place after the signing, he knew that if anyone wanted to see something in Hall H, they either had to get lucky, or get in right away. He'd played that game the previous year and missed pretty much everything else the con had to offer because he didn't want to forgo the panels. This year, he would only seek out what he could on the show floor or attend the smaller and more accessible panels about the comic industry. If he was lucky, maybe he'd get to see the movie early, but he certainly wasn't going to pass up the chance to meet the one and only Marie LeBeau. His friends, however, didn't share this sentiment and chose to head to Hall H. So this time, Chris would be flying solo.

As Chris stepped out onto the show floor, he watched the swarm of fans spread out like locusts. He had thankfully already gotten the information on where the signing was being held and speed-walked toward the booth. Navigating the crowd could be tricky, as it moved like a river. The one time you could be sure there wouldn't be any need to travel upstream was in the morning, since everyone was more or less fanning out from the open doors. Chris found his mark thanks to the massive *Black Berenice* banner hoisted up above the booth. There was also a poster positioned next to the signing table, announcing the time the stars of the film would be there. Chris would have loved to be waiting there first in line, but he ended up much further back than he preferred. Still, he seemed close enough to make it in time for some autographs, and maybe even a picture with Marie.

Of course, getting a place in line was only half the battle.

Nobody arranged for signings the second the con opened. It would be another hour before the stars were slated to appear. And while waiting in line with a friend was no big deal, your bladder could make or break success when alone. Chris was smart, though, and had avoided any liquids that morning. He'd need them outside later—the sweltering San Diego heat would make sure of that—but at least the con was air-conditioned. And so, Chris did what any solo flyer did while waiting in line.

He got comfortable.

Pulling out his Nintendo 3DS, Chris picked up where he left off in *Dragon Quest VIII*, his all-time favorite of the series. Aside from his love of comics and movies, Chris was an avid gamer, and especially loved exploring the world of retro video games. For him, it wasn't just a nostalgia trip—he genuinely loved finding the diamonds in the rough, the things he'd missed along the way by being too focused on the popular titles. But today, he was only interested in satisfying his appetite for comfortable nostalgia.

As Chris grinded away on the terrible beasties of *Dragon Quest*, he would compulsively check the time almost every five minutes, until a light shined on the small stage at the booth and a man in a *Black Berenice* T-shirt appeared to announce the cast. Others had crowded around the stage just to get a close look at some of their favorite actors, but of course the media was closest. After the actors posed for a quick photo op, they all took their seats at the table, ready to sign whatever the fans wanted them to.

Other than Marie, Chris was familiar with the rest of the cast to varying degrees. Former teen heartthrob Philip Dalton had taken the role of Berenice's partner and eventual lover, Merus. Meanwhile, the villainous Arastis was being played by screen legend Martin Conroy. Chris had been a fan of his for years, dating back to his time on the ever-popular series of spy films that followed the character of Harry Fairfield. As he'd gotten older, Martin started taking on villain roles more frequently. It seemed he'd grown tired of always playing the hero and appeared to love chewing the scenery much more as a well-written antagonist. Finally, there was the ill-fated young sidekick Fenrir, played by relative unknown Kirk Lamont.

The line seemed to barely move as Chris pocketed his 3DS and tried to remain patient. He planned to have his copy of *Black Berenice #1* signed by the cast. He'd already gotten the writer and artist of the comic to sign it the previous year. Naturally, there were also large stacks of posters for the film that the cast could sign, but Chris didn't really want to drag one around all day—he'd made that mistake his first year at Comic-Con and ended up with a damaged poster. At least his issue of *Black Berenice* was reinforced in his backpack.

Soon the line shrank before him and he was ushered up to the table where a limited number of fans were permitted to approach the cast for autographs and pictures. First up was Kirk Lamont, who seemed very excited to talk to anyone who'd bothered to approach him and though Chris couldn't call himself a fan of Kirk—let alone the character Fenrir—he still tried to act excited to meet the young actor. Then it was onto Martin Conroy, who first tried to sign a poster for Chris, until he saw the comic book being shoved in his face. He seemed intrigued by this and as he signed the front, he asked Chris, "So you are an *original* fan, I take it?"

Chris laughed at this and said, "I can't say I was there at the beginning, but I've loved this since I discovered it."

"Well, I hope you enjoy the film. I think you'll be *very* pleased."

"I'm sure I will be. I just had to say, I am such a huge fan of your work in the Fairfield series. I mean, to me, you're still the only real Fairfield . . . the others after you might as well have been some other character."

Martin laughed. "Kind of you to say, my boy, but alas I don't control these things. The work, as they say, speaks for itself. If my performance meant that much to you, that will always keep me warm at night. Anyway, I just hope you feel I do justice to Arastis. He was quite the challenge if I may say so, but I did have fun playing him."

"I'm sure you're fantastic in it. When you were cast, I immediately thought, 'This sounds perfect.'"

"Wonderful. Well, it was very nice to meet you . . ."

"Chris."

"Chris, have fun the rest of your time here, and I hope you enjoy the film when you see it." Martin stuck out his hand, which Chris shook and was a little shocked by the firm grip. Then it was onto Philip Dalton, who was all smiles and happily signed the comic presented to him, no questions asked. He said something to Chris, but in that moment, the fanboy found himself unable to focus on anything except the goddess sitting next to Philip.

There she was, mere feet from him and even more beautiful than she seemed in her films. Chris found himself at a loss for words in that moment and wondered what the hell he could possibly say to Marie that wouldn't sound like the stupidest or most pathetic thing she'd heard all day. Before that could happen though, Philip proceeded to serve up the embarrassment of Chris' life.

Nudging Marie with his elbow, he said, "Seems you've enchanted another young man over here."

As she'd finished saying her farewells to the fan who'd been talking with her, Marie turned her gaze to Chris and smiled sweetly. In that moment, he felt the world around him vanish, and things grew dark.

When Chris awoke, he was on the floor, staring up at none other than Marie LeBeau. She looked relieved that he was conscious and someone working for the studio ran up to take over for her. "Are you okay?" the man asked, as Marie stepped aside. Chris nodded and heard a few snickers around him.

Marie said to the studio man, "He just fainted ... I'm ashamed to say this isn't the first time I've seen it happen." Chris found her French accent just as pleasant to his ears as it had been in her films. It sent a tingle from the base of his skull down to his toes. He nearly fainted all over again.

The studio man kept his eyes fixed on Chris, observing him closely, as if he was a doctor in his spare time. "What's your name, kid?" he asked.

"Chris."

"You okay to stand up?"

"Yeah, I think so."

The man helped him to his feet and some cheeky folks in the crowd gave him a round of applause. Marie then handed Chris back the issue of *Black Berenice* he hoped she'd sign with the rest of the cast. "I signed it for you. It was the least I could do after what happened. Would you like a picture as well?"

Chris felt like he was in shock, in a dream or something— this couldn't be reality—but amidst the euphoria, he nodded and the woman of his dreams cozied up to him. The studio man asked for Chris' phone and he managed to get the camera set up so a picture could be taken. Once it had been, Marie smiled and said, "I'm sorry about all that, but as I now feel a little guilty, I think Lawrence here could fill you in about the party this evening?"

Lawrence, the man who'd helped Chris, seemed irritated that she'd mentioned the party and then insisted, "They're supposed to do the scavenger hunt for that, Marie."

"Hasn't this young man been through enough?" She waved her hand in dismissal as she added, "Just give him some passes."

Lawrence seemed trapped between a rock and a hard place. After a moment, he relented and urged Chris to follow him to a bag containing two stacks of cards. He removed four from each stack and said, "You haven't seen anyone get on Marie's bad side, so even though I'm not supposed to do this, I'm choosing to make an exception." Handing Chris the first four cards, he said, "Those will get you into the screening tonight. I gave you four in case you have some friends. I'd just as soon give you one, but I don't want any further problems with Marie. You can find the time and place on the cards. Just don't be late." Then handing the remaining four cards to Chris, he added, "These other ones will get you into the after-party. Again, details are on the cards."

"Wow, thanks. I don't know what to say."

"Best you don't say anything. This incident was a bit embarrassing for everyone."

Chris nodded, still in shock of everything that had transpired in the past minute. Then Lawrence was helping him exit the signing area.

Moving back into the surging river of fans that passed between the booths on the show floor, Chris carefully secured the first issue of *Black Berenice* in his backpack. For the next few minutes, it almost felt like he was floating around the con. His feet weren't touching the floor—they were stepping on clouds. He had been touched by an angel, and he'd never forget it for as long as he lived.

2

That evening, Chris sat at the hotel bar stewing in mixture of elation and embarrassment. He sipped his drink slowly, attempting to avoid getting too tipsy before the party he was attending with his friends Dan Lopez, Nick Leung, and Melanie Cooper. But the alcohol did little to settle his nerves as he mulled over the events of that morning. On the one hand, fainting in front of all those people had probably been the most humiliating experience of his life. On the other hand, it had paved the way for him to be able to attend the advance screening and after-party for *Black Berenice*. Despite making a fool of himself in front of Marie, the after-party would provide him with a chance to make a better impression. A chance to prove that he wasn't the loser the rest of Comic-Con now saw him as.

"So . . ." Mel asked, "Any thoughts on what you'll say to Marie if you see her again at this party?"

"Maybe she'll remember you from earlier," Dan chuckled.

Chris shrugged. "She's a celebrity. I doubt they remember anybody they meet."

"You'd be surprised," Nick said. "If something is memorable, I bet they do. And your whole episode this morning was *definitely* memorable."

"Speaking of which . . ." Dan quickly whipped out his phone and Chris wondered for a moment what he was doing. Then he realized Dan had to be looking for a clip of Chris at the signing for *Black Berenice*. None of his friends had been present there with him, and he'd been thankful for that, but now his nerves went on edge as he realized he was going to have to relive that nightmare all over again.

"Nice, found it!" Dan exclaimed with glee and hit PLAY on the video.

Chris leaned in to see for himself what had really happened earlier, hoping it wasn't as awful as he'd remembered. Unfortunately, it went down exactly as he expected. There he was, getting an autograph from former teen heartthrob Philip Dalton, ready to move on to the real reason he was there . . . Marie LeBeau. And like a marionette with his strings cut, Chris suddenly lost consciousness and dropped to the ground. Dan and Nick laughed briefly at Chris' fall, but that joy quickly became tinged with jealously. They watched in shock as Marie leaped up from the table she'd been sitting behind and ran over to Chris. There was concern in her eyes, as if nothing was more important to her than the safety of this lone fan.

Dan's eyes went wide at this. "Damn, dude. She's like right up on you."

"Yeah," Nick added, "I kinda wish I had thought of something like this!"

"Except I wasn't faking it!" Chris confessed, "I had to eat something after just to get my blood sugar back to normal."

Shaking his head, Dan said, "You and your damn blood sugar, dude. As ridiculous as you looked fainting like that, it's pretty cool that she pitied you enough to give us tickets to that screening and after-party. Besides, you got nothing to complain about when you got one-on-one time with someone like Marie LeBeau." And honestly, any of them would have felt blessed to simply be in close proximity to her.

It had been less than an hour since Chris had left the screening of *Black Berenice* and the film had not only met his expectations—it had surpassed them. All he could think about was Marie and how magnetic a presence she was. It was akin to seeing Sigourney Weaver's masterstroke of acting as Ripley in *Aliens*. He thought it was just as possible Marie could end up with another Oscar nomination for her performance. In fact, he felt like it was worth telling this to Marie if he saw her at the after-party—more than anything just to apologize for being a complete idiot at the signing.

"Well, I'm sure you'll all have a chance to speak to Marie at this party," Mel said, before correcting herself. "Oh, who am I kidding? None of you will probably get within twenty feet of her."

"What? You don't think I can use my charms to get close?" Nick asked.

Mel laughed, "What charms?"

Nick waved his hand in dismissal.

As ridiculous as his friends could be, Chris felt lucky to have them. Most of his friends from college had moved away only a year after. Now that he was in his mid-twenties, these three were the only ones who still resided in LA. Nick was Chris' best friend in college. The two had quickly bonded over their mutual love of horror and martial arts films. As a result, Nick's primary focus at Comic-Con was film-related. He was interested in *Black Berenice* as a film, but would likely never pick up the comic. The fact they were all able to attend Comic-Con for free each year, though, was thanks to Nick. He worked at a toy company his uncle owned and got the hookup every year for free tickets. They considered it a company expense or something. Chris didn't really know the details or care to ask; all Nick had to say three years ago was "free Comic-Con", and Chris was immediately in.

Dan didn't have to be convinced, either. Aside from being

Chris' current roommate, he was also his only friend who was seriously into comics. Being an avid reader and lover of all things fantasy, he was the one who introduced Chris to *Black Berenice* back in college. While mostly a knock-off of the fantasy series *Red Sonja*, what set it apart was the incredible writing. Dan could always be trusted to recommend well-written material.

Finally, there was Mel, who admittedly had not attended college with Chris. In fact, she was several years older. They'd met during casting of his senior thesis at film school and the two had immediately connected over zombie movies. Mel's taste wasn't quite as broad as Nick's, but she was the only girl Chris knew who was into horror. The important thing to Chris was they were both movie buffs and that made hanging out easy when everyone had a shared passion.

After Dan had put his phone away, he decided to get one more jab in. "Maybe you should try and get Marie's phone number."

Mel smacked him on the arm. "Is everything a joke to you?"

"No, but you were acting like he has a chance with her or something." Turning to Chris, he added, "I mean, why do you care so much, Chris? I know what happened was embarrassing for you, but do you really think it'll make a difference meeting Marie again at this party? I mean, meeting celebrities is always awkward. To us, it's a big deal, but to them, it's just another day."

Chris shook his head. "I don't know. I'm not expecting anything here, and I can't say I'm going to this party just to meet Marie again, but you know, back in film school, I had all these big dreams, thought I'd be knee-deep in filmmaking by now. Yet here I am in my mid-twenties and I haven't gotten a single project off the ground since college. So yeah, sure, going to this party isn't likely to change things, but they always told us getting into the industry was all about who you know, right? So, if I have the chance to rub elbows with the kinds of people who will be at a party like this—people I look up to—shouldn't I try my best to make something of that? Anyway, even if nothing comes out of this, the movie was at least great. And that was all I really cared about. Anything that might happen at this party, that's just like a bonus, right?"

"And we *gotta* discuss the bonus situation," Nick chimed in enthusiastically. Any chance to quote his favorite horror film, *Alien*, was an opportunity he seized. "Brett and I, we think we deserve full shares. Right, baby?"

Playing along, Chris laughed and said, "Right."

Mel shook her head. "Yeah, you guys aren't making any connections tonight."

3

Chris wondered what time it was when he finished his drink. Checking his phone, he saw it was just past 11 p.m. "Looks like we're good to go, if you guys are done."

Dan finished off the rest of his drink in one gulp and said, "Yeah, let's blow this popsicle stand."

And go they did, Ubering over to the Hard Rock Hotel to save themselves any sweating. San Diego had been particularly hot that day and a change of clothes back at their hotel wouldn't save them from making things bad if they exerted themselves too much on the way over to the party. But soon they were inside those air-conditioned walls and a quick elevator ride took them up to the rooftop lounge where the most glorious sight awaited them.

The entrance to the party was roped off with security all over the place to stop paparazzi or crazed fans from getting past. But beyond them was something Chris had only witnessed in the movies before. There were various themed decorations placed about to give the environment a more sword and sorcery vibe. A stage had also been erected at the far end where a band was likely to be coming out shortly. Numerous couches adorned the space, and even a pool had some guests gathering around it with drinks in their hands. The place was packed, but not too packed. There was likely a guest list to keep it from turning into the usual crowded mess you'd see in the LA bar scene. The music playing was the film's score by Mogwai and everybody seemed to be having a great time. Chris supposed anyone at these exclusive parties had a good time, but he was never the kind of person to be truly comfortable at a large gathering.

Chris had always had a bit of social anxiety and LA was just about the worst place for him to attempt socializing. He'd do fine in smaller environments like the homes of friends, but any time they chose to go out to a bar or club was an event he absolutely dreaded. At the same time though, Chris hated the idea of missing out, and usually suppressed these feelings as much as possible in an attempt to have a good time—however unlikely that might be.

Approaching the employee at the entrance, Chris presented the four passes he'd been given and the woman looked them over before smiling back. "Enjoy the party, guys." She then stamped their hands in case they needed to leave and cleared the rope for them to proceed inside. Chris and his three friends thanked her before making their way past the velvet roped gates into a crowd of unfamiliar faces. Chris wasn't sure who most of these people were. *Possibly press,* he thought, *or folks considered important enough to be rubbing elbows with the Hollywood elite.* He didn't know, and frankly, he didn't care. He just wanted to find somebody worth talking to there.

"Anybody specific you're going to try and chat up?" Dan asked Chris as he surveyed the crowd.

"Well, I met some of the cast already at the signing, so the big one would probably be Tony Martínez. Been a fan of his since junior high. What about you?"

"Well, I mean, I gotta try and talk to Marie, right? Though I'm sure she's currently surrounded by people—and security."

Nick shrugged. "You never know. I'm sure any nerds like us here are just as intimidated to talk to her. Or, worst-case scenario, you could wait a bit and they'll have moved on. Not like you can sustain a conversation with any famous person here past a few comments. Probably gonna be weird."

"Well, I can tell you who I *won't* be talking to," Dan said with a chuckle.

"Milton Humphreys?" Chris suggested with a grin.

This got another laugh out of Dan. "Jesus, you see the fucking plain white T-shirt he was sporting at the screening? I saw him talking with Tony after the Q&A on their way out."

"I must have missed him."

"I couldn't miss him. Think he had a fucking mustard stain on it. Like classic wife-beater look."

"Gross," Mel said.

Chris added, "I don't think he's married."

"Well yeah," Dan clarified, "He looks like too much of a creeper."

"Oh my God!" Mel squealed in delight. "That's Philip Dalton! I've had the hots for him since middle school. God, he still looks like he's twenty."

"Isn't he forty?" Nick scoffed.

Mel didn't even bother to respond, she just shot off like a rocket toward its target.

Not that Chris cared, he knew everyone was destined to separate at the party as they all found people they wanted to meet. And Chris had finally found the first person he was eager to compliment.

Black Berenice director Tony Martínez was chatting with several people who looked like fans, and Chris beelined for the location. Dan and Nick apparently noticed and followed closely behind. When they got near Tony, Chris waited patiently for his chance to approach the director.

Nick wondered why they were waiting and asked Chris, "Aren't you going to say anything?"

"Just didn't want to be a dick, since he's talking with those people."

As the fans began to break off, Nick quickly said, "Now he's not," and swooped in before anyone else—even Chris. Holding out his hand to the surprised filmmaker, he said, "Mr. Martínez. Big fan, loved the film by the way."

"Thanks," he said, noticing Chris and Dan approach as well. "You guys fans?"

Chris nodded and said, "Yeah, it's my favorite comic."

"Hey, it's mine too!"

"I loved that you used that song from *On Dangerous Ground*, by the way."

Tony looked confused for a moment, perhaps having a hard time understanding Chris over the music—which was rather loud. But then his brain seemed to process what was said and he laughed, "Oh yeah, *On Dangerous Ground*. Love that one. Thanks for noticing."

Pulling out his phone, Dan asked, "Could we possibly get a picture with you?"

Tony didn't seem to like this much and scoffed, "C'mon, it's a party!" Then he turned and walked away, leaving the three friends rather deflated.

Nick shook his head. "Thanks for blowing that, man."

"Hey, it's not my fault he's a dick," Dan said.

"Well, we probably shouldn't be asking anyone for pictures at this party. They get that shit a lot, I'm sure they don't expect it here."

Shrugging, Dan put his phone away. "Whatever. I'm gonna go see what kind of food they're serving. Looks good whatever it is." He licked his lips as he broke off to approach one of the servers walking around with a tray of something edible.

Nick then said, "I wanna see what kind of drinks they're

offering. Don't even have a strong buzz going yet. You gonna be good here?"

Chris nodded and said, "Yeah . . . I guess I'll just look for the next person to embarrass myself in front of."

Nick laughed at this, "Hey, this time wasn't on you. That was all Dan. You're cool, man. Just have a little more confidence."

Nick's words didn't exactly have much of an effect on Chris. At this point in his life, he wasn't sure anything would. He'd been beaten down emotionally so many times, with so many failures, not much was going to shake him out of it. But he was still at a party, and determined to try and make a good impression on at least one celebrity. So he did as much as he could muster—which meant wandering around, hoping somebody might pull him out of his funk. Looking around, there were quite a few faces Chris recognized. Not that it helped make it any easier trying to approach them—until someone approached him.

No sooner had the firm hand fallen on Chris' shoulder than a voice he recognized asked, "Doing all right now, kid?"

Chris turned in shock to see Philip Dalton standing before him, the very actor he'd fainted in front of that morning. "Oh, uh, hi."

"Didn't think I'd see you again after the signing. Just thought I'd say hi, seeing how you're the one fan I couldn't forget. Not every day you see a guy faint like that. At least for me, it's usually the ladies." Philip laughed at his own joke.

"Yeah, I'm fine. Guess I was just too excited about meeting all of you."

Philip waved his hand in dismissal. "Pfft, c'mon man, be honest, it wasn't *us* that got you so hot under the collar. It was *her*." Pointing to his right, Philip acknowledged the presence of Marie LeBeau, who was standing by the edge of the roof not too far from the pool, talking to some fans. She was illuminated by the lights surrounding the pool in a kind of heavenly glow that didn't seem to have the same effect on anyone else around her. It was as if the lights had been adjusted just for her at that very spot.

Much to his shock, Chris watched as if she had somehow sensed his gaze on her, and turned her head to look directly at him. Though it was possible she was really looking at Philip, who waved to her before she waved back. "Marie just has this power over men. We're putty in her hands. Most fans tend to lose their ability to speak around her. But if there's something she wants, nothing will stop that woman from getting it."

"You make her sound like she's got superpowers or something," Chris said, feeling rather uncomfortable as the words left his lips.

Philip laughed at this. "Maybe she does." Taking a sip of his drink, he saw someone else familiar and waved to them. "Well, I'll see you around, kid. Enjoy the party."

Philip made a path away from Chris and the lonesome fanboy was trying to decide where to head next. But he couldn't seem to take his eyes away from Marie. As if a tractor beam was pulling him toward her, he slowly moved in her direction. Before he could reach her though, someone took to the stage and announced that without further ado, the main attraction for that evening was about to perform—none other than the band who did such a magnificent job scoring the film, Mogwai. At this news, the entire party erupted in applause. He wasn't sure who all there knew about this, but it was a *huge* deal. Mogwai started into their classic song, "Hunted by a Freak," and everyone lost their collective minds.

Except for Chris.

His attention was still fixed on Marie. He watched as the group talking with her broke off to watch the band and suddenly, she was left alone. Chris then noticed something odd out of the corner of his eye.

While the rooftop lounge was encased in a wall about a dozen feet high to provide some semblance of privacy, there was a small gap where a stairway let out to the street for anyone wanting a quick getaway. It was as Chris was passing this, he noticed what appeared to be a shadowy figure running across the adjacent roof of the Old Spaghetti Factory. But in a flash, the shadow passed from view. Chris blinked his eyes, convinced it had to be a trick of the light, but the moment still disturbed him, leaving a small knot in his stomach that only fueled the fear he felt at approaching Marie.

Somehow, though, all this concern melted away in an instant as Chris neared her. She turned in his direction with a smile, as if knowing he was coming and said sweetly, "Hi, Chris."

He was taken aback by this greeting, which felt so intimate and personal to him. Yet it came from someone who didn't know him at all. "Um, hi . . . Marie."

"Surprised I remembered you?" she said with a devilish grin.

Once more, the soothing sound of her French accent sent a tingle through Chris' body. But he tried his best to maintain his cool and shook his head, saying, "No, no. I'm sure my fainting was probably the worst part of your day, or week, or whatever."

She giggled at this and said, "No, I'd call it the *highlight* of my day. Not that I thought your fainting was a great thing, it was awful. But to think I had that power over a fan, well, I could tell meeting me meant a lot to you, and that felt good. I hope you enjoyed the film."

"Oh of course. I mean, you were perfect. Everything about the film was perfect and it's my favorite comic so I had every reason to be critical." Chris felt stupid at that last comment and wished he could have taken it back, but instead of being put off by it, she giggled again.

"I'm sure you do. I know fans can feel a sense of ownership over something they love."

Shaking his head, Chris said, "No, it's stupid. I mean, of course it's not ours, someone else created it, they should call the shots, but I . . ."

"You care about it. That's what matters, right?"

"Yeah, you're right." He was surprised how easy she was to talk to. All the jitters he had before and during the party up to this point somehow had melted away in the past minute. He felt like he could just stay there, right in that spot, and keep talking to her for hours. The way she looked at him, it was as if she truly cared about what he had to say. Perhaps he was projecting, but it almost felt like there was some kind of connection between them. It was something he would have given anything to pursue further.

Unfortunately, someone had other plans.

A slim shadow crept silently over the wall at the edge of the roof and dropped to the ground right behind Marie. Chris knew in that instant it was the same figure he'd spotted on the adjacent roof and suddenly fear consumed him that he'd made a terrible mistake not telling somebody about it. Luckily, a fight or flight response within him kicked in. Marie's safety was the only thing on his mind and he quickly pushed himself in front of her.

Chris might have been a nerd, but sometimes that came with certain advantages, like the fact that he was shit at team sports and in love with martial arts films. Having a natural talent for gymnastics, this led him to take up mixed martial arts in third grade. For over a decade he'd become proficient in karate, judo, Jeet Kune Do, and Filipino martial arts. Up until this point, he'd never had to use these practices in the real world. But as he stared at the black-clad figure—who also had their face covered—he noticed their hand move to what he thought was a sword on their back and panicked. Perhaps Chris had watched too many movies, but his brain immediately went to *ninja*.

There would be a split-second to act before this person

harmed Marie or someone else at the party. However, instead of throwing a punch or kick, he tackled the ninja to the ground. They didn't see this coming, but wouldn't make the same mistake twice. They kicked Chris off their body. He fell back hard against the ground. Marie gasped and ran for help. The ninja said, "Shit." Chris sprang up into a sweeping kick, but they hopped right over his leg.

The ninja threw a front kick at Chris. He deflected it and threw an elbow strike. It was blocked. They went in for a punch. Chris blocked this before they traded several more blows. None connected and security was on their way with guns drawn.

As Chris noticed this, he lost his concentration. A single blow struck him in the face, knocking him back to the ground. His hazy vision caught a brief glimpse of the ninja leaping over the wall and out of view. It seemed like they might have committed suicide, but he couldn't tell. At least he had kept Marie safe. That was all that mattered to him.

4

After saving the life of one of Hollywood's hottest celebrities, Chris wouldn't have been crazy to expect a party in his honor. Instead, he got a night at the police station. After all, this was nothing the San Diego Police Department took lightly. Comic-Con wasn't just the biggest event of the year for the city, it was something that they prided themselves on keeping orderly and safe for all visitors. So, when an attack is seemingly made on an actress like Marie LeBeau during a party loaded with security and witnesses, all of whom—apart from Marie and Chris— seemed unaware of the attacker? They want to know *everything*.

Marie was the initial person they questioned since Chris had reported the attack was intended against her. However, Chris was second, and they took their time with him. It seemed like they wanted to know his whole life story leading up to that point—as well as what the attacker looked like and how he managed to fight them off. The things they insinuated almost made it sound like they believed he was in on it with the attacker as some kind of stunt to impress Marie. His story just seemed too ridiculous— even Chris had to admit that. The black-clad killer with their face covered, and a sword on their back? It was basically like every ninja movie he'd ever seen. But it was *real,* and whether or not they believed that, he knew it to be true.

After losing his interrogation virginity, Chris was spent, but he was happy to see his friends all waiting for him outside the station. Apparently, they didn't want to wait inside, and he didn't blame them for that. Chris wasn't sure how much his friends knew, but he was sure they all had seen the commotion at the party.

Dan was the first one to run up to him, looking very concerned. "Jesus, dude, what the hell happened?"

Chris sighed, "I figured you guys heard the story already."

Nick said, "We heard somebody tried to attack Marie and apparently you stopped them? How the *hell* did you do that?"

Shrugging, Chris said, "I guess all those years of martial arts paid off."

Nick laughed at this, but Dan didn't look too amused. "I didn't honestly think you were serious about all that when you told me. I mean, I never saw you take any classes in LA."

"Admittedly, I am a little rusty, but was amazed how quickly that stuff came flooding back when I needed it."

"And you're sure you're okay?" Dan asked.

Nick said, "He's fine, Dan. You worry too much."

"Well, if you guys are done," Mel asked, "Why don't we go somewhere not directly in front of a police station where all manner of creeps are coming out?" She then quickly attempted to correct herself. "Not that I'm calling you a creep, Chris. I just mean, well . . . you know."

He did, and didn't put up a fight as they walked back toward their hotel. Once they got there, he was ready to get some sleep. Unfortunately, as they were all sharing a room, his friends ordered room service and seemed bent on staying up the rest of the night to discuss theories about what happened.

"So you're serious? They were like a ninja?" Mel asked in disbelief.

"I know what ninjas look like—better than most—and I

don't know what else you'd call someone clad all in black, with a sword on their back, and moves that'd make Bruce Lee blush. Honestly, if security hadn't shown up, I'd probably be dead along with Marie right now."

"Why the hell would anybody wanna kill her, anyway?" Dan wondered.

"Beats me. I mean I don't even know if they really wanted her dead, or if it was a warning, or maybe even an attempted kidnapping. All I knew was that this ninja was bad news. Still, even if Marie had made some enemies in Hollywood, I don't see how a ninja is anywhere in the sphere of what I'd consider reasonable action against your enemies. Unless you're the yakuza or something."

"Could it have been?" Nick wondered.

Mel smacked him on the arm. "Don't be an idiot."

"What? You think they operate exclusively in Japan?"

"That shit doesn't happen in the real world. You've just been watching way too many ninja movies with Chris."

Shrugging, Nick said, "Just 'cause it happens in movies doesn't mean it doesn't happen in real life. Hell, I think what happened to Chris proves that, right? So like Holmes said, 'If you remove everything impossible, whatever remains, however improbable, must be the truth.' Which means the person Chris saw *was* a ninja, and for some reason they were looking to harm Marie LeBeau."

"Or somebody paid them to do so," Dan added.

Mel sighed. "You guys are ridiculous, and I've had enough of this shit. I'm gonna hit the hay."

As Mel took her time in the bathroom, doing whatever girls do before bed, Dan finished off the pizza they ordered. The boys then got ready to go to sleep themselves—what little sleep they could get in the remaining hours before the sun came up. Perhaps they'd all sleep in and just leave without hitting up the convention center on Sunday. At this point, Chris wouldn't have cared. All his thoughts were on Marie and the ninja. His friends were no help in solving the mystery, so he supposed he'd have to do it himself.

If he ever got the chance.

5

Firm knocking on the door snapped Chris awake that morning. He checked the time on the hotel alarm clock and wasn't surprised to see it was already 11 a.m. His first thought was the maid was at the door, though he doubted they would knock before entering. It could have been the police—a thought which naturally sent a cold chill down his spine. Regardless, he wouldn't have been crazy to assume whoever was there had come to see him and this caused Chris to bound out of bed, quickly slip on his shirt and pants, and try not to trip over anything on the floor.

When he cracked open the door, Chris realized he probably should have at least checked the peephole first, but as he saw the person standing there, whatever fear taking hold instantly melted away. In his doorway was none other than actress extraordinaire, Marie LeBeau.

Yanking open the door the rest of the way in a wave of pure euphoria, he was struck by the fact that she was even more beautiful than the previous times he'd seen her. Bathed in the warm light of the hotel hallway, Marie didn't appear quite as movie star-like wearing a pair of skinny jeans, a loose-fitting T-shirt with the sleeves cut off, and a Dodgers cap. Maybe she was trying to keep a low profile, or maybe this was just her in a more natural state that wasn't trying to attract the press. Yet she was still as stunning as ever. Chris doubted it was possible for her to not exude that sense of loveliness that seemed to make up her natural aura. But the way she looked somehow made her seem more attainable, even if she was still way out of Chris' league—this quality was what he found so intoxicating at that moment.

"Hey," she simply said with a rather shy-looking grin. *Was it possible she was nervous?* Chris seriously doubted this and put the thought right out of his head.

"Hi, um, Marie . . . what brings you here? I mean, how did you know I was here?"

She giggled softly and said, "It wasn't too hard to find out. I had someone call around until they found a hotel room under your name."

"I didn't think they gave out that information to just anybody."

Shrugging, she said, "I guess I'm not just anybody."

Chris, suddenly feeling stupid that he was leaving her standing out in the hall, asked, "Would you like to come in? I mean, my friends are still sleeping I think, but I'm sure they'd love to meet you."

Marie shook her head and said, "I wouldn't want to intrude. Could I buy you a coffee, though? It's the least I could do after you basically saved my life."

"Is that the best idea? I mean, I'd assume the paparazzi is like crazy around here."

Marie shrugged. "Let them take my picture. I've got nothing to be ashamed of."

"And if they want more than a picture?"

Smiling with a mischievous grin, she said, "Well, I'll have you there to protect me, right?"

Chris laughed lightly. "I'm pretty sure whoever you got for security would do a better job."

"They didn't help much last night. I gave them the day off."

"You can do that?"

"I can do whatever I want." And there was the grin again, the one that told him she could be playful when she wanted to be, forceful when she had to be, and more than anything was interested in having a little fun with Chris that morning. Something he could hardly believe until she took his hand and led him out of the room. Of course, he had to pop back in for his shoes, but then they were off on an adventure. One Chris was sure to never forget.

Hopping into Marie's BMW, they drove about twenty minutes north to a small coffee shop by the beach called Bird Rock Coffee Roasters. Marie said she'd never been, but had heard it was great. Once they had their coffee in hand, Chris could confirm it was one fantastic cup of joe. And the location being so close to the beach was a bonus, as they decided to take a stroll on the sands while they enjoyed their coffee.

After taking a sip of her drink, Marie said, "You must think my life is pretty crazy, Chris. But it's not. I wanted you to know that what happened last night, it's something I thought might be coming for some time, but I was too ashamed to tell anyone. I guess I didn't think they'd believe me if I did."

"So what the hell *was* that all about? Were they trying to kill you?"

"Yes. At least I think so. I didn't always live in America, as you probably know. Aside from Canada, I spent some time in Japan and fell for a man there. The *wrong* man. His name was Hiro Nobunaga and he was anything but a hero to me. Not like you. Things started great, but then he turned cruel, possessive. I couldn't stay with a man like that, and eventually I left him. But it wasn't easy. He'd make threats, tell me things like I wouldn't live long without him, make me believe I needed his protection—whatever that was supposed to be. But the truth of the matter is that I was far safer outside his presence. I knew he had dealings with the yakuza and other bad apples, but I honestly thought they'd kill him before he could ever enlist their help in coming after me."

"So you think that ninja was . . . who? Somebody he sent after you?"

Marie nodded and Chris wasn't sure what to make of this. Her story honestly sounded like something out of movie, yet he couldn't deny that this fantasy had to have some basis in reality if that ninja was to be believed. And he could tell from his fight that they were not some cheap stuntperson hired to put on a show.

They were out for blood.

"I'm sorry about all this, Chris. I honestly never thought something like this could really happen, and I wouldn't have wanted to involve anyone else, but now . . ."

"Now it's too late. Look, Marie, whatever happened with this guy, it sounds like you made the right decision to get out of there. But there are people who can help you. With someone like you, cops would be falling over each other to find and stop anyone involved in this."

Shaking her head, he could see tears welling up in her eyes and fear seizing this woman who appeared so strong only a short time ago. "I can't tell this to anyone. Nobody would believe it. I mean, I wouldn't even think you'd believe it if not for what happened last night. You talked to the police, right? Did you tell them everything that happened?"

"Yeah . . ."

"And what did they think?"

"They thought I was crazy. They didn't say that, but I could tell. I'm assuming you told them the same thing?"

Marie nodded. "I thought about stretching the truth, making

up something more believable, but I didn't want them to think you were a liar."

Chris sighed. "No, they just thought we both were."

"I'm really sorry, Chris. Really." She stared deeply into his eyes and in that moment, she looked so wounded, so fragile. He wanted to comfort her, to hold her and tell her everything would be okay. But the reality was he barely knew her . . . and it just didn't feel right.

"You have nothing to be sorry about. I just wish there was more I could do to help."

"But you can."

"What do you mean?"

"I saw the way you fought. I've never seen anyone move like that. You're like a martial arts expert or something?"

Shaking his head, Chris laughed. "I'd hardly call myself an expert."

"But you've been doing it a long time?"

"Over ten years, yeah. I thought I was a little rusty, to be honest."

"You didn't look that rusty to me."

"I got lucky. I wouldn't want to try my luck again. Especially if they had that sword out."

"What if I paid you?"

Chris was taken aback in that moment. Stopping cold, he pondered what she meant. She couldn't seriously be suggesting paying him to . . . *protect* her? It was too silly to be true. Or was it?

"To do what?" he asked.

"Find the person who's after me."

"You already know who that is."

Marie shook her head in frustration. "You can't go after Nobunaga. He's in another country. My problem is *here*, and that's where it's going to stay."

"But that's what you've got security for, right? Even if the cops don't believe you, your guys are armed. I'm sure a ninja isn't going to stop bullets."

"I'm not getting rid of my security. But what if I added you to the team? Off the books. You wouldn't be with the team proper . . . you'd be closer to me."

Chris could feel his heartbeat speeding up at the thought of being close to Marie for an indefinite amount of time. It was almost like a dream come true—if that assassin didn't have the potential to turn the whole thing into a nightmare. He wanted so much to say yes, but instead he said, "I'm sorry, but I really think there are others more suited to this, who could keep you safer."

Marie clearly was disappointed by this, but then asked, "Would you do me a favor then?"

"What?"

"Just take a week . . . to think about it."

"And if that ninja comes back before the week is up?"

Marie laughed nervously at this. "Well, then you'll know whether or not I needed your help after all."

Chris sighed. "Don't do that. Now you're making me feel like an asshole here."

Shaking her head, Marie said, "I don't want you to feel like there's any pressure on you, Chris. But if I'm being honest . . . I just like having you around."

He could hardly believe this, and whether or not it was a ploy to get him to join her security team, Chris *wanted* to believe it more than anything. "Really?"

Smiling, she nodded. "Yeah." And in that moment, she moved in closer and he thought she might kiss him, but instead, she gave him a hug. It was long and gentle and when she broke away, she was holding a card with her phone number on it. "Don't lose it, okay? And *don't* give it to anyone else, please."

"Of course," Chris said and then pocketed the card.

"Now, let's get you back to your friends."

And with that, Marie drove him back. They had talked a bit casually on the way to the coffee shop, but the drive to the hotel was more uncomfortable. Chris was worried if he started talking about anything, Marie would sway the conversation back around to him working for her. So he mostly stayed silent, except for the few times she asked him something. Once they arrived back at the hotel, she dropped him off out front. He thought of asking once more if she'd like to meet his friends, but he could tell after the way things went on the beach, that wasn't happening. Maybe things would change if he took the job. A lot of things could change if he took the job—he knew that to be true. The question was, would his life change for the better, or the worse?

6

After his joyous, yet slightly concerning morning with Marie LeBeau, Chris had decided he was ready to head back to LA. Most years at Comic-Con, Chris would use Sunday to take advantage of last day sales, but currently he had little interest in that. Perhaps it was because he was emotionally spent, or perhaps it was because all his thoughts were locked on Marie and her proposition. Despite his hesitancy to take a job on her security detail, he never even bothered to ask how much she'd offer him. He could only assume it was a lot, and certainly more than his $10 an hour tester job at Apollonia Games. Still, at least he knew his life was safe at that job.

When he'd initially spilled all the gory details to his friends, Nick thought he was bullshitting. Which was fair. After all, what were the odds that an A-list celebrity would turn up at the door of their hotel room? Yet, as Mel rightly pointed out, it's no small thing to save someone's life—especially when that someone was Marie LeBeau. She personally felt that Marie owed Chris a hell of a lot more than a cup of coffee and a job opportunity. Meanwhile, Dan was fascinated by the whole account, wanting to know every detail to the point that Mel felt he was bordering on creepy. And perhaps she was right, but she also had no idea just how insane the whole time with Marie had felt. That sense of euphoria was far greater than anything he got from smoking a joint. Regardless, it was time he wished more than anything he could extend. If only he didn't have to contend with the potential of coming face-to-face with a killer once more. A mysterious assassin who could end Chris' life in a nanosecond if he made the wrong move.

After they'd finished discussing Chris' morning with Marie, the group agreed to skip the Sunday festivities at Comic-Con and head home to LA. Yet even after making it back and dropping off Mel and Nick, Chris still couldn't shake Marie from his thoughts. When he pulled up to his apartment complex in El Segundo, Dan had to snap him out of it.

"Hey, Earth to Chris!"

Chris turned to see his friend outside the car, already holding his bags pulled from the trunk. "Sorry, guess I drifted off there for a moment."

"Hey man, I get it. I'd probably be the same way if I spent the morning with Marie LeBeau, but I'm just glad you didn't space out on the road."

Chris shrugged. "Honestly, I kinda did. Guess I was on autopilot."

"Then thank God your autopilot is a better driver than you tend to be when you're talking to all of us. I swear, I was nervous a few times on that drive down to San Diego."

Finally exiting the car, Chris moved to the trunk to retrieve his own bag before shutting it and locking his car. Dan waited for him at the gate leading into their apartment complex. When Chris approached, Dan asked, "So I assume if you're still thinking about Marie, you're considering taking that job?"

Chris shook his head. "I don't know, man. I mean, yeah, the job would probably pay a lot. It might even help get my film career off the ground, either from the money or from meeting people around her. But taking a job like this could get me killed. Somebody is still after Marie; they haven't gone anywhere."

Working his keys in the gate lock, he opened it up and held it for Dan.

"Yeah, but you're forgetting the biggest perk of that job. Valuable time close to Marie."

"That won't mean shit if I'm dead, man."

"Stop looking at the negative, dude! What if you save her life again? I mean, saving it once should have at least gotten you laid. But saving it twice? She should be fucking *proposing* to you."

Chris waited for Dan to unlock their apartment door and followed him inside. Plopping down on their couch in an attempt to relax, he said, "It's a nice dream, Dan, but I have to live in reality here. Shit like that doesn't happen."

"You told us all about your martial arts experience though, and you *did* successfully fight off that ninja."

"And if they bring friends next time, I'm fucked."

"So then you track them down and stop them at the source."

"What? Like set a trap?"

"Is that the worst idea in the world? Run it by Marie. If she's okay being used as bait, it's worth a shot, right? Besides, you're going nowhere at that fucking game company."

And that was one fact that Chris couldn't argue with. He'd been at Apollonia almost three years and been laid off at least three times since he started. Of course, it wasn't really a lay-off as much as they considered his contract ended. That was the whole problem with contract work—there was *zero* job security. Which was something that Chris craved more and more with each passing year. He figured maybe Dan was right about his dead-end job, but if he was wrong . . . he'd be dead wrong.

7

The next morning Chris woke up early, like he always did for Apollonia Games. He was supposed to work forty hours a week, but more often than not that was extended due to necessary overtime—ten hour, even twelve hour workdays. Sure, he'd get overtime pay, but it didn't make it feel any better when a job he usually hated felt like it was consuming his entire existence. The one thing that made it bearable was the people there. His coworkers didn't seem to change much project to project, even though they almost all went through the same unfortunate lay-off process. There were of course the lucky few who seemed to hop from game to game when they were in a late alpha, early beta stage, but the rest seemed to get dumped on the project as it was approaching the end of its lifecycle. This meant overtime hell.

Speaking of hell, the room that Apollonia Games shoved the testers into felt not unlike hell in the summertime. There was no AC in there, despite AC being in just about every room of the building the company occupied. Rumor had it that originally the testing room had been a storage room and they converted it by moving the junk out and the people they treated like junk in. He supposed management considered that a fair trade. Besides, these people were willing to work a contract position for near minimum wage, of course they'd be willing to put up with the seasonal heat too.

Being back among his work friends, Chris wanted to share

stories of his Comic-Con exploits, but he kinda figured none of them would believe him. His one friend there who was a cinephile like he was, Bobby, naturally asked if Chris saw any upcoming movies there and Chris was inclined to share the news of seeing *Black Berenice*. Not more than a minute after sharing this though, somebody dropped their phone into the conversation.

"Is this you, Chris?!"

Looking at the phone, he spotted a fairly hazy picture of him with the cops and a headline that read, MAN SAVES THE LIFE OF A-LIST CELEBRITY, MARIE LEBEAU. Chris was a little shook; he didn't think anybody would know, but of course people would find out, as that's what happens in the world of constant media bombardment. He was stupid to think he could keep it to himself.

"Holy shit, bro! Why didn't you start with this?!" Bobby asked, clearly recognizing Chris in the photo. "I heard about this shit, but never thought it was anybody I knew. I mean, you were there with Marie? Wait, *how* were you even there?!"

"Well, I got tickets to an after-party after I fainted at a signing."

Winston, the big guy with the phone, seemed focused on bringing that incident up as well, asking, "Man, what the fuck happened to you this weekend? I just found a video of you fainting in front of Marie, but there's also paparazzi photos of you two on a fucking beach! People are talking about this shit all over the internet!" He showed everyone his phone and now a crowd had gathered, something the team lead, Ron, had taken notice of and was none too happy to see.

"Hey, what the hell are you guys doing? You're supposed to be testing games!"

Everyone quickly moved back to their testing spots and pretended to play the game they were all checking for bugs, but they really wanted to hear more from Chris. Bobby was the first one to prod him for more. "C'mon, bro, you gotta spill here. You hook up with Marie? What the fuck happened?"

Chris sighed, trying to figure out himself how this whole thing started, but something made it feel like fate. He could never admit this to his co-workers, but it all sounded so ridiculous as he told them everything that happened. If it weren't for the photos and videos, he knew telling them anything would have been pointless. Yet the evidence spoke for itself, and as a result, they hung onto his every word as he told them of his embarrassing morning encounter, the scavenger hunt, the screening, and then the after-party. How he never in a million years would have expected to find himself able to talk so intimately with a woman as beautiful as Marie LeBeau and that if he hadn't spent all those years practicing martial arts, it likely would have been his last day on the planet. Finally, he told them about the next morning and the job she offered him.

Naturally, Bobby was the first to speak up. "Damn bro, I knew you were all into kung fu movies after I lent you those Shaw Brothers flicks, but I had no idea you possessed the moves to kick ass like that. So what the fuck are you doing back here? You're gonna take that job, right?"

Chris shrugged. "I don't know, man. I mean, I'm sure it pays well and—"

"Fuck the pay, bro. You get to be close to *Marie LeBeau* every fucking day! What's there to think about?"

"Yeah, he crazy," another coworker laughed.

"I was thinking about staying alive, maybe? Jesus, it's like everyone I talk to about this forgets the fact that some ninja motherfucker wants her dead! If I fuck up, I'm dead too."

Bobby shook his head. "Shit, you gotta do something. You just gonna toss her to the wolves?"

Sighing, Chris threw up his hands. "I don't know! Alright?

I'm kinda fucking scared here. I mean, yeah, it's Marie LeBeau, I'd give my right arm to get with a woman like that. But this ain't my arm, it's my life and I'm twenty-six years old. I don't have any desire to end my life this early."

Winston shook his head. "Man, you got it fuckin' easy. Some guys don't got a fucking choice out there. My best friend always tried to keep out of danger, stay away from the gangs in our neighborhood. Two years back, he died from a stray shot in a fucking drive-by. Staying out of danger might seem the smart thing to do, but that ain't no way to go through life. Sometimes, you gotta take a risk. As they say, 'no risk, no reward.'"

"Dayum, Big Win dropping those truth bombs," Bobby laughed.

Chris took Winston's words to heart. He knew that accepting the job with Marie was crazy, maybe even stupid, but like Dan had pointed out, he was going nowhere at Apollonia Games. Testers never had any upward trajectory—team lead was the ceiling for them. That's why most people who quit did so to go back to school in hopes of trying to aim a little higher. But Chris had been coasting by for three years.

And it was three years too long.

8

As everyone broke for lunch, Chris told his boss he was quitting and then promptly left. No notice given, as he felt there was no reason to give them the courtesy they never gave any of their employees. On his way home, he called the number Marie had given him. He expected a voice mailbox, or even an agent to answer the phone. Certainly not her directly. But when he heard the voice on the other end say, "Hello?" he knew that it was Marie's personal number. No wonder she didn't want him sharing it with anyone.

"Hi Marie, it's Chris."

With a hint of pleasure in her voice, Marie said, "Chris. Lovely to hear from you so soon. So I take it you've had enough time to consider my offer?"

"Yeah, I'm in. Whatever it takes, I'm your man."

"You certainly are." Those words sent a tingle down his spine. He waited for the next ones with bated breath. "Can you start tomorrow?"

"Of course."

"Good. You'll need a nice suit. Do you have one?"

He had a suit, but certainly didn't think it was up to Marie's standards, so he said, "No."

"I figured as much. We'll have to take care of that tomorrow. Which is perfect, as my schedule is quite light. In the meantime, I can't have you by my side in just anything, but I may have a few things lying around that fit you. As for other things you might need during your stay here, bring what you think you need."

"Okay." He was surprised to hear she kept any men's clothes on hand, but then again, he wasn't too familiar with the super-rich and didn't know what they tended to keep around.

"Good. Then I'll see you bright and early tomorrow morning. Let me text you my address. I want you here at 8 a.m. sharp."

He could tell this would be his foreseeable future—becoming Marie LeBeau's fateful servant at her eternal beck and call. And he had zero issues with this. He doubted many men would. Especially if they were being paid to do so.

After pulling over to save the address she texted him onto his phone, Chris returned back to his apartment and wondered for a moment if this might be the last time he saw that place—or Dan—for some time. If he was working security closer than anyone else, that had to mean staying at Marie's house, as the killer could strike again at any time, day or night. He felt nervous at the thought that they might strike that night before he even started, but took a small measure of comfort in the thought that no killer would strike again so soon, as their target would still be on high alert.

9

Milton Humphreys had been reclining on an outdoor lounge chair by his pool for the better part of the afternoon, doing business calls on his phone and sipping mai tais in the sun. He'd had eleven so far. It was safe to say one more and he wouldn't be able to conduct any business.

A week ago, Milton would have drunk half that amount and been good, but lately he'd been feeling better than ever, stronger even. He wasn't sure if that was due to the birthday retreat he took at his girlfriend's behest or something else. Now it was taking a few more drinks to get him to a happy place. That was the way he liked his evenings: a little tipsy and a lot of fun. Fun that was easy to come by in the company of his girlfriend and latest 'discovery', actress Jyll Masters. She'd been staying with him on and off for the past few months. As she was a working actress, she wasn't exactly living with him, but didn't seem shy about taking advantage of the comforts his mansion provided. And he likewise didn't mind taking advantage of the comforts she provided with that tight twenty-three-year-old body of hers.

Milton's stomach began to rumble, and he had the overwhelming urge to eat something soon. Despite feeling great the past week, something had happened in the wake of his return from San Diego Comic-Con. He was not quite feeling himself and suspected he'd caught a cold from that sweating mass of nerds.

Which was why he was so determined to get drunk that day—better to not notice you're sick than to feel the worst of it. Or at least that's how he preferred it. But hunger was driving him crazy at the moment and he couldn't wait any longer for something to eat, so he called out for his butler Juan.

But Juan did not answer.

Not after the first time, nor the second, not even the third when Milton found himself screaming so loud his neighbors were probably quaking in fear. Just the way he liked them to be. Nothing worse than neighbors wanting to get up in your business. *Keep them afraid and they'll never cross you.* He'd applied that same philosophy to his time in Hollywood, even if his brother didn't fully agree with his tactics. Though he would eventually fall in line.

"Juan! Where the fuck are you?!" His patience had run dry, just like his mouth was starting to. He didn't just want food, he wanted another cocktail, neither of which was possible if his damn butler couldn't do his job properly. As he slid his overweight body off the lounge chair, the swim trunks he was wearing were pushed up his legs a bit and exposed the two spots on his inner right thigh. He'd almost forgotten about the spots that had appeared a few weeks back. At the time, he assumed they were pimples. But they were still there, and he tried to make a mental note to set up an appointment with his dermatologist.

If he could actually remember that note when he was sober.

Scooping up his robe, Milton draped it over his hefty frame and then slid on his slippers before making way to the door of his basement. He kept a fully-stocked bar down there, out of the sun and easy to access while he worked outside—as he was prone to do when the weather was nice.

Opening the door, Milton's nose was immediately assaulted by the scent of rum and blood. The bottle had shattered on the ground, spilling its contents all over the sandalwood floor behind the bar and working its way toward the door. But the blood seemed to have come from Juan, whose legs were suspiciously sticking out from behind the bar. They were still, and his butler was clearly unconscious. But what had caused the accident? Had Juan slipped or had a stroke? He didn't know and didn't much care, except for the fact that he had become exceedingly reliant on the man to do almost everything for him. *And* he was being paid quite well for the work.

Well, if the man needed medical attention, that was one thing Milton would *not* be paying for. The position did not come with health coverage.

Moving around the bar, Milton approached Juan cautiously to check for a pulse. He almost expected some kind of horror film scare like something his brother would have produced. Juan leaping up to attack, maybe in zombie form. But as his fingers reached Juan's neck, he felt a pulse immediately. It was normal and calm. Juan was fine apart from collapsing due to some unknown means.

Milton was in the process of thinking how stupid the whole scene looked when the world around him began to spin, like he was back in one of those human gyroscope rides he tried once in college. Except as the world stopped spinning, he saw his headless body several feet from him, collapsed on top of Juan, and a dark figure hovering above it. Then everything went dark . . . forever.

10

The dead body of Milton Humphreys had been discovered behind his bar at 6:33 p.m. by his butler, Juan Sánchez.

It was several feet from his severed head.

Detective Liz Gutiérrez didn't like the case from the get-go. Something felt off about it. The butler had apparently been knocked unconscious sometime prior from a blow to the head. The killer then must have snuck up on Milton as he was checking on the butler—or so she assumed. The estimated time of death was around an hour earlier, sometime between 5 p.m. and 5:30 p.m. The butler was helpful in this regard due to his recollection that he'd checked the time shortly before preparing Mr. Humphreys another mai tai.

Liz confirmed with Juan, "So the last time you saw Mr. Humphreys alive was prior to 5 p.m.?"

"Yes, I had checked the time just before preparing his next drink. Mr. Humphreys can drink too much sometimes, and with dinner soon approaching, I knew that this would have to be his last one. I would have told him as much when I served it to him, but well, I don't remember anything after starting to mix the drink."

"So you never got a good look at the killer?"

"I never saw them, which is surprising, as the bar faces the door. They must have been hiding somewhere in the room and I guess, being focused on the job at hand . . ." He shrugged.

"Any idea who might have done this? Anyone who wanted Mr. Humphreys dead?"

Juan shook his head. "No, everyone loved Mr. Humphreys." *Everyone you know, maybe.* It was possible the butler was still a little out of it and not thinking clearly enough to know for sure, but Liz figured if he really knew much about Humphreys' life outside of his home, it wouldn't be too hard to remember. From what she'd heard, Humphreys had something of a reputation in Hollywood, not just throwing his weight around to get what he wanted, but several other things that turned her stomach.

As a detective who'd been on the force for over a decade, she'd seen plenty of stuff she wished she never knew about with these Hollywood types. What was worse was when they could buy someone's silence. She'd heard things, but thankfully hadn't had to deal with them herself—nor had her late husband, Óscar. He was a cop like her, righteous and determined to be that shining star on the force. It worked up until it got him killed in the line of duty a little over a year ago. That still hurt to think about. She wished she had been there to back him up, but she was his wife, not his partner. And his partner had died along with him. When it came to being a cop in the LAPD, half of what kept you alive was instinct and experience—the other half was luck. Everyone's luck could run out sooner or later. Some people seemed determined to test that luck at every opportunity.

Liz's partner was one of those people.

Detective Chuck Lawson was exactly the kind of cop she wished she wasn't saddled with. He always sought out the worst cases, the ones with the highest profile and most risk involved. He was a thrill seeker who wasn't shy about letting the department know of his extracurricular activities. He was one of those guys you'd see on a motorcycle on the freeway racing between the cars stuck in gridlock. She'd seen plenty of those people scraped off the pavement before. Some dark part of her hoped one day she'd find Lawson in a bloody mess on the road. It would be better than both of them ending up that way due to a mistake he made in the line of duty.

Since the death of her husband, Liz had tried to stay away from as much danger as she could within the confines of her job, while working as hard as possible to get promoted. Her hope was to one day hit captain or higher. Anything that would pay more and keep her off the streets. She needed to stay safe and stay alive, if for no other reason than for her son.

Freddy was a good kid—shy, but with so much love to give. She always told him he wore his heart on his sleeve because for those he shared his emotions with, he was an open book. This made him more susceptible to being hurt, which is why she supposed he'd become more introverted with each passing year. There were only a few people he'd ever opened up to completely. Three were family—his mother, his late father, and his Uncle Hector, who Liz hadn't really seen since her husband's death. It wasn't that she was avoiding him, but they had never gotten along great. It didn't help that Hector had never reached out in those trying times after his brother died. The only person outside of his family that Freddy had opened up to was his babysitter.

Lydia Sinclair came from a good family in a nice neighborhood in Santa Monica. It seemed part of her upbringing was her parents' insistence on paying her own way instead of the handouts most of her friends got at that age. Liz admired that about Lydia, that she had no qualms about working through high school. It was at times like these that she wished she could travel back in time to Lydia's age, when things were much simpler. Now there were too many things to worry about, bringing in money was only one of them. Staring down at the decapitated body of Milton Humphreys, she thought death in its own way was the ultimate release from all the burdens of this mortal coil. But Liz was never the type to give up easily.

"Gutiérrez, they find the murder weapon yet?" Lawson asked from behind her.

"No sign of it yet." Liz answered without turning away from the body. "I doubt the killer was sloppy enough to leave it behind. This looks like a professional hit."

"How many professionals chop off people's heads?"

"None that I've seen in LA."

"You thinking this might have been an out-of-town job?"

Turning to Lawson, she said, "I don't know. We need to look into Humphreys' recent business, anything he might have been involved in that could have led to a hit being placed on him."

"You think he owed money to someone? I'd have thought a big shot like him could have paid off anybody."

"We don't know anything yet, Lawson. Don't make assumptions till you have all the facts. I've seen guys living in greater luxury than Humphreys who were up to their ears in debt. The fancy house, clothes, cars, women. Sometimes it's all a façade."

"No way. This guy was producing pictures crossing a billion dollars. I don't buy it."

"Well, I'm open to other ideas."

"Jealous lover, maybe? Who was this guy seeing?"

"According to Mr. Sanchez, Humphreys was seeing actress Jyll Masters. But things were good between them. No fights at his home, or anything Sanchez was aware of at least."

"Holy shit, that's right! I saw 'em in the tabloids."

"You read that trash?"

"Well, I wouldn't say *read*. Some of it is hard to miss on the web. I see ads and shit on my phone all the time."

"Whatever. Let's talk to the girlfriend, see what she knows, then talk to his brother. They produce films together, so any business that might have gone sideways he should know about. We'll also have to get a look at his finances and see if anything is amiss there."

Lawson took a long look at the body once more. "Just don't know what kind of financial trouble leads somebody to chop your head off."

"That's why we check every possibility, Lawson. Something will turn up. Something always does."

11

When Dan arrived home that evening, Chris spilled the details about his new job. It was clear Dan was a little jealous—or maybe he just wanted the chance to meet Marie, but Chris knew that friendly introductions like that could wait until he was comfortable requesting them.

For the rest of the night, Chris was a bit of a mess. His nerves had him on edge, turning his digestive tract into a war zone. The only thing he could do to alleviate this stress was to smoke a little weed. Unfortunately, all that did was make him even more nervous. Popping one of his favorite albums onto his turntable, he lied back on his bed and listened to A Tribe Called Quest's *The Low End Theory*. It helped calm his nerves as his mind escaped into those soothing jazz hip-hop sounds.

Chris woke the next morning in shock.

Having fallen asleep to his music the previous night, he'd forgotten to set his alarm and saw his PaRappa the Rapper clock reading 7:06 a.m. He thanked God he was a naturally early riser. Knowing with LA traffic there was no way he'd make it to the Hollywood Hills from El Segundo in thirty minutes, he had to skip the shower. Throwing on a clean pair of clothes, he grabbed his bag of bathroom supplies and other essentials that he at least had the forethought to pack the previous night. Then he headed out the door and toward his new normal.

The drive to Marie's house was the typical LA nightmare he'd experienced before. Thankfully, he wouldn't have to make this commute every morning, but for today, it made him extra nervous the whole way. Despite what his phone was telling him, he was sure he was going to be late. Yet when he pulled off the 101, he was amazed at how light things had gotten. It was like driving through a ghost town. Perhaps this was what it was like when you had enough money to afford the luxury of sleeping in. Or perhaps all these people were already at their high-paying jobs? He didn't care; he was just thankful that he managed to arrive at the gate to Marie's home a good five minutes early.

When he hit the buzzer, an elderly yet distinguished voice called out, seemingly knowing who he was already. Chris suspected there was a camera somewhere that was aimed directly at him, but he couldn't spot the thing. "Welcome, Mr. Hart. Please pull up to the front, I'll let Miss LeBeau know you're here."

The gate slowly creaked open on its automated hinges, allowing his passage up the winding driveway to the mansion. At least, he assumed it was a mansion. It was certainly the biggest home he'd ever seen, but not quite the sort of thing seen in the movies. Still, the structure stretched over a significant chunk of property and had a spectacular view of the valley. He suspected there might even be a pool around the back. But that would have to wait—if he ever had the opportunity to use it.

Instead, Chris was focused on making a good first impression—if that was even possible, having not taken a shower. Thankfully, he at least had one the previous evening. He did a quick sniff of his pits to make sure he smelled decent, and was satisfied by the result. Then he stepped out of his car and approached the front doors toward an unknown future.

One of the doors was opened by an elderly man who seemed all business and called Chris "Mr. Hart." He reminded Chris a bit of Alfred from *Batman*, or maybe just any stereotype of the English butler. He was definitely English, about as proper English as you could get in his perfectly pressed uniform complete with white gloves. One of those gloves waved Chris inside and he did as the man instructed.

Waiting in the main foyer, Chris took in the sights before him. He was standing on a perfectly polished white marble floor that led to two lavishly decorated staircases with brass handrails. They twisted around the sides of the room toward the upper floor—which he assumed was likely the third floor since the house was on a hill. Everything was shockingly pristine white, with only the brass to break up the monotony.

The butler excused himself from the foyer by saying, "Miss LeBeau will be with you shortly. If you need anything, my name is Thomas."

Chris thought of asking how the man might hear him in another room, but before he could, Thomas seemed to glide out of sight as if he was on a pair of roller skates. And then Chris was alone, feeling awkward as he waited for his new boss.

But he didn't have to wait long.

The first thing he heard was the clack of heels against the steps leading down toward him. Looking up, he saw Marie, decked out in a luxurious ruby red dress accompanied by a matching lipstick. Her hair was done up in a way that made him wonder if she had a live-in stylist. The whole look was to die for, and all he could think was that she must have had some fancy event to attend that morning. It couldn't be merely his presence that would require such an effort. Yet, as he later learned, she simply liked to dress up when she was expecting guests.

As she approached the bottom of the stairs, Marie smiled. "Chris. So glad to see you made it on time. We said 8 a.m., correct?" Checking her watch—which resembled jewelry more than a functioning clock—she said, "I've got one minute past."

Chris nodded. "I always try to be on time."

"That's good to know. If I'm being honest, I didn't expect you to be on time, but it tells me something about you at least."

"What's that?"

"That you're dependable. Meaning I can trust you to do your job."

"Speaking of that. You didn't exactly go over everything I'd be doing."

"Well, I thought it was fairly obvious, you'll be in charge of my safety, working alongside my security team."

"And what do they think of working with someone who has no experience in security?"

Shrugging, Marie said, "I don't care what they think. They're not paid to give me their opinions, they're paid to keep me safe. I'm adding one more body to help, so they shouldn't have any objections to that. If they do, they can take it up with me. Satisfied?"

Chris couldn't disagree with that. So he simply nodded.

"Good. Now, you want a bit more detail about what you'll be doing? You'll be by my side every hour of the day, from dawn till dusk. Do you have a problem with this?"

A shudder seemed to pass through Chris' body at the idea of spending all day, every day, with someone like Marie. If he could have been her slave, he'd probably have said yes. So he really didn't care what she requested of him. "No."

"Good. Now aside from staying by my side, you'll naturally need to keep an eye out for anyone who might be meaning to do me harm. I know you can handle yourself, but have you ever fired a gun?"

He had, a few times at the shooting range run by his friend's dad. But he'd hardly call himself an expert, so he honestly answered, "Yes, but I wouldn't expect myself to be able to hit a still target, let alone a moving one. If that's something you need from me, I suggest you look to the other guys on your security detail."

Marie seemed satisfied with this answer and said, "Good. That is what they're there for. But none of them are as quick as you and if someone is at my throat with a knife, I expect you to be able to stop them. Do you have a problem with this?"

"No."

"Good, then I think we've got that settled. If there's anything else I need of you while you're in my employ I will let you know. Now I must say, this isn't some kind of binding contract you've entered into here. If you feel uncomfortable at any time you may leave, but I really hope you don't."

When she finished that last sentence, the woman who seemed all business a moment ago instantly melted away, and he was staring back at the vulnerable woman he'd spoken to on that beach in San Diego. The same woman he'd so quickly fallen for. In that moment, he was unsure what he should do next—he wanted to kiss her, to hold her, to tell her she had nothing to worry about ever again. Instead, he simply said, "You can count on me." It sounded stupid saying it out loud, and he wished he'd come up with something a little better. But it seemed to be acceptable to Marie.

"I'm sure I can." Smiling back at him, she turned and led him up the stairs to the top floor. "I suppose I should give you the tour, but I do have things to do today, so to start, we'll get you settled in."

At the top of the stairs, Marie moved down the hall, past a collection of paintings and statues that looked like they were worth a fortune. Perhaps she could afford it all, or perhaps she had some very good connections. He wasn't one to judge or question her lifestyle at this point. When she reached the double doors at the end, she opened them up and led Chris into the most extravagant bedroom he'd ever seen, with even more expensive art and a lavish design that would make an oil baron blush. Extravagant didn't even begin to cover it. It was unlike anything Chris could have expected.

Leading Chris over to the walk-in closet, Marie said, "You can set your things in the corner." She then began to rummage through the various outfits hanging around the closet. Chris thought it was a little odd she hadn't taken him to his room, so he asked, "I thought you were going to start by showing me my room."

Turning back, Marie laughed in disbelief. "I thought I was clear; you'll be by my side at all hours. That includes in my bedroom at night. Or do you expect to make it to my room before the killer strikes?" He couldn't argue with that logic, only wonder when exactly he was supposed to sleep if she wanted him watching her at all hours of the night. As if she was reading his mind, she said, "Don't worry, I don't expect you to turn into an insomniac. You'll sleep by my side; I have motion sensors in my room. They won't miss anything."

Chris was certainly caught off guard by this news. So he asked for clarification. "By your side, you mean . . . *in your bed?*"

Marie raised an eyebrow and said, "Surprised by this? Don't worry, I'm sure you can remain a gentleman and keep your hands to yourself."

He knew that he could, but worried more about his tendency to roll excessively in his sleep. Waking Marie up with an erection that accidently happened to bump into her in the night was akin to his worst nightmare. Yet he could never reveal this embarrassing thought to her and just mumbled, "Of course."

"Good, now let's find you something to wear while we go out to the tailor."

An actual tailor, making a suit for him. He could hardly believe it. He'd never even been able to afford a decent suit, let alone something tailor-made to fit him. The whole experience so far had been surreal, and he could only imagine at that point it would continue to be so for the foreseeable future.

Just like Chris imagined, the rest of the day was like he was wandering through a very elaborate, very detailed dream. It was a life he always thought was only in the movies, nothing any normal person could ever achieve. And yet with every shop they hit on Rodeo Drive, he witnessed those around him waiting on him hand and foot. All at the command of his new boss, Marie LeBeau. She needed only snap her fingers for the employees to come running like well-trained dogs.

When Chris emerged from his dream several hours later, he was carrying multiple large shopping bags filled to the brim with shirts, slacks, shoes, and even underwear—all the highest-class merchandise money could buy. His tailored suit he'd have to wait for, but Marie bought him two others—backups, she called them. They wouldn't offer the same perfect cut of his tailored one, but they'd get the job done. She even did Chris the courtesy of purchasing him a new Rolex from their very own store. He wasn't aware Rolex had stores. But he supposed when enough of the super-rich are around, they can afford to have a specific retail location.

Flying high on cloud nine, Chris rode home with Marie in the back of her Rolls Royce. If he was to guess the previous day, he assumed he'd be driving her, or she'd be driving her BMW again. Yet now he'd seen her garage of cars, with at least a half-dozen high-priced automobiles, shiny, chrome, and clean as if they were just off the lot. He had to admit the gearhead in him was jealous, but if he played his cards right, maybe she'd let him drive one someday. For now, he had to settle for her driver—who also happened to be her butler, Thomas—escorting them around.

In their talking over the course of the afternoon, Marie didn't mince words about her expectations of him and his salary. She would pay him $100,000 a year for as long as he'd stick around. It was more money than he could ever dream of making in his normal life. But was he really worth it? He supposed the answer to that would arrive the next time that killer made an attempt on Marie's life. If they ever did again.

12

Jyll Masters was filming an episode of her hit series *You Go, Girl!* when she got the news about Milton Humphreys' murder. From what Liz had heard from the woman's agent, she was beside herself and production had shut down early. The detectives arranged to meet Jyll back at her home in Sherman Oaks, but had to pick up some food on the way since Lawson started complaining. The guy ate more than anyone Liz knew— even her son Freddy who was still a growing boy. Lawson not only shoveled down larger quantities of food than a man of his frame could be expected to, but he was prone to getting hangry if he went too long without sustenance. Still, it could have been worse; they were at least close to an In-N-Out Burger, and even Liz couldn't say no to that.

So after picking up their burgers and fries—and a chocolate shake for Lawson—they found their way to Jyll Masters' home. It was a very nice-looking house, nothing like Humphreys' mansion, but what one expected a fresh star and lead of a popular television show to afford. When Jyll opened the door, her eyes looked puffy like she'd been crying—and that wouldn't be a surprise to anyone. She welcomed them in, even though her general attitude didn't make them feel welcome.

Liz was used to that.

Part of the job was going where you usually weren't wanted.

If anyone was ever gracious, it was because they had personally called the police there. Detectives didn't have that luxury, but Jyll did her best to seem a good host and offered them fresh coffee. Somehow Lawson hadn't hit his limit after two burgers, Animal Style fries, and a shake. Liz refrained from any, since she found caffeine made her jittery on the job. She only had it when she *really* needed it. Now was not one of those times. What she needed at that moment was her wits, not to be bouncing off the walls.

Once Jyll was comfortable, Liz began to ask the questions she'd jotted down in preparation. "Miss Masters, you—"

"You can call me Jyll," she said as she began to pet the cat who'd just pounced up on her lap from the ground. Liz preferred to keep things formal, but before she could even respond, Lawson decided to jump in.

"Jyll, I just had to tell you how much I love *You Go, Girl!* I've been telling all my friends to check it out."

Jyll seemed surprised by this. "Most of my fans are female. I didn't think a guy like you would be into a show like that."

Lawson shrugged, "Hey, good writing is good writing and funny is funny, am I right?"

This got a smile out of Jyll and she said, "Yeah, I guess you are."

Liz thought this little moment of levity might help ease her worries, but as she knew from experience, the second she went back to business, Jyll would be reminded of why they were really there. "Jyll, can you tell us how long you were dating Milton Humphreys?"

Like she suspected, Jyll snapped back into the same mode she'd been in when they arrived. She also seemed to have some kind of itch irritating her inner thigh. Liz wouldn't be surprised if she caught something from Humphreys. "Well, we'd been seeing each other for about six months, I think."

"He helped you land your role on *You Go, Girl!*, right?" Lawson asked.

Jyll nodded. Liz wouldn't pry further, but knowing who Humphreys was, she wouldn't be surprised if Jyll had to do something for him to help her land that role. There always seemed to be some young fresh discovery of his every few years; they'd get all the big roles for a while and then he'd move onto something younger. She wondered if Jyll knew the man's *real* history. It was no big secret, just one of those things that didn't seem to be talked openly about. Liz didn't even follow Hollywood that closely, but she'd have to have been blind to miss it.

"So would you say things had been good with you two up until now?" Liz asked.

Jyll nodded. "I mean, we'd fight every now and then, but for the most part things were good."

"Fight about what, exactly?"

"Just stupid stuff, you know." She did, but had to ask anyway.

"He ever get physical with you?"

Jyll laughed at this. "No way. Milton loved to shout, but he couldn't hurt a fly. All that bravado was a smoke screen. Anyone who was ever really close to him could see that. Ask Carlton if you don't believe me."

Carlton was Milton's brother, as well as his producing partner and closest confidant. He would have to be their next stop—unless they heard back from the medical examiner first. She wished he could find something helpful on the corpse, but wasn't holding out hope. They didn't find any real evidence at the scene. The killer seemed very prepared, in and out like the wind.

"We plan to follow up with Mr. Humphreys later, but we're just trying to understand if Milton was the kind of man who might have gotten in an altercation or angered someone who might have wanted to hurt him back."

"And you think *I* might have done this?"

"Frankly, no. But I have to look at this from every angle. You're our first stop, so hopefully you can help us narrow the search."

"I wish there was more I could tell you, but Milton's business was just that . . . *his* business. He never involved me, and I never wanted to be involved. So if something happened there, Carlton would know better than me. Better than anyone else, to be honest. Our relationship wasn't that far along. As you can see, I'm still living here. Nothing I ever saw when I was with him would lead me to believe anyone wanted to kill him, but you never know in this business. People make enemies all the time. Just never thought he'd end up dead over it."

"So you weren't living with him. Can you tell us the last time you saw him, then?"

"Yesterday, I knew he wasn't feeling well after getting back from Comic-Con, so I brought him lunch."

"He was sick? Sick how? Like a cold or—"

"I think it might have been a stomach bug. He didn't have much of an appetite, basically just pecked at the meal I prepared, and it wasn't anything too fancy. Meatloaf and mashed potatoes— his favorite. He looked weak too. Whoever it was that killed him, I doubt he would have fought back. Was it quick, at least? Can you tell me that?"

"Yes. From the look of things, they caught him from behind. I'd rather not get into details, but I don't think he felt any pain."

Jyll nodded and seemed to be on the verge of tears. There were still a few more questions, but Liz decided to save them for Milton's brother, Carlton. There just wasn't much point to grill Jyll any further. Not until they had a better reason to. The woman needed some time to grieve. So Liz let Lawson finish his coffee and fanboy a bit more before they finally left. Then it was on to see if they could meet with Carlton Humphreys. He was apparently still working that day. No rest for the wicked, it seemed.

Before they could get there, though, she got a call from the medical examiner, Hank Morris, about the body. It seemed there was something strange about it. *So* strange in fact, that Hank didn't want to discuss it over the phone. He said she wouldn't have believed him if he did. So, the two detectives turned around and made their way over to the morgue. Liz had no idea what could have been more surprising than a decapitated movie producer. But as a Los Angeles police officer, she always tried to keep an open mind.

13

Hank was waiting for them when the two detectives arrived. This was unusual for him, as he usually felt dealing with the police was nothing more than a distraction. But there was something he'd found that day which must have truly disturbed him because he looked paler than normal and a bit jittery. Though she supposed Hank could have been drinking too much coffee in the wake of his discovery—he always seemed to have a fresh pot brewing when they arrived.

"Detectives, if you could follow me."

"You wanna tell us what you found, Hank?" Lawson asked.

"Not here. Let me show you the body first." Liz could see Lawson's curiosity was as piqued as her own, so they had no choice but to do as instructed.

After following him to where the body was covered by a sheet on the autopsy table, Hank lifted it back to reveal Humphreys' corpse. "You notice anything odd?"

Liz moved around the table, looking for anything that stood out from what she'd seen earlier. Lawson decided to add his two cents first. "His head is missing. I'd call that odd."

Hank didn't look amused. "I'd prefer if you could keep the smartass comments in check, Chuck. I'm being serious here."

Liz stopped and shrugged, having noticed nothing new. "Can you enlighten us?"

Moving closer to the body, Hank spread the legs a few extra inches and pointed to an area on Humphrey's inner thigh were two reddish spots resided. At first glance they looked like pimples, but it was odd to have two so close together.

"What is that? An STD?" Lawson mused.

"I thought so at first, but closer inspection revealed them to be puncture wounds that haven't fully healed."

"Puncture? Like a bite?" Liz asked.

Lawson laughed. "So his girlfriend got a little kinky and it got infected, big deal. It had nothing to do with his cause of death."

"Wait, we don't know that," Liz said. "Remember, Jyll mentioned he'd been sick. Maybe the killer did something in advance to weaken him."

"What? Like poison? I guess it kinda looks like a snakebite."

Hank stepped in and added, "I thought it could have been poison too, only when I ran his blood, I couldn't believe what I saw. Not only was there no evidence of poison, and no drugs in his system other than alcohol, but the results made no sense."

Liz narrowed her eyes. "What do you mean?"

"I mean the way his blood looked, it was like he wasn't . . . *human*. Biconvex red blood cells, binucleated PMNs . . . the panel I ran had numbers way out of the normal range for everything."

Lawson sighed, "Can you translate that for us?"

"In layman's terms, no normal human could have had results like that."

"You trying to say Humphreys wasn't human?"

"That's *exactly* what I'm saying."

This got Lawson to laugh. "That's a good one, Hank. You want to tell us what you *really* found now?"

"I'm being serious here, Lawson. I don't joke about my work. I even called up his doctor to check the results of his last physical. It was a little over a week ago, before his birthday. Everything was as it should be. The man had an excess of fat, high cholesterol, and high blood pressure . . . but nothing like this. You can see why I didn't say anything over the phone. I knew you wouldn't believe me, just like I know you don't right now. But I'm telling you that unless all my equipment is broken, as well as my own two eyes, then something fucked-up is going on here. No way does a man go into his doctor a week ago looking fine and then show up on my table as some kind of freak of nature."

Liz didn't understand any of this, but she was trying to, opening that door in her mind usually reserved for the fantastical movies her son was so fond of. "Say we want to entertain any of this. You're trying to say Milton was what? Swapped out by an alien in disguise or something?"

Hank shook his head. "I don't know. He certainly looks human, not like I found something hidden under fake skin or a little guy piloting the inside of his body. All his organs appear normal. But something is *very* wrong with his blood."

The thought turned Liz's stomach, making that burger from earlier suddenly not sit too well with her. She wanted to take a seat, better yet she wanted to go home, back to somewhere safe and normal and far from whatever can of worms they had potentially opened with this case. Her years on the force had prepared her for anything she thought LA could throw at her, but not this. What did it mean? Were there more people out there like Humphreys? Were they a threat? Who had killed him, and why? These thoughts were enough to drive her crazy. She still had no answers, but hoped that somehow Carlton Humphreys might have something for her. At the very least, he'd better be prepared to give them a blood sample.

14

Detective Gutiérrez and her partner had managed to catch Carlton Humphreys in his office at the end of his workday. Carlton had a lot of calls to make that day in the wake of his brother's death. He wasn't even sure he'd be able to meet the detectives, but as they stressed the urgency and importance of whatever information he could provide to the case, he agreed to meet them half an hour before he left for home.

They were let into the office by a very attractive female assistant, that if Liz had to guess, had been hired by Milton. Carlton wasn't known to be getting in as much trouble as his brother with the opposite sex, but then again, Liz had been at her job long enough to know that nothing would surprise her—especially what the quiet ones got up to when nobody was watching.

"Please have a seat," Carlton said as he motioned to the two comfy-looking chairs in front of his desk. Liz and Lawson sat down and she took a moment to size up Carlton Humphreys. He had kind eyes, something that made her suddenly feel sympathy for the loss of his brother. She only knew Milton by reputation, but from his media appearances, he didn't ever look happy. Most of the time he appeared to be scowling, and if there was any love in him, she had to guess it was for his only brother. That love, at the very least, seemed to flow one way from the puffiness of

Carlton's face. He'd been crying that day, clearly not too long before they arrived and had attempted to erase the evidence. She thought of saying something comforting in that moment, perhaps if for no other reason than to make their questions go down a little easier. But before she could, Lawson flew off half-cocked, as he was prone to do.

"So you and your brother made a lot of big films together?" He was staring at the various award-winning film posters that adorned the walls of the office.

"Five Oscar winners, three for best picture."

"That's a pretty good track record by my standards. I'm not the biggest cinephile out there, but I've seen all these. I'd have given them awards too."

Carlton nodded. "Thank you." Liz thought Lawson's attempt at small talk was going to backfire, but for once, she was surprised that it seemed to lift Carlton's spirits a bit. "We were certainly proud of them. Good to know people still appreciate them."

"Yeah. I'm sorry for your loss . . . we both are," Lawson said, pointing at Liz. She nodded, not knowing what else to do in that moment. She could see that this didn't make it any easier on Carlton and he smiled in appreciation, but then seemed to revert back to business.

"I assume you have some questions for me? About my brother?"

"Yes," Liz said, seizing her opportunity to enter the conversation. "You've been here all day, I assume?"

"That's correct."

"And your brother was working from home yesterday?"

Carlton nodded. "He wasn't feeling well after getting back from Comic-Con."

"That's what his girlfriend Jyll had told us as well. What was he out promoting in San Diego?" Lawson asked, clearly interested for personal reasons.

"*Black Berenice.* There was a panel and an advanced screening for the fans."

"Oh yeah, that looked pretty cool from the trailer," Lawson said, "Based off a comic book, right?"

"Yeah, the graphic novel is pretty popular. We're expecting an opening weekend gross of over a hundred million."

Lawson whistled at this. "That's like Marvel money."

Carlton nodded, but Liz could see that talking about the film's prospects wasn't lifting his spirits much. "Projections are strong so far. We'll see, though. International is a whole different matter."

Steering things back to the matter at hand, Liz asked, "So you didn't go with Milton? To Comic-Con?"

"I had other things to take care of here. The premiere is next Tuesday, so a lot of prep work on my end."

"Did you see your brother when he got back at all?"

"No, I talked with him on the phone yesterday morning, but that was it. Last time I saw him was Thursday. A day before he left."

"Did he seem nervous or scared of anything at the time?"

Carlton appeared confused by this and asked, "What do you mean?"

"Well, we have a theory that your brother's death might have been from something he was involved in."

"Like illegal activities?" Carlton seemed wounded by the notion that his brother might have been crooked, so Liz attempted to back off a bit.

"I don't want you to get the wrong idea, Mr. Humphreys. We just want to bring your brother's killer to justice, as I'm sure you do. It's not our job to assume anything, but we have to look at these matters from every angle, until we have all the facts. If there's anything you can tell us about your brother's recent business dealings, we'd really appreciate it. Anything that could be relevant."

Carlton took a deep breath before exhaling. "I wish I had some idea who might have killed him or why, but Milton made enemies easily. He was also good at turning enemies into friends when it was necessary. The way that guy could work people—work a room even—it always blew me away. I was better at the creative side of things, but him? *He* was the real brains behind everything. Our company never would have gotten off the ground without him taking charge the way he always did."

"You said he sometimes made enemies. Any he made lately that come to mind?"

"None that I can think of. But we weren't always together when we did business. Like I mentioned with that Comic-Con thing."

"Any other recent business? A new film he was involved in?"

"Well, a few weeks ago Milton briefly flew out to Japan with Gareth Morello. They were location scouting for his new film, *The Righteous Dragons.*"

Lawson seemed to perk up at this news. "I read about that in *Variety.* Supposed to be a yakuza film, right?"

Carlton nodded. "That's right, but it's not like they went over there to interact with the mob or something, if that's what you're thinking."

"It could be possible, though?" Liz asked. "I mean, if he was scouting some seedy areas?"

Carlton shrugged. "I don't know. I mean, you'd have to ask Gareth. I was still working here."

"Can you put us in touch with Mr. Morello?"

"Of course, anything you need. Did you have any other questions?"

Liz had plenty of queries after their talk with Hank Morris, but she couldn't come out and say anything directly without Carlton laughing them out of his office. She was thankful Lawson hadn't done anything embarrassing either, so she tried to phrase her next question carefully. "Was there anything else *off* about your brother the past week?"

"I don't follow," Carlton said looking rather confused.

Liz could feel Lawson's eyes on her. Clearly, he was concerned with where her questions were leading, but he stayed silent. "Well, like I mentioned before he could have been nervous about something. Just anything that maybe was out of the norm for him. Someone could have threatened his life prior to his murder. Maybe he was more irritable than normal?"

Carlton gave this some thought for a moment, then he said, "You know, it had been a little strange. His girlfriend, Jyll Masters, she'd taken him to this birthday retreat for several days out in Palm Springs right before Comic-Con. Some kind of spiritual thing she was into. I don't know the details, but he seemed better after. Not like he wasn't okay normally, but he could be surly at times and this was the healthiest he'd ever looked, his attitude was better than normal too.

"After he got back from Comic-Con, he must have caught something. He called me yesterday to say he was going to work from home because he wasn't feeling too well. Milton could pull that stunt on occasion just as an excuse to work from home. I don't fault him for it. I like coming into the office and it's important one of us is present here for anyone important who shows up, but yeah, I don't think he was faking it this time. He sounded tired, like he hadn't been getting enough sleep. Was hoping he'd recover soon, but I guess he never got the chance." Carlton seemed to drift off in that moment and Liz thought he might start to cry, but he then composed himself enough to go on. "Anyway, that's all I can say about him in the past week."

Liz wasn't sure what to make of any of that new information. Somebody getting sick after a major gathering like San Diego Comic-Con was probably pretty common. His mental state prior to that also made sense if he had cleared out some of the cobwebs at that retreat. But none of it helped them in figuring out why the man had died a medical mystery. She didn't know if that body in the morgue was truly Carlton's brother, but all signs pointed to yes apart from his extremely abnormal bloodwork. For the moment, she'd have to just keep that information in her back pocket. Part of being a detective was trying not to read into things too much—not until all the cards were on the table. And her deck was missing far too many cards to come any kind of conclusion.

After Liz finished her last few questions about Milton's recent activities, Lawson decided to ask a few more movie-related questions and Carlton indulged him, even offering to let him attend the *Black Berenice* premiere. Lawson just about leaped at this opportunity. He might have said he wasn't a cinephile, but the man had a hard time containing his inner geek amongst one of the Hollywood elite. Unfortunately for Lawson, Liz politely turned down the offer for the both of them, explaining that it could be considered as a bribe and it wasn't worth jeopardizing the investigation.

When they left the Humphreys Brothers' offices, Liz went over their list of people they still needed to interview. There were currently no real suspects—which bothered her more than anything—but at least they had some names. There was the director Gareth Morello, who'd traveled to Japan with Humphreys, then the actress Marie LeBeau, who was producing *Black Berenice* alongside the brothers. Finally, there was still Jyll Masters, who it seemed had to know more than she was letting on. They didn't have any real reason to believe this other than the fact she was closest to Milton and if he had gone through some change, or possession, or whatever caused his funky blood, she had to know something beyond the fact that he was sick. They might even have reason to believe her blood might be weird like that of her boyfriend. *Especially* if it was due to some kind of contagion he picked up. The only question was why she didn't appear sick like him.

"Shit, we never asked for his blood," Lawson said as he slapped his leg in the car.

Liz shook her head and said, "There was no need. I didn't want to alert him what we found with his brother unless he gave me reason to believe he had recent contact with him or knew something, but you heard what he said—Milton got sick after getting back from Comic-Con. He hadn't had any contact with his brother since. If we're going to go around asking for anyone's blood who was close to him, we're better off asking his butler or the girlfriend."

"So you really think he didn't know anything about the blood? Or why his brother was murdered?"

"I don't know, honestly. But I didn't get that impression. You were there too, what'd you think?"

Lawson shrugged. "He seemed like a nice guy. I know his brother had a bad reputation, but Carlton seemed cool."

"Not how you feel about him as a person, Lawson. As a fucking *suspect*."

Shaking his head, Lawson said, "No way. Could tell he loved his brother."

"That's the impression I got too. Just wish we had a bit more to go on."

"So let's pay a visit to Morello. I mean, Milton's head was cut off, that could have been yakuza-related, right? All those kung fu fuckers have swords and shit."

Lawson didn't always have the brightest observations, but

she couldn't fault him on this one. A sword was not out of the question. It didn't help at all to explain Milton's strange blood, but him getting mixed up in something with the yakuza was starting to feel like their best bet for solving this case. Still, Liz always took things one step at a time. So, the next step would be to visit Morello and see what he had to say.

15

Liz counted her lucky stars that Gareth Morello could see them that evening. Usually with these Hollywood types you had to go through their agents just to get a hold of them, then things could get drawn out from there. Maybe they were busy, maybe they were out of town for work. Who knew what could get in the way of a case? But thankfully, Carlton Humphreys had given them Morello's personal number and the guy just happened to pick up when Liz called. He was polishing his script for *The Righteous Dragons*—which he apparently liked to do up until the cameras rolled on each of his films.

Morello was surprised they thought he could provide any helpful information on Milton Humphreys' death, which Liz took as a bad sign. This typically meant either the guy had something to do with the death, or he really knew nothing helpful and their trip would be a waste of time. Now, with the former, you'd think Liz would consider it a good thing; however, trying to interview someone when you know they're lying is typically a pain in the ass. There is this little dance you have to do, in an attempt to outmaneuver the person who clearly thinks they're smarter than the police, and any detective can tell you it rarely works in their favor. Unless they have a warrant to search the suspect's home, or can get them down to the station for a proper interrogation, it almost never leads anywhere and only serves to sour the investigation.

After getting comfortable in Morello's home, where he served the two detectives some espresso, their suspect prepped himself for the inevitable questions. If Liz didn't know any better, she'd think Gareth was studying the two detectives as they spoke, looking for details that might someday end up in one of his award-winning screenplays. She tried not to let this get to her, though, and kept her eyes on the ball.

"Carlton Humphreys told us earlier that you were with his brother, Milton, a few weeks ago in Japan?"

Morello nodded and said, "Yeah, we were there for about a week back in late June. A lot of *Dragons* is filming on stages in LA, but we needed some exteriors there. I fucking hate using the backlot for foreign locations. It always looks so fake, you know?"

"And can you tell us where exactly you went? Or if perhaps Milton ever traveled anywhere without you?"

"We were primarily scouting in Kobe and Tokyo. I'm not sure if you know, but Kobe is home to about half the yakuza in Japan with the Yamaguchi-gumi family."

"Did you two have any interactions with the yakuza while you were there? Perhaps anger them in some way?"

Gareth laughed at this. "If I did, don't you think my head would have been severed along with Milton's? To answer your question, no. We had zero interaction with the yakuza. I did my research for the film, but that's it. This is a *fictional* story—I wasn't about to involve any real gangsters in it. I'm not that crazy."

"So you don't believe that's why Milton was murdered?"

Gareth sighed and shrugged his shoulders. "Shit, I don't know. I mean, Milton wasn't with me that entire time, so anything is possible. I really don't think I can provide you with much else on this, though. Milton was my producer and friend, but he still lived his own life and if he had any skeletons in his closet, I had no fucking clue what they were."

Lawson didn't have anything else to add and Liz knew they'd hit a dead end with the yakuza angle. Maybe it was too much to hope that there might have been a connection to something as simple as a film Milton was working on. While the way Milton was killed still looked like some kind of a professional hit, the detectives would have to look elsewhere for answers to who killed him and what was going on with his bloodwork. Morello hadn't even seen Milton in the past week, so it was clear that whatever had changed the guy's blood, Morello wouldn't have a clue about it.

They still had to question *Black Berenice* producer and lead actress, Marie LeBeau, but as it was getting late, Liz and Lawson decided to call it a day. They'd get in touch with the actress the next day and hopefully she'd be able to give them some more useful information than Gareth Morello.

16

After a busy afternoon, Chris and Marie had settled down for dinner prepared by her butler, driver, and apparently also personal chef, Thomas. They were seated at her long and elegant dining table, adorned with various candles housed in candlesticks that looked like they'd come from somewhere very expensive in Europe. The food was all laid out, fresh from the oven, or stove, or wherever it had been prepared. As silver covers were removed from each dish, steam floated up, sending signals to Chris' brain of divine taste sensations awaiting his tongue. The final touch from Thomas was a bottle of wine which he carefully poured for Marie and Chris. It was ornately decorated and missing a label. Chris knew nothing of wines, but felt compelled to ask about it. More than anything because his stomach had a hard time handling red wine.

"The wine, I'm sorry, but how acidic is it? It's just my stomach has trouble with red wine. I'm not familiar with this and I didn't see a label."

"It's from my own vineyard. Started in Napa Valley a few years back. It's not in mass production yet, hence the lack of a label, but I think you'll like it, and hopefully your stomach will approve as well. If not, I'm sure we can find something else for you to drink."

Chris said, "Thanks. Sorry if I'm being a pain."

With a smile, Marie said, "Not at all. I was just pleased you were willing to have dinner with me. I know it might seem a little strange now that I'm your employer, but I really would like to get to know you better."

"Well, ask whatever you'd like." Chris went to try the wine while waiting for her questions and as soon as the first sip hit his lips, it was like fireworks going off in his brain. The wine was, for a lack of a better word, perfect. There were so many flavors that seemed to be assaulting his taste buds, and he was far from being any kind of wine connoisseur who could pick these things out at wine tastings. His palate was the furthest thing from refined. But this wine she had made somehow hit all the right buttons for him. It tasted somehow different than any wine he'd had before, not too sweet or sour, but with a slightly salty aftertaste. Chris almost wanted to call it the Gatorade of wines, but doing so would do it a disservice. All he knew was that he was craving more of it even after their meal was done and Marie had her fill of asking questions. It felt like he'd covered nearly his entire life story by the time they were done.

After dinner, they relaxed on Marie's luxuriously supple leather couch in her living room. She wanted to watch the evening news, but unfortunately their eyes were assaulted by the first story concerning the fate of Milton Humphreys. FOUND MURDERED, the headline read. The newscaster said he'd been killed by an unknown assailant the previous evening. Decapitated, to be precise. There were only a few weapons capable of decapitating a human, and while Chris' brain would always go to a sword first, Marie's recent brush with death made this unquestionably the murder weapon. He was there to protect Marie and Marie alone, but she had only ever presented *herself* as a potential target based on her history with a jilted lover in Japan. She never suggested those she worked with or was close to could be targets. That seemed to open up a whole new can of worms for Chris.

"This is him, right? The guy you said wanted you dead? That same ninja assassin son of a bitch?"

Marie kept staring at the news, apparently just as shocked as Chris was. She didn't snap out of her trance until he grabbed her shoulder so she'd turn to him. "What?"

"How is this the first you're hearing about this? Humphreys executive produced *Black Berenice*."

Marie stammered as she tried to find the words, "I-I silenced my phone today, even told Thomas not to disturb us. I didn't think . . ."

"That the killer might go after those close to you? Jesus Christ, Marie!" Chris launched himself from the couch and started to pace back and forth. "How am I supposed to protect you if you're not going to take this seriously?"

Tears started to well up in Marie's eyes. "I'm sorry, Chris. I didn't know, didn't think Hiro could, could go after other people just to try and lure me out. I mean Milton and I, we'd worked together, but weren't that close, I don't know why—"

"It doesn't matter why, Marie! We were exposed *all day*! If that killer had been following us, we'd be dead!" Chris could feel his anger pouring over, his head feeling several sizes too small from all the wine and he thought for a moment he might suffer another panic attack and collapse right there, but before he could, he felt the soft warm touch of Marie's hand on his arm as she had risen to meet him.

Turning him gently toward her, she said, "I'm so sorry. I was stupid to do what I did. But if I'm letting down my guard it's only because you make me feel safer."

Chris began to feel his nerves relax and focus return to his brain, a sense of clarity telling him that he needed a plan, something to focus on moving forward so the fear didn't creep back in. "Well clearly if we made it through today, that means the killer wasn't prepared. Which gives us a bit of an advantage, but we can't make that mistake again. No more trips outside until we resolve this. They won't try to attack you here if they haven't already. There was a reason they struck during that Comic-Con party. Milton's funeral could be the perfect place to try again, so that's off the table."

Marie nodded, but still seemed nervous about something.

Chris could tell and didn't want to guess. "What is it?"

"Just the idea that I should stay cooped up in here for who knows how long. I don't like it." He couldn't disagree. He thought waiting for an attack was a terrible plan. He could grow complacent, relax, and slip up. Then Marie would be the one paying for his mistake with her life. "If that killer is waiting for me to make a mistake, then we have to beat them at their own game. Set a trap for them."

"With you as bait?" Chris asked.

Marie nodded.

"No way. There are too many things that could go wrong, Marie. You can't—*we* can't take that risk." But as his fear for Marie took over, his brain desperately tried to locate an alternative, until, like a fog dispersing, the answer presented itself clear as day. "What if we set a trap for them somewhere else? With someone else as bait."

"What do you mean?"

"I mean, if the killer still can't get to you, they'll move onto someone else you know. Someone you were closer to than Milton, perhaps? If we work with that person, maybe, just maybe we could get lucky and nab this bastard." The only question was who that next target might be. So, Chris did what anyone without the necessary knowledge of the situation would do—he asked. "They had to have targeted Milton because of your time together in Hollywood, since he's the one person you've collaborated with on multiple projects. From an outsider, that would appear you two were close, right? So who might the next target be then? Who else might they think you're close to?"

"Well, you are a fan, right? Who else did you know I was close to?"

Chris felt like an idiot. Maybe it was the fact that *he* was now close to her, but he'd let all his time reading about Marie's career drift out of his thoughts and had failed to let any of that prior knowledge float to the surface until that very moment. Now that she'd mentioned it, all the news he'd read in the past few years came flooding back. And one name that immediately sprang to mind was, "Philip Dalton."

Marie smiled, pleased that he remembered her most recent relationship. She'd started dating Philip during production of their film before *Black Berenice—Burning Passion*, an erotic thriller from acclaimed director Raymond Trainor. Like any hot and heavy romance that seemed to blossom between budding stars, it flamed out almost as quickly as it began. They were through after only a year, but remained friends, and that was how Dalton ended up with a leading role in *Black Berenice*. Now it seemed his life might be in danger, and if he wasn't made aware of this, he would be quite easy to pick off.

Chris knew he had to do something and fast.

"So you *are* a fan," Marie said.

"Yeah, but that's not important right now. If Philip could be next, you need to contact him. He needs to take this seriously if we're going to have any chance of stopping this killer."

"Philip doesn't take much of anything seriously, I'm afraid. But I can probably get him to listen to reason. He'll want to meet with you, naturally, before agreeing to be our bait."

Chris was confused and asked, "Why would you tell him he's bait?"

Marie laughed at his question and clarified, "I won't, but if I tell him his life is in danger, he still has to agree to let you guard him. Otherwise, he might go to the police."

"Is that the worst thing?"

Marie shook her head. "We don't want to involve the police. You saw what they were like in San Diego. They'll be even worse here. And I . . . I don't have the best history with them. So, the truth is out of the question. If we tried to make something else up, like a conspiracy, or worse, some kind of illegal thing we were mixed up in? That would just get me in bigger trouble than I'm already in. Trust me, this is the safest course of action."

"And if Philip disagrees?"

Marie smiled. "I'll make him see reason."

Chris shook his head. "It doesn't seem reasonable to me . . . or very smart. I worry that you're not giving this assassin enough credit."

"Don't sell yourself short, Chris. We've already been over this. I trust you. I think Philip will too. And he has a hard time saying no to me."

Chris laughed at this. He doubted anyone had an easy time saying no to Marie. Perhaps she'd never heard anyone deny her something. But in this instance, she didn't seem amused.

"You can do this, Chris. It isn't a joke. My life is in your hands, as you know, but now so is Philip's. So don't let us down."

Chris felt his stomach turn on him, as it usually did when he was nervous. Right now, he was feeling a weight crushing him down into the ground. If he was ever going to get out from under it, he knew he'd need to man up and throw that weight off of himself.

17

After Marie called her old flame to alert him of the situation, Chris drove to meet Philip Dalton at his home. Marie naturally stayed behind with her security team, as she was safest in her own place. When Chris arrived, Philip was all smiles as he approached. Chris wasn't sure exactly what had been said when Marie called Philip—as she'd stepped out onto her balcony and he'd given her privacy—but Philip didn't seem too concerned. Approaching Chris, he came in for a big hug and said, "Chris! Great to see you again, pal."

Chris felt the air squeezed out of his lungs from the strength of the hug and yelped out, "Nice to see you too." When Philip released him, Chris breathed in a deep lungful of air.

With a laugh, Phillip said, "I see you didn't waste any time making a move on Marie, but hey, I'm not here to judge. Me and her are ancient history."

Chris went flush with embarrassment and was quick to correct Philip. "It's not like that, *really*. Strictly professional. She asked for my help . . . to keep her safe."

Philip laughed again. "Yeah, sure, buddy. Look whatever helps you sleep better at night. It's not my place to ask anyway what has or hasn't happened, but I know a thing or two about Marie, and I highly doubt she hired you *just* for your martial arts skills."

Annoyed, Chris spat back, "She trusted those skills enough to keep your ass safe. Or should I just turn around and head back? I'm sure you're capable of keeping your head attached to your neck all on your own."

This got Philip to grin. "I'm impressed. If you can protect anyone half as good as you can verbally spar, I'm sure I'm in safe hands. Not that I fully believe my life is in danger, otherwise I probably would have called the cops, despite what Marie had told me about San Diego."

"You think they'd believe a ninja was killing those close to her?"

"Well, Marie clearly doesn't. So maybe she's right, but she's got her own reasons for not trusting the police."

"She mentioned something about a bad history with them, but didn't elaborate."

Shaking his head, Philip said, "It's not my place to tell you. Maybe she will if you ask nicely, but for now, why don't we step inside? If I'm gonna die, I'd at least like it to be in my home and not on the driveway."

The two stepped inside and Chris saw that Philip had his TV on, playing what looked like *Apocalypse Now*. The film geek in him couldn't resist commenting on the film, let alone the massive screen it was being played on. "*Apocalypse Now*, nice. And that TV is seriously impressive."

"Bigger than Marie's?"

"Yeah." It was true, Marie may or may not have had more money than Philip. Chris was sure their lifestyles were comparable, but she kept her televisions strictly under seventy inches. They felt more like decorations than functional electronics. Mostly she just left the news playing on them, or looped videos of fireplaces or fish.

"Well, just more important to me I suppose. I'm not just in

this business for the money, although there is plenty to be made. I'm a film fan, and can tell you are too. This is one of Brando's best, right? Fucking Kurtz, man."

"What about Sheen? Gotta be like a career best. He actually got drunk and punched a mirror, you know?"

"Yeah, I heard about that. Watched *Hearts of Darkness,* too. Heard people say it's better than *Apocalypse Now*, but fuck that. *Apocalypse* is a goddamn cinema classic. Still the best Vietnam movie ever made. Nothing else ever seemed to capture the madness of that war, you know? My uncle was in Nam. Came back all fucked-up. The shit he told me you wouldn't believe. At his core, every man has a demon inside, and that place was like the Devil's fucking playpen, I tell ya."

Chris didn't really know what to say. He didn't know anybody who had been in Nam and he certainly wasn't up to hearing secondhand war stories, so he just nodded, uncomfortably waiting for Philip to say something else.

"Hey, you want a drink? I've got this aged bourbon. The fucking best, I tell ya, man."

Chris wasn't much of a hard alcohol man, but could tell there wouldn't be any saying no as Philip was already on the way over to his bar. Not wanting to be an ungrateful guest, he stepped over and waited as Philip poured him a glass. Chris thought it might have gone down easier with ice, but wasn't about to potentially offend his host by asking for some. He was surprised, however, when Philip poured in a few drops of water.

"Helps open up the flavor—or so I've been told. I like it either way." Holding up his glass, he was clearly waiting for Chris to take his own and once he had, Philip clinked them together and said "Cheers."

Drinking down his bourbon, Chris was shocked at how much the alcohol stung his throat going down. He tried not to wince, but clearly Philip noticed and had a good laugh at his expense.

"Has a bit of a bite to it, but you get used to it." Moving out from around the bar he said, "Now, I know you're here to watch my back, but what kind of a host would I be if just left you sitting around? I'm gonna continue my movie. You can watch if you want, though not too closely, want to make sure you're keeping an eye out for anything out of the ordinary. I do have a camera out front, so my phone will alert me of anybody out there, but I'm sure you wanna check the windows, look around the house, and so on, right?"

Chris nodded. He didn't think the killer was already inside, but knew it couldn't hurt to check. So he began looking around. He didn't like leaving Philip in the living room, but could tell the guy wasn't going to budge. He was clearly tolerating Chris' presence for Marie, but wasn't going to go out of his way to make things easier.

The rooms on that floor were all clean, with nothing surprising in the closets, or in the garage. When Chris made his way to the bedroom on the other side of the house, he freaked out for a second at what he thought was somebody hiding by the door, but it was just the shadow of a plant too close to a light. He felt like an idiot when he realized this. Part of him wished before arriving there that he had a gun, but as he wasn't licensed to carry a firearm, he wasn't about to risk jail time trying to save this guy's life. And seeing how on edge he already was, he knew it was good he had no weapon, as he might have killed a plant in fear—or worse, a person. No, if he wanted something to defend himself with other than his fists, he'd have to see what kind of items Philip kept around his home that could be used for defense.

Thankfully, he found that Philip was into baseball, and a bat was all he needed for the moment. When he returned to the living room to give Philip the all-clear, Chris was surprised to find that

Philip wasn't on the couch. His heartbeat skyrocketed in that moment and his eyes and ears became hyper-alert.

Then the toilet flushed.

Whirling around to the sound, Chris saw Philip exiting the bathroom down the hall and breathed a sigh of relief. As Philip approached, he asked, "You feeling okay, buddy? You look a little pale."

Chris could admit, at least to himself, that he was *not* feeling okay. In fact, he was turning into a nervous wreck. He was there to a protect a man and he couldn't even protect himself from his own nerves. At that point, he knew he was in for a *long* night.

18

The next day, Liz woke to her phone ringing. Another headless corpse had been found early that morning. At some point late in the night, Jyll Masters, girlfriend of Milton Humphreys, had driven down an alley off Hollywood Boulevard and her head had been chopped off. Nobody knew why she went down the alley—if she'd been forced to drive down it, out of view from the street, or if she'd purposely chosen that desolate route.

As someone who'd been working the Hollywood area as long as she had, Liz knew that sometimes johns would pull into an alley for a little business with any of the working girls they might stumble upon. But typically, any murders that happened in those alleys were either those same girls or an unlucky soul robbed and killed under the cover of darkness. It was literally unheard for an actor to wind up dead in one of those alleys—especially a well-known and reputable up-and-coming actress. Liz couldn't wrap her head around it and when she showed up at the scene, it was even more alarming than she anticipated.

The car hadn't just pulled off the road, it had driven far enough down the alley that most people passing by wouldn't have noticed it at night, or if they had, might have thought it was just another parked vehicle. The car had been turned off and for some strange reason had all the upholstery covered in plastic wrap. It was an odd sight to behold. She couldn't figure out why the hell

Jyll Masters would have done this to her own car. Either she suffered from extreme OCD, or she was planning a murder herself. It would have made more sense to Liz that the car was stolen . . . if Jyll's body hadn't been discovered only a few feet from the car.

The victim's head had been severed by a sharp blade—exactly the same manner as her boyfriend. It appeared to have rolled under a nearby dumpster, which had to be slid out a few feet to retrieve it. There were no cuts or bruises on Jyll's face, apart from whatever marks she'd sustained as her head went rolling along the pavement. Her body likewise showed no unusual marks. Liz was fresh out of ideas until she noticed that the dress Jyll was wearing must have slid up as she hit the pavement. From her revealed thighs, Liz immediately took note of the two small red marks on her left inner thigh.

Like lightning had struck her, Liz flashed back to the same red marks on Milton's inner thigh that Hank had shown the detectives at the morgue. It was in that moment of revelation that Liz also realized it must have been the same spot Jyll was scratching when they'd questioned her the previous day. Liz felt sick, and it wasn't from the sight before her. It was from her own stupidity.

How could I have missed this? she wondered.

It wasn't totally ridiculous; she'd visited Jyll before seeing Milton's body. But still, she wasn't one to typically overlook anything and somehow this major clue had slipped past her. Now it was too late for Jyll Masters, but she suspected there could be more victims. Liz was just angry at herself that she hadn't come up with any suspects or signs that might lead her to why these people were being killed in this way.

When Lawson finally arrived, she didn't even wait for him to reach the body, she moved right up and said, "We need to test her blood."

"Why?" he asked, still looking a little out of sorts. She figured he hadn't had any coffee yet.

"Because I've already looked at the body, and she's got those same marks on her inner thigh as Milton Humphreys. It's got to be connected. I can't see any other reason they'd have the same damn marks. The fact that she was killed a day later, the same way as her boyfriend, is just too coincidental to overlook. Right?"

Lawson seemed to be trying to regain his senses as he took a deep breath and closed his eyes. When he opened them, he said, "Yeah, this is starting to get pretty fucking weird. Anything else you noticed?"

She led him back toward the body. "The interior of her car is covered in plastic wrap. That's pretty fucking weird too, right?"

He nodded and peered into the car. The passenger and driver door were both open, as they had been since she arrived at the scene. "Was anything stolen? From the car, I mean."

"Not that I could tell. Didn't look like anything valuable was in the car, though, so we'll have to see if there's any fingerprints or DNA left behind."

"Was she traveling alone?"

"Far as I can tell, but her purse was missing."

Lawson shook his head. "No surprise there. If there was nothing worth stealing in the car, any vagrants that happened upon the purse would have naturally taken it. Would have been good to have, though. I'd liked to have seen who her last call was to."

"We'll have to look into her phone records."

"That'll take time. We could have another murder before we get those back—if they even provide anything helpful."

"We should check her house, see if there's anything we might have missed when we visited her yesterday."

Lawson nodded. Then he pointed down below the dumpster. "You see this?"

"What?" Liz asked, trying to focus on where he was pointing. That's when she noticed what appeared to be a soggy hairball. Looked like it had gotten caught under the dumpster when the police moved it to retrieve the head. "Is that a wig?"

"Looks to be."

"So a notable actress was wearing a wig and driving down a seedy alley late at night. Any thoughts?"

"Only one. She came down here to do something illegal and didn't want anybody to notice."

"Yeah, but what was she trying to do? Most people come down these alleys for a good time out of view from prying eyes. She was the type of girl who could have afforded an expensive escort if that was really her thing. So why come down here?"

"You saw that plastic wrap all over the car. I've only ever seen somebody do something like that when they've got premeditated murder on the brain."

"She had no criminal record, though. No history of violence. People don't just up and decide to go kill-crazy."

"Who said she went kill-crazy? Maybe she knew more than she was telling us the other day. Maybe she knew who murdered her boyfriend, planned to lead them into this alley with the intent to exact revenge, and her plan backfired in a major way."

Liz shook her head. "I just don't see it. It's a wild theory, but no sane person would do something like that."

Lawson raised his eyebrows. "They might if they were no longer human."

19

Liz's stomach felt off the rest of the morning. It was like some horrible monster had crawled into her gut and was trying to tear out her insides. But she knew better. It was just nerves, and the damn case she was on was threatening her well-being now. Something she could not tolerate. For her son's sake more than anyone else.

When she arrived back at her house, Liz found Freddy in the living room watching TV. He turned and said, "Good morning, Mom. I made some pancakes if you wanted any. They're in the fridge, you just have to nuke 'em."

Moving to her son, Liz kissed him on the head. "Thanks, mijo, I appreciate it. Don't worry about the dishes, I'll get them."

"Oh, I already cleaned them," he said with a big grin.

Liz found herself shocked that he'd cleaned up all on his own and when she peered into the kitchen, she could see the skillet drying on the rack next to the sink. She almost found herself tearing up, realizing her son was no longer a little boy. He was eleven years old and starting middle school in the fall. Sometimes Liz forgot how independent he'd gotten. If it wasn't for his insistence on keeping Lydia around to watch him in the evenings, she'd probably think he'd be fine alone. It also didn't help how much Liz doted on him, but with her husband gone she couldn't really help it.

"I guess I'll take you up on those pancakes. Haven't eaten anything yet." Which was mostly due to the state of her stomach when she'd arrived home, but thankfully her appetite was beginning to return in the presence of her son. As she microwaved the pancakes, she also brewed up a fresh pot of coffee. For a moment, she wondered if Freddy might want some, but his revulsion to the question told her all she needed to know. He still wasn't much of a coffee drinker, but she was sure by high school, he'd acquire a taste for it. Maybe she'd be holding onto that little boy just a while longer.

As she sat down to eat her pancakes, Liz checked her phone and saw she'd apparently missed a call from Hank. Listening to her voice mail, she heard him explain that during the night, the corpse of Milton Humphreys had somehow been stolen. She normally would have thought it had just been misplaced, but after everything they'd seen so far, she was pretty sure somebody was trying to cover this whole mess up.

Unfortunately, security hadn't picked up anything—not the guards, nor the cameras. But at least there wasn't anything else to be learned from Milton's corpse. As for the recently deceased Jyll Masters, Hank said he'd take a blood sample from the body when she arrived at the morgue. It would be a few hours till Liz heard back, though, since that body could not take priority over the others.

Once Liz had finished her breakfast and taken care of the dishes, she gave Freddy a kiss goodbye and made her way over to the station to meet up with Lawson. It seemed he'd already gotten a hold of Marie LeBeau via a number provided by Carlton Humphreys. The actress was free to meet around noon, so that gave them a few hours to handle some much-needed paperwork and check out the home of the late Jyll Masters.

No sooner had the two detectives entered said house, their

noses were assaulted by a foul odor of some kind. It was hard to tell where the odor was emanating from with the lights off, but once they'd turned them on, it was a simple process of elimination and the kitchen made it abundantly clear. Leaking from the bottom of the refrigerator door, a dark red substance had pooled up the floor. Liz didn't need to get any closer to know it was blood. Approaching the fridge, she could see the door hadn't fully closed. A furry tail had gotten in the way. Pulling open the door, Liz almost retched from the horrendous smell she knew only too well from her job.

It was the stench of decay.

A dead cat was taking up space in the fridge, its throat torn out and whatever blood was still in it at the time of death had leaked all over the floor. "Jesus Christ," Lawson said as he stepped out from behind Liz, his arm covering his mouth and nose. "Is that her fucking *cat*?!"

Liz was close enough to know for sure. The animal was in bad shape, but she still recognized it as the same ginger one that Jyll was snuggling up to during their first visit. It wasn't clear if Jyll had killed the cat herself, or some other animal in the neighborhood did, but what was clear was that Jyll had tried to preserve it in the fridge (and quite poorly).

"Why wouldn't she have stuck it in the freezer? Or at least bagged the damn thing?" Lawson asked.

Liz shut the door completely, making sure not to catch the tail this time. She hoped to reduce the smell. "Beats me. But we knew she wasn't in her right mind. You said it yourself, no sane human would have done what she was attempting to do in that alley. This only backs that up."

"So who killed her cat then? That doesn't look like something our killer did. Looks like it was attacked by some animal."

"It's possible, but let's keep looking. I'm not here to

investigate the murder of a cat. The poor act of preservation on Jyll's part helps us understand she wasn't thinking too clearly before her death, and that's all we need to know right now."

Lawson nodded, ready to get out of the kitchen. He pushed past Liz and made his way over to a window, which he promptly opened and sucked in a lungful of fresh air. Meanwhile, Liz made her way over to the living room, where she looked for any other clues. That's when she spotted the bloodstain on the couch and floor. "Think I got something here. Dried blood, from the look of it."

Lawson stepped over to where she was pointing and asked, "Is it from the cat?"

"Seems likely."

"If it *was* the cat, then it was killed in her home. That doesn't match up with some animal doing the deed, unless she let it in."

"Or did it herself."

Lawson narrowed his eyes at this thought. He didn't seem to think it was a viable option.

"We'll need CSU down here to confirm, but we know she wasn't in her right mind. Who knows what she was capable of?"

"Then why'd she bother putting it in the fridge?"

Liz shrugged. "Beats me. Let's check out the rest of the house."

After putting a call in to get the crime scene unit over there, the detectives made their way through the rest of the house, taking notice of every small detail that might be important. Unfortunately, not much was until they arrived at the bedroom. The curtains were drawn, which wasn't uncommon for anyone who didn't want sunlight to wake them in the morning. But what was odd was the fact that duct tape had been used to seal off any gaps that would have let sunlight through the sides, top, and bottom of the curtains.

"Okay, that's *definitely* weird," Lawson said at the sight. "And a bit extreme, if you ask me. Why wouldn't she have just bought better curtains? Not like she couldn't afford it."

"I'm more curious why she felt the need to prevent any light from coming through the window. It's extreme, like you said, but what the hell compelled her to attempt something like this?"

"Same thing that compelled her to eat her cat and wrap the shit out of her car." Things were getting weirder and weirder, and Liz's stomach was beginning to turn into a roiling volcano. Regretting the pancakes and coffee she'd recently ingested, she made a mental note to grab something simple for lunch.

While waiting for the crime scene unit, Liz received a call from Hank back at the morgue. He said he'd checked the blood and the results were the same as with Milton Humphreys, but that didn't shock him as much as what he found when he examined Jyll Masters' head. He refused to tell Liz what he'd found over the phone once again, and requested she come there with Lawson as soon as possible. She had no idea what he could have found that shocked him more than the blood, but wanting to know herself, she rushed to the morgue as soon as CSU got to Jyll's house.

Hank once more led the detectives to the back as quickly and quietly as possible. He clearly didn't want anyone else seeing or hearing what he had to share. Liz found herself anxious and scared for the first time in years, and it wasn't even in a hostile situation. There was nothing to fear from a place where everyone who wasn't working there was dead. Unless, of course, she was secretly in a zombie film. But as she came to find out, she might just be in something worse.

Approaching the still-covered body, Hank said, "I take it from our conversation on the phone, nobody looked too closely at the head?"

"I mean, it had been collected, so yeah, people saw it up close, including me."

"But nobody opened her mouth."

Liz was confused by this and asked, "Why?"

Hank didn't waste words, knowing that seeing would be the only way for them to believe. Pulling back the sheet from the severed head of Jyll Masters, Liz and her partner now had a clear view of the corpse's open mouth. Her clean white teeth practically glowed against the soft fluorescent lights shining down on them. And where any normal person might have had shorter, worn-down upper canines, she had razor-sharp fangs that extended about half an inch past the others.

"What the fuck?" Lawson spat in disbelief. He got in close, reaching out the touch the fangs, just to make sure they were real. When one of them pricked his finger, he reeled back in pain, sucking at the wound. "Son of a bitch. Those things are sharp!"

Hank finally spoke with a mixture of excitement and fear, "I'm no monster movie expert, but I don't have to be a genius to know what those teeth mean. This lady was a vampire."

Liz was stunned, standing in shock and disbelief at what had finally been revealed to her. Yet, as she went back over the various puzzle pieces of the case, she was finding that they were quickly forming a picture in her mind. It had been right in front of her the whole time, just too ridiculous to have been considered. But the dead cat, the plastic-wrapped car, the red marks, they all pointed to the same thing. "So her and Milton? They were *vampires*?"

Hank nodded. "I'm not a betting man, but if I was, I'd put all my money on that."

"Wait, but Milton didn't have fangs like that," Lawson said, between sucks on his still bleeding finger.

"If I had to guess," Hank added, "These things only reveal themselves when the person is ready to feed."

"Which would explain why Jyll's car interior had been smothered in plastic wrap." Liz pointed out.

Lawson shook his head. "But we found her in the daylight. Aren't these things supposed to, you know, explode in sunlight or whatever? Same with Milton. He was killed when it was still light out."

Hank shrugged. "Like I said, I'm no expert, but you're going off of movie knowledge. As far as I or anyone else knows, these things don't exist, except in fiction. Yet we definitely have something here that defies logic. Any media outlet would be in a frenzy to get proof of supernatural forces like this. But who would really believe it without proof? Why do you think I asked you down here? You'd never believe me on the phone. What we've got here is something that you're believing because I'm telling you and you can see and feel and smell it for yourself."

"You think that's why Milton's body disappeared? To get rid of the evidence?" Liz asked.

"That would be my guess. I wouldn't be surprised if Miss Masters here mysteriously disappears in the night too. That's what scares me the most, not the existence of these things, but what kind of trouble they could bring down on all our heads if the person or persons who stole that body knows that we know. We have no idea how deep this goes."

"So then we find out."

Hank shook his head. "Did you listen to nothing I just said? You know me, Liz. I don't scare easily, and this shit scares me to my core. I'm telling you as a friend and someone you can trust that you need to let this one go. If we dig any deeper, or try and sound the alarms to the general public, we might as well be signing our own death warrants. Now, I can't tell you two what to do with this information, but I hope you'll be smart. For all of our sakes."

"Jesus, Hank. We're talking about people's lives here. How can you expect me to walk away from this?"

"By doing the same thing we'd have been doing if we didn't

stumble onto this," Lawson said. "Our jobs. Which last time I checked involves the living, not the undead."

"Seriously, Lawson?"

"Yes, Liz. I am not dying because you're desperate to get to the bottom of some fucking vampire conspiracy in LA."

Liz.

He called her by her first name. Lawson never did that. She knew he was serious, and afraid more than anything else. He was usually the first one through the door in a dangerous situation, but at that moment, he looked like a frightened little boy who'd made the mistake of sneaking downstairs while his parents were watching a horror film.

Liz knew it was crazy to stay on this case, but she was worried more people could die, and not vampires this time. "As long as things like this are out there, people are going to keep dying."

"People die every day. But so far the last two corpses we picked up were the same things you seem adamant about hunting down. If somebody is doing that for us, why should we get in their way?"

"What if the next body we find is this headhunter? What then? How long before the city becomes overrun by these things?"

Lawson shrugged. "How do we know it isn't already? Like Hank said, there's no way to know how deep this goes. There were no real signs these two were vampires. Hell, there could be some in the department for all you know. Maybe even the government. Jesus, saying all this out loud, it's just too crazy."

Liz knew there was no real way to win the argument. Maybe Lawson was right, maybe they'd already lost and just didn't know it yet. But she felt like they had to do something now. They couldn't just sit on this information. She also knew she couldn't just tell Captain Ford. He was a no-nonsense type of guy. Even if they showed him what Hank had found, he'd dismiss it as a practical joke before even looking close enough to see it was real. For that matter, she doubted at this point anyone would believe her. Hank was right—it was better to keep this to themselves.

"Maybe you're both right. But what the hell *do* we tell Captain Ford? This is still an open investigation and we don't have any suspects. Unless another body turns up with a sword, we have to keep looking like we're still working the case. At least until something comes along that allows us to close it."

Lawson sighed. "So then we keep doing our job, or at least look like we are, but we keep our distance. Unless something falls into our laps, we let this one go cold. Any other time I'd hate the thought of an unsolved case, but I don't want to catch the motherfucker who's killing these things, and I don't think you do either now. Right?"

She was a police officer and therefore believed nobody was above the law, but how the hell does the law make any difference when dealing with undead creatures playing at being human? For all she knew other people were aware of the vampires, people in high places, bought and paid for and ready to eliminate anyone who threatened to push the truth out into the light. In that moment, those thoughts drew her to Freddy. He was still young, vulnerable . . . how could she protect him from this if she couldn't even protect herself? There was no real choice other than the one she finally had to admit was the right one.

"You're right. We need to let this one go cold. Let's do our interview with Marie LeBeau and tell Ford we're out of leads." Lawson nodded and Liz said goodbye to Hank. The two detectives headed out to their car and had a quick, quiet drive back to the station.

20

Chris had spent the past night at Philip Dalton's home, watching over the man while he was awake and asleep. By morning, he was physically and mentally exhausted from the stress of the ordeal. The looming threat that never came was driving him mad without Marie. She faced the same threat, possibly more so than Philip, yet when he was in her presence, he felt calm and sure of himself. For the first time in his life, Chris didn't feel quite so much like a loser; he felt like he was capable of much more than he could have ever dreamed. But when Marie asked him to watch Philip, something changed.

That safe warm blanket that she provided him had been stripped away, leaving him exposed to so many horrible inadequacies. In the face of potential danger, they were turning him from an unmovable oak into a withered tree ready to crack in two from any potential attack. He needed that strength back, the confidence that only Marie was capable of providing. He had to get away from Philip, or he was liable to fall to pieces.

When he called her that morning, she didn't seem the least bit surprised to hear from him. "Chris. How are things going? Philip treating you well?"

"Yeah," Chris admitted, "Things have been fine over here."

"Maybe a little *too* fine?" she asked playfully, as if reading his mind.

"Yeah, I . . . I'm going a little crazy, if I'm being honest. I don't think I'm really cut out for this. I can't tell if Philip is really in any danger, and the thought of an attack coming at any moment? It's too much. At least with you, there's additional security. I know I thought I was ready for this, but I'm not. If you don't want me to come back at all, I understand. But I don't think I can stay here another night."

He heard her sigh. "Oh Chris, you worry too much. If you really don't think you can be of any further help to Philip, then I want you back here as soon as you're able. Provided you still want the job."

"If you'll have me back, of course. Anything you want."

"Anything I want . . . I like that. I want you back here, Chris. Can you be here in an hour?"

"Yeah, no problem, Marie. But what about Philip? You think he'll be okay?"

"Philip is a big boy. He can take care of himself, or get assistance from elsewhere if he so desires. Now I don't want you worrying about him another second. Just hurry back."

"I will, see you soon." After he hung up the phone, Chris felt a warm feeling fill his body. If he didn't know any better, he might think it was love. He couldn't say he'd really been in love before, but there was something about Marie that made him feel something stronger than anything he'd ever felt. It was like gravity; he was drawn to her and couldn't get away if he tried. She was now everything to him and he'd do anything to keep her safe. Keep her his.

When he broke the news of his departure to Philip, the guy didn't seem like he could be bothered with the news. He was too busy dealing with a work-related situation, contract negotiations with his agent or something. So Chris left without much fuss and a short time later, was pulling up to Marie LeBeau's house. The place looked just as magnificent as it had when he left it a day earlier. As he approached the front doors, they parted open, and Marie stepped outside to greet him. She was in a robe, but still looking great enough to walk the red carpet.

"Chris, so glad you're back." She surprised him with a hug, and Chris felt his body instantly relax. It was like she was transferring some of her life force over to him, instantly revitalizing his worn-out spirit so he was ready to get back to the task at hand. When she broke from the hug, she stared deeply into his eyes, as if studying him to make sure he was in fact okay. In that moment, he wanted nothing more than to kiss her, but knew that would be beyond unprofessional.

"I'm glad to be back, Marie. I've missed you." He instantly felt his face go flush at what he said and tried to quickly cover up what he meant, "I mean, I missed being here. You know, Philip's place just doesn't have the same warmth as yours does."

Marie laughed at this, clearly aware of his ruse and finding it charming. "Please, you don't need to lie to me, Chris. I've missed having you around too." That warm feeling rushed back through his body and Chris thought he might just melt right there on the cobblestone driveway. Instead, Marie waved him onward and began to walk back into her home. He followed like the loyal dog he'd become.

After settling back in, Chris heard Marie take a call. When she was finished, she informed him, "Two detectives will be stopping by around noon."

He asked, "Are they coming because of Milton's murder?"

"That they are. Just some routine questions, I assume, since by my estimation, I was one of the last people to see Milton alive."

"But you don't know anything, right?"

"Nothing that could help them, but you know how thorough the police can be. They just want to be sure."

"Should I make myself scarce when they arrive? Do you need privacy?"

Marie shrugged, "It's up to you. If you'd rather not have to deal with them, you don't have to. But, if you want to stay with me, to keep me safe, that's also on the table."

He thought for a moment about what she'd said, but knew deep down, there was only one course of action that made sense. "I'm here to protect you. No point in sending me away again. Besides, I'd like to hear what these cops have to say about Milton."

Marie rolled her eyes at his last comment. "If you're thinking of telling them about what's really going on, don't bother. I told you they won't believe it."

"But how can you know for sure?"

Moving in close to him, she spoke slowly and deliberately, so he'd know she was serious. "Trust me, Chris. I know." When he stared into her eyes once more, that certainty became crystalized. Suddenly, he didn't feel a need to press the issue.

"Well, I'm still sticking around, at least until I'm sure the cops aren't a threat." This got her to smile in approval.

"That's good to hear, Chris."

<h1 style="text-align:center">21</h1>

Liz arrived at the house promptly at noon. She wanted to get this over with quickly, so they could report to Captain Ford and put this whole spooky mess behind them. Hopefully, they'd never have to think about it again. But perhaps that was too much to hope for. Lawson also seemed in a rush—or perhaps just hangry, since they weren't planning to eat until after questioning Marie.

When Lawson knocked on the door several times, it was opened before he could finish. His hand was left in mid-air, trying to knock on a surface that had moved several feet. Standing in its place was an elderly and well-put-together man, who said, "Please come in, Miss LeBeau is expecting you. My name is Thomas. If there's anything you need while here, please let me know."

Lawson gave the man a nod and moved past him, while Liz said, "Thank you," before entering the house. When she stepped inside, the look of the place was shocking if nothing else. She was no stranger to homes in the Hills, but somehow this one put them all to shame. It wasn't just lavishly decorated; it possessed some of the finest craftsmanship she'd ever seen. Paintings decorated the walls and small ornaments adorned surfaces, but these weren't just ordinary things one could find in an LA art gallery. These looked very old, antique—almost what she'd call relics. The kind of things you'd expect to find in a museum, slowly falling apart.

Yet everything in Marie's home was pristine. She didn't even want to think how much all of this must have cost, or how Marie came to acquire it.

Before Liz could finish admiring the hall of wonders, Marie stepped out from the living room and greeted her guests. "Detectives Lawson and Gutiérrez, correct?"

"That's right, Miss LeBeau," Lawson confirmed.

"Marie, please." She waved them toward the living room. "If it's all right with both of you, I figured we could do this in the living room. It's the most comfortable place in my home, and I'm sure you two could use any relaxation you can get while on the job."

Lawson seemed giddy at this prospect, but even more so when he saw that Thomas was carrying in a tray of some rather unique-looking hors d'oeuvres. Liz found the smell of them intoxicating, and not just because she was hungry. In fact, the smell seemed to make her even hungrier than before.

Making her way into the living room, Liz passed several large men obviously working security for Marie. As she approached the tray of food, Lawson had already grabbed four of the things before plopping down on a very plush-looking leather sectional couch. Liz eyed the food closely, which appeared to be bacon wrapped around an assortment of other things smashed into a kind of paste. She almost reached out for one, but then stopped herself, wondering what was in them. She was allergic to several tree nuts after all, and decided she'd best just pass.

"Not hungry?" Marie asked as she took a seat across from the couch.

Liz shook her head, and politely said, "Sorry, didn't want to spoil my lunch."

"These are amazing, Gutiérrez, you gotta try them." Lawson stuffed another in his mouth, savoring the taste as he chewed in heavenly bliss.

"Would you like to sit down?" Marie asked, pointing to the couch where Lawson had perhaps gotten a little too comfortable.

As a sort of reflex to her partner's lack of professionalism, Liz said, "I can stand—we won't be here long. Just a few questions we needed to ask you about Milton Humphreys."

"Ask away," Marie said with a smile.

Liz fumbled in her pockets for her notepad. She'd written down a few questions to ask that hopefully wouldn't dig too deep into things, but would at least work for her report when she told Captain Ford how they'd hit a wall. At the moment she pulled it out, though, she caught a young man clocking her from across the room. He had wandered up behind Marie and whispered something in her ear, which apparently pleased her, then she nodded and he took a seat nearby. The man looked well-dressed in a very expensive-looking suit, but it didn't quite fit him. He was attractive enough, yet clearly not Marie's boyfriend, and he also didn't fit the bill for security. She'd passed a few guards on her way in who were much bigger than him. This man—who honestly looked more like a college boy—must have been in his twenties, appeared to have some muscle on him, yet didn't look too athletic. In many ways, she found him a bit nerdy-looking.

"This is Chris Hart, my head of security. I hope you don't mind him sitting in with us. He just wants to make sure everything is okay."

"We're the police, Miss LeBeau," Liz assured her, "You have nothing to fear from us."

Marie looked rather embarrassed and said, "I'm sorry, I didn't want to give you the wrong impression. I've . . . well, I've had this stalker. I'm not sure if you heard about my incident in San Diego, but Chris is just here to keep me safe in case they return. As is the rest of my security team, of course. I just . . . feel safer with him around." She shot him a smile and he smiled back. If Liz didn't know any better, she'd think they were involved romantically. But for the moment, she put that thought out of her head.

Lawson asked, "I remember reading about that incident at Comic-Con. Papers didn't have a lot of details, but they said you were attacked, right? Like an attempt on your life?"

Marie nodded. "I'm lucky Chris was there to protect me."

"Has the stalker returned since?" Lawson asked out of curiosity. Liz realized she might need to steer the conversation back to the reason they had come there. Unfortunately, there was no wrangling Lawson when he got starstruck.

"No," Marie said.

"Maybe we should get back to the reason we're here?" Liz chimed in, but Lawson continued with another question.

"Strange, and the San Diego police didn't catch them?"

"They didn't seem to care much, frankly, I don't think they believed me. Thought maybe it was staged or something."

Lawson shook his head. "That's fucked-up. Pardon my French. I mean, we'd never do that here. LA cops have seen too much, so we tend to believe almost anything."

Chris looked at Marie, suddenly concerned, and then said, "Maybe they *could* help. Shouldn't you try to explain—"

Marie snapped at Chris, shouting, "No!" Turning back to the detectives, she smiled sweetly again and said, "I'm sorry. My head of security is overstepping."

Lawson seemed confused and even Liz found her interest piqued as she ended up asking, "Help with what? Your stalker?"

Marie shook her head, looking ready to shut down, when Chris suddenly moved in close and whispered something to her. She then said, "I'm sorry, would you excuse us for a moment?"

Liz and Lawson both nodded before Chris and Marie left the room.

Turning back to Liz, Lawson said, "Okay, *that* was weird."

"Maybe the stalker is a sore subject?"

"Ex-boyfriend, maybe? Or just another nut-job fan."

"Who knows? But if she's not comfortable sharing it, let's not press the issue. It's not why we're here, remember?"

Lawson seemed a little disappointed he wouldn't get to share in the juicy gossip, so he just nodded and turned back around on the couch.

When Marie returned, it was without her head of security. She once more sat down on the chair across from them and said, "Please continue with your questions. I apologize for my outburst."

Liz then proceeded down her list of topics pertaining to Milton, such as the last meeting Marie had with him. Turned out it was just to discuss details surrounding the premiere of *Black Berenice*. Nothing too interesting, though Lawson was hooked on every word. They asked if Milton appeared okay or if he was nervous or scared about anything. She said he seemed his normal aggressive self. Finally, Liz asked a few questions about whether or not Marie was friendly at all with Milton outside of their business relationship, but she admitted it was strictly business between them and she didn't know Milton too well personally. If he was in any kind of trouble, she didn't know about it.

The end of their questions was a wall that Liz was thankful to hit. Lawson seemed a little let down that they were apparently done there, but decided to take two more of the hors d'oeuvres to go. They both thanked Marie for her time and then made their way to the front door. Security seemed to still be lurking at various places around the house, and this time it felt a bit more ominous compared to when they'd entered. Liz wasn't sure why it bothered her, but it did.

When they stepped outside into the warm afternoon sunlight, Lawson took in a deep breath and said, "I swear the air is just fresher up here than down in Hollywood proper, right? Almost like all that money flowing up here keeps it clean or something."

"Or it's just above the smog," Liz said.

He nodded in agreement to her observation before moving back to their car to get in. Before either of them could get in the car though, Chris Hart was moving quickly to their location. It wasn't clear if he'd come out the front door or somewhere else, but Liz never heard his approach. If she hadn't seen him, she never would have noticed.

"Detectives, can I have a quick word?"

Liz looked at Lawson, who appeared just as confused as she was. He shrugged and Liz said, "Sure."

"Marie would likely fire me if she knew I was telling you this, but I think she's stubborn and has some kind of bad blood when it comes to the LAPD. The thing is, I'm worried that her stalker is connected to Milton Humphreys' death."

This immediately froze Liz; she was seized by terror that the case she was trying to let go cold had heated up so fast it might as well have burned her. Lawson didn't look pleased either, but still asked, "What are you talking about?"

"That incident in San Diego. It wasn't a stalker, it was . . . well, like a ninja. I know that sounds crazy, but before you say anything, Marie confessed the whole mess to me afterward. How she had a bad break-up with this guy in Japan who was connected, and she thinks he's trying to kill her, that he, like, sent people here to do what he couldn't do himself."

Lawson held up his hand and said, "Look . . . Chris, right? That first bit didn't sound nearly as crazy as everything that came after it. It's no wonder somebody as young as you is working for her, she's clearly got you wrapped around her finger. I don't know what the truth of the matter is, but trust me, that person who attacked her *can't* be connected to Milton Humphreys' death."

Liz was very nervous about what Lawson might be about to admit to Chris and not wanting to put him in any danger, she quickly stepped into the conversation. "Don't, Lawson."

He stopped in his tracks, realizing the potential consequences of his actions, but Chris was interested now and asked, "What? How can you know it wasn't connected? Do you know who did it?"

Lawson sighed and shrugged, saying, "Do what you want, Gutiérrez." He then climbed into the car.

Taking a deep breath, Liz attempted to calm her nerves a bit. To tell herself that there was still the possibility whoever attacked Marie had nothing to do with their vampire killer. She needed to not jump to any conclusions and framed her answer as delicately as possible. "We don't know, okay? But the chances are very slim, trust me. The person who killed Milton? It looked like they also killed his girlfriend. She was found dead this morning. We think they were tied up in something bad. I highly doubt it had anything to do with this attack on Miss LeBeau."

"You know that for sure?"

Liz wanted to say yes, but she was never a person that could lie easily. Part of her was still nervous the guy could be working for a vampire. Worse, he might know it and be fishing for the truth to take them out if they posed a threat. Or perhaps she was just being extremely paranoid for her own safety. But when she looked into Chris' eyes in that moment, she saw concern, and perhaps even love for his employer. Nothing that she'd expect from someone who was willingly working for a creature of the night. If her worst fears were true, she felt a small amount of pity for the poor fool. "How long have you been working for her?"

"Two days," he admitted. "Is it that obvious?"

Liz let out a small laugh, "You stuck out like a sore thumb."

"To be honest, I wonder at times why she hired me."

"She said you saved her in San Diego. I just assumed that you were working for her at the time of the incident."

Shaking his head, Chris said, "No, I was just a fan at a party. Right place, wrong time . . . or right time, I guess. When that ninja popped out, I thought I was going to die, but all my years taking martial arts, I guess they paid off. Next thing I know, security is charging in and this attacker jumps off the roof. Craziest thing I ever saw. Guess I'm just lucky they didn't pull the sword on their back."

Liz felt her blood go cold once more. It was the one piece of information she needed to cement her growing concern that Marie LeBeau was, in fact, a vampire. It also scared her how many others in Hollywood could be among the undead. How connected they might be, and how hard it could be to escape if they discovered Liz knew of their existence. In a way, she almost wished Chris hadn't said anything. But he had and now there was no turning back from the truth. "Sword?" she asked for confirmation.

"Yeah, I said they were dressed like a ninja. Figured you got the full picture, but I guess not."

Sighing, Liz abruptly grabbed Chris by the shoulders, letting him know she was serious, and saw him flinch. He was clearly frightened and confused as she said, "That woman you're working for is dangerous. I can't tell you why right here, and you might not even believe me if I did, but I can explain everything. We just need to get away from this house."

"What?" Chris seemed to be trying to process what Liz told him. "I don't understand."

"I can help you understand, but you have to trust me."

"How can I trust you if you won't tell me why?"

Releasing his shoulders, she said, "I will, but it's not safe here, please just come with us right now."

"If I say no, are you going to force me?"

Liz knew she couldn't as an officer of the law, but she wasn't in a position to argue about it, so she lied. "Yes. It's that important. Now get in the car." To drive the point home, she reached for her sidearm, just to show she was serious.

Chris didn't need to be told twice and moved into the back seat of the vehicle.

When Liz climbed into the driver's seat, she saw Lawson looking confused and alarmed at their new passenger in the back. "Did you just arrest him?"

"You see him in cuffs?" Without wasting any more words, she started up the car and drove off. The whole way out onto the road, she kept her eyes on the rearview mirror to make sure nobody was following them off the property. The security cameras at the gate might notice Chris in the back, or Marie would likely just notice his absence in a few minutes, but as long as they went somewhere that she didn't expect them to go, it seemed they would be safe for the time being.

"So can you tell me what the hell is going on now?" Chris asked with growing concern.

"Okay," Liz said, trying to regain her composure. "You'll probably think I'm insane for saying this, but that woman you're working for . . . I think she's a vampire."

Chris heard this and she expected him to laugh, or call her crazy, but surprisingly, he just sat there in silence. When she looked at Lawson, Liz saw he was a bit in shock. "Jesus, you just tell him like that? Now we gotta worry about this kid dying on us."

"I didn't have a choice, Lawson. He said the so-called ninja stalker had a sword. It *has* to be our vampire killer."

Chris started shaking his head. "Vampire killer? You can't be serious. I mean, this is all too crazy. How can you expect me to believe Marie is a . . . a *vampire*? I mean, I'm kind of a horror nerd, and even by my standards that seems nuts. Everybody knows vampires can't move around in the daylight. Marie isn't exactly walking around in one million SPF sunscreen."

"I know how it sounds, Chris," Liz said. "But have you ever seen a vampire in real life or are you just going by what you heard in movies? I mean, I can say for myself and Lawson, we'd never seen a vampire until we saw Milton Humphreys and Jyll Masters. The medical examiner said their bloodwork was unlike anything he'd ever seen, and Jyll had fangs that I've never seen on a normal human who wasn't doing cosplay. I'm telling you, as crazy as it sounds, it's the God's honest truth. I wish it weren't, but you seem like a good person. I couldn't just leave you there if you didn't already know."

Chris remained quiet for the next minute, clearly trying to process everything he had been told. Finally, he asked, "Can you show me? At the morgue. Are the bodies still there?"

Liz looked at Lawson and he seemed like he no longer cared what she did. So she said, "Yeah, we'll show you. But once you see, you know you can't go back there, right?"

"Even if I wanted to go back, would you let me? I mean, if she knows you know, you'll both be dead, right?"

Lawson said, "Yeah, that's exactly why I was ready to let you go on believing your stalker wasn't connected. It was safer for everyone if you didn't know. But now that you do? Shit, I don't know what to do. But I am not going to let you get us killed, that's for damn sure."

"Then we'll need to think up a plan," Liz said. "Chris, does Marie know where you live?"

"It wouldn't be hard for her to find out if she didn't," Lawson said.

Chris admitted, "Yeah, I think she knows, but I have a friend in Santa Monica I can stay with. She doesn't know him, hasn't even met him."

"Do you have any roommates?" Liz asked.

"Just one."

"Tell them to go out of town for a few weeks, stay with family or something."

"That's easier said than done."

"Well unless you want them in danger, or to get involved further, it's all I can think of. They'll be safer out of the way."

Lawson started shaking his head. "We don't even know how or *if* we can resolve this situation now. You've put a target on all of our backs, Gutiérrez. If this doesn't stop with Marie, we could be fucked."

Liz found herself at the end of her rope with Lawson and finally snapped. "I'm doing my fucking best, Chuck! You got any better ideas, spit them the fuck out or shut up! Or maybe you'd like me to just leave you on the side of the road up ahead and you can figure your own plan out?"

He was clearly taken aback by her verbal lashing, and even Chris seemed stunned in the back seat. But Lawson didn't respond and kept quiet the rest of the car ride. Liz just hoped she'd made the right call. Because this was one situation where the wrong choice would certainly end in their deaths.

22

Chris couldn't believe what he'd been told by the detectives—but more than that, he couldn't believe what he was shown at the morgue. The medical examiner told Chris everything he knew and showed him the severed head of Jyll Masters. Chris promptly threw up upon seeing the gory truth for himself. He felt like he couldn't walk, like his body wanted to shut down. The immediate fear of what had been revealed took hold and he wanted to curl up into a ball somewhere warm and safe where nobody could find him.

Worse than anything shown to him, though, was the odd pull he still felt toward Marie. He couldn't just wash away his feelings for her, yet what scared him more than anything was how he felt now that she wasn't around. Similar to his night with Philip Dalton, he felt depressed without her in his company—weak, even. She was like a drug he'd become addicted to and attempting to quit cold turkey could cost him a high price. Still, he didn't want to become one of the undead, or throw his life away. He wished in that moment he'd never met her. That he'd stayed with his other friends at Comic-Con and not gone to that signing, or the screening, and *definitely* not the after-party.

But the damage had been done, and he'd been shown the horrible truth. What mattered in that moment was what he chose to do next. The first thing he did was to call up Dan. He had to come up with a good excuse for his friend to leave town. And what he ended up saying was a lie. That the person after Marie had been tracking Chris and now Dan's life was as in as much danger as his own since they lived together. Dan didn't need to be told twice and took a two-week vacation from work, planning to drive home that night to his parents out in Redlands.

Meanwhile, Chris now had a time limit on trying to resolve this mess. If there was even a way to resolve it. From what he'd been told about the bodies, they were connected to Marie, so it was possible she turned them, but it was also just as possible a whole lot of vampires existed around Hollywood and had recently set their sights on those in higher positions of power to take control of the city . . . if they hadn't already. Chris couldn't help but think this could even be a *Blade* scenario, where vampires already ruled things behind the scenes and simply knowing about them meant there was no escape. They'd be on the run for the rest of their lives. But he couldn't surrender himself to this thought until it was proven true. For now, they had to work with what they knew and figure out what to do next. And what came next for Chris was to lay low with his friend Nick while the detectives who'd uncovered the whole conspiracy did the heavy lifting.

Nick was surprised to receive a call from Chris mid-week and though he was at work when Chris called, Chris told his friend that he was in a bad state and needed help. Nick couldn't just skip work, but said he could meet him after. Chris was a little nervous about waiting around for several hours and therefore asked Nick if he had a spare key hidden anywhere. Thankfully, Nick did, in one of those old fake rocks. Outside Nick's home was a little garden filled with stones, and hidden among them was an inconspicuous one that he'd hidden well. It took Chris a minute to find it, as he had to actually feel the surface to recognize the fake. Once he found it, he retrieved the key from inside and moved into Nick's home. The two detectives followed.

The three of them had agreed in advance that it would be best if they weren't around when Nick arrived home, as it would likely scare his friend and they didn't want him panicking and doing something stupid. What they did need to do before Nick got home, though, was discuss what their next move was going to be. Chris wasn't exactly a master strategist, but proposed, "Why don't we just send that body at the morgue to the press? I mean, we don't know where the vampires could be hiding, but I'd put my money on government or police. Certainly, not the press."

Liz shook her head. "Normally I'd say the press is a good option, but not for this. No credible paper would touch this with a ten-foot pole. Doesn't matter how real the body looks. They'd still be in denial. The only papers that would print this are the tabloids running stories nobody is gonna believe."

"But if we don't do anything, isn't Jyll just going to end up vanishing like Milton's body?"

Lawson said, "Yeah, but that won't matter, kid. We might not make it to tomorrow at this rate. That vampire you were with might not have seen you leave with us, but if she has, we're fucked. She has our names, and it won't be hard to find us now."

"Or that vampire killer might get her first. She seemed pretty adamant that she needed me around for protection. Without me there, she's exposed."

"We don't even know why she hired you," Liz said. "Maybe she was being honest, maybe she did believe you could protect her, but if you'd bothered to talk with anyone else about this, I'm sure they would have thought she sounded crazy."

Chris shrugged. "I mean, yeah, it seemed weird, but I truly believed she thought I could help. I did manage to fight off this so-called 'vampire killer'."

"You might have gotten lucky, Chris. Point is, we can't go assuming anything. Safest thing may be for Lawson and me to blow town. We can't fight her when she's got the advantage."

"Fuck that, Gutiérrez," Lawson spat. "We need to take the fight to her. I say we find this vampire hunter and form some kind of alliance."

"We're still cops, Lawson. We can't just go vigilante."

"These fuckers aren't even human, Liz! We gotta do *something*. We can't run forever. Same with the kid here. I mean, he's got a life to get back to."

"I know we can't run, Lawson. I was only saying that would be the safest thing to do. But I also got a little boy to look after. I need to get him somewhere safe first. I think his babysitter's family might look after him for a bit—they're pretty close. As for us, we should get a motel. I don't think this vampire is going to be tracking us that well. At least I hope she's not that connected."

"And the captain? What do we tell him about the case?"

"Same as before, it's gone cold. We still got a job to do, we can't run from that, but we're going to have to work this on the side somehow."

"That's a lot to ask."

"Well, do you have a better idea?"

"Yeah, I already pitched it to you."

"We don't know the first thing about this vampire hunter. How could we even go about finding them?"

"Maybe we'll get lucky and they'll find us?"

"I got a crazy idea . . ." Chris started and was a little taken back when the two detectives turned to him, like he'd just said something absurd. "I mean, hopefully not *too* crazy. But I got an idea where this person might strike next."

"We're not going back to Marie's place, kid," Lawson laughed. "That would be suicide."

"No, Marie seemed to think her co-star Philip Dalton might be the next one killed. Now, the only reason I can think she might have thought that is if he's *also* a vampire. So, what if we staked out his place and waited for this vampire killer to show up?"

Liz said, "It's not a terrible plan, but the only *we* here is Lawson and me. *You* are staying here with your friend. Staying safe, so we don't have to worry about you."

"C'mon," Chris argued. "I can help."

"No fucking way, kid," Lawson said. "Liz is right, you're staying here. We'll fill you in when we know more. But we can't have a civilian tagging along."

And with that, Lawson and Liz prepared to head back to the police station. Chris wasn't sure exactly what their plans were, since they didn't want to share too much with him in case he felt like following. Not that he had his car anymore, but still, he knew even if he did head to Philip's house, they'd probably spot him and just drive him right back to Nick's. So for the time being, he'd do as they instructed and sit tight.

He just wasn't sure what the hell he was going to tell Nick . . .

23

"Philip Dalton? The actor?" Captain Patrick Ford asked with visible confusion.

"That's right, sir." Lawson had just broken the news to him that Dalton was their prime suspect in the Humphreys and Masters murder investigation. It was a complete lie and likely was the reason for the confused expression on Ford's face. But with the press breathing down his neck for information, Liz figured he'd be relieved to have any leads, even if they seemed to be wrong.

"You've got to be joking. The guy's record is as clean as they come. He's got one DUI from a decade ago when he was partying as much as can be expected from a twentysomething actor. But no assaults, gambling, drugs, nothing that would make me think of him as our sword-swinging slasher. So you've gotta give me a *little* more to go on here. You haven't even questioned him yet."

Liz knew Ford had them there. Under normal circumstances, they would have questioned Dalton, except he was never a suspect and if Ford prodded further, their lie would quickly fall apart. So Liz pivoted. "We were going to do that, but we wanted to speak to you first. If we could just get some surveillance gear, we—"

"I can't approve that on a hunch, Gutiérrez. You know that."

"You know he used to date Marie LeBeau, right?" Lawson interjected.

"Yeah, everybody knew about that. Hot and passionate before a quick flameout. You saying she's involved somehow?"

"Possibly, but we're unsure. She didn't give us any answers today that would lead us to believe that, but we know she was close with Milton, perhaps closer than she wanted anyone to know. Dalton was the jealous type when they were together too. Not much got to the press because he was never physical, but there were incidents where he'd get drunk and lose it a bit in public places." This was news to Liz, but whether or not it was true, she wasn't about to interrupt her partner. Lawson continued, "If something was going on with Marie and Milton, I could see Dalton offing him. Perhaps a sword was all he had available—we don't know. That's why we'd like to run surveillance on his place, see if we can find anything that could net us that search warrant."

"And Miss Masters?" Ford asked, leaning forward with curiosity.

Liz decided to step in to make it look like Lawson wasn't completely off-base with his theory. "It's possible she saw something that convinced her Dalton was responsible. We still don't know why her car was all plastic-wrapped to hell. Perhaps she lured Dalton there, wanted to kill him and it backfired."

"Hmm." Captain Ford pondered everything they'd handed him for a moment. Then he said, "Look, I'm not going to say you're way off-base here, but what you've given me still only amounts to a few hunches. I'm not going to approve surveillance on Dalton. If you two want to watch his place, it'll be from your vehicle with whatever you have on you. Unless you'd like to question him, which frankly you should have done already. But if you can't get me anything solid in forty-eight hours, I want you to move on. Got it?"

"Of course, Captain," Lawson said with a nod.

On their way out of the station, Liz took a call from her son's babysitter. For the past several hours, Liz had become quite concerned that Marie or other vampires could go after her son. It wasn't clear yet if they knew about Freddy—or that he was home alone—but she wasn't about to lead anyone back there while he was still inside. Calling Lydia to pick him up and let him stay with her for a while seemed the most sensible option. Unfortunately, Lydia, being the busy teenager she was, didn't respond immediately to texts and Liz's call went straight to voice mail. So Liz left one asking Lydia to call her back ASAP. Thankfully, by the time they'd finished with Captain Ford, Lydia did just that.

Since Liz never really told Lydia the particulars of any of her cases, she made up a story close to the truth. "All I can tell you is that my life is currently in danger. I think I can resolve the situation soon, I just don't know when—and I think it's safer for Freddy if he stayed with you for a few days. If you need anything you can call or text me, but right now you're the only one I trust with my son." She knew if Freddy's Uncle Hector heard her say that, he'd have been furious, but having not spoken to him in as long as it had been, she just didn't feel comfortable calling him about this.

"I understand, Mrs. G. It's really no big deal. Though when you say a few days, do you know how many, exactly?"

"I don't and I'm sorry for that, but I'll double your rate if it'll help."

"Oh, it's not for me, but my parents. Asking them to take in Freddy for an open-ended amount of time isn't the easiest thing to drop in their laps. However, with my brother away at college, I'm sure they'd like having another young guy around the house."

"Got it, so you just want the normal rate?"

"You bet." Liz's bank account was thankful Lydia declined her offer for double. "Anyway, I'll swing by your house in a little bit. Does Freddy know I'm coming?"

"I'll let him know. Thanks again, Lydia, you're a literal lifesaver here."

"No problem, Mrs. G. Anytime."

With that item out of the way, Liz caught up with Lawson at their car and the two headed back up into the Hollywood Hills to find Philip Dalton's home. When they arrived at his address, they went over the plan. As Ford didn't approve them for any surveillance gear, they had to make do with some binoculars, but despite his insistence they watch the house from the car, the detectives knew they weren't going to see anything from the road. They'd need to find a better vantage point.

Parking the car a good distance past Dalton's property, the detectives then navigated their way around the rear of his house. There wasn't any easy way to get close without tipping their hand or having his neighbors freak out. They ended up finding some bushes just past the edge of his pool area where they were able to stay safely hidden. Through their binoculars, it gave them a great view of the two floors of his home which had massive floor to ceiling windows from one end to the other. Liz thought it must have been a nightmare to keep cool in the summer, but she supposed someone as rich as Dalton could afford the best air conditioning money could buy.

For the next several hours, the two tried to not let their limbs fall asleep. Constantly shifting how they were sitting to get more comfortable was a challenge all its own. Liz wished they could have just stayed in the car, but the front of Dalton's house was mostly obscured and the street behind his home was far enough down the hill they'd be too low to see anything clearly. So creeping in the bushes was unfortunately their best option. She was just glad they picked up some food on the way there. But bathroom breaks were not an easy feat when one had to trek halfway down the hill to make sure they were clear of any onlookers who'd suspect the detectives were trying to break into their home.

It seemed for a while like their trip there might have been a waste of time, but then a thought struck Liz like a lightning bolt to the brain as she witnessed Dalton getting dressed after a shower. He already had his pants on when he stepped out of the bathroom—the only spot obscured from their view—but it got her thinking, wondering about something that perhaps the killer was also wondering. "Shit, I think I know why that killer hasn't struck yet. Providing they *are* watching Dalton."

"Enlighten me," Lawson said.

"Think back to when Milton and his girlfriend were killed. He was just at the pool, while she was trying to feed on some poor soul in an alley. In both cases the killer struck. For Jyll, it made sense. They had to step in. But why Milton? Why at that time?"

Lawson shrugged. "No idea."

"The red marks on his leg, *both* their legs, remember? What if the killer had spotted those while he was at the pool? From their perspective, that'd be a pretty good confirmation he was one of the undead, right?"

Lawson thought about this for a moment and admitted, "Yeah, I guess that makes sense. So what, you think they're waiting for Dalton to get down to his skivvies?"

"Yeah, or try to kill someone. Whatever the case, he's either not a vampire, or he's being very careful. If Dalton hasn't gotten sloppy feeding on people or taking off his clothes, the killer would have no choice but to wait or seek out other targets. We haven't had any dead bodies drained of blood, so if he's getting blood from somewhere, he's not leaving a trail."

"Then what the hell can we do about this? Should we just head home if this is going to be a waste of time?"

"No way, the sun's almost set, so it's the perfect time for this killer to strike. We just need to make sure they leave a trail this time." And with that, she stepped out of the bushes and made her way toward Dalton's home.

"Liz, what the fuck are you doing?!" Lawson sprang out after her, clearly afraid for her safety, and his own. "You can't seriously think about going in there. If he *is* one of the undead and he's talked to Marie, we're fucked."

"We're not totally defenseless here, Lawson. Besides, if he's dumb enough to start any shit, that killer is bound to show up, just like we wanted."

"And if they don't and he fucking kills us? Jesus, what about Freddy?"

Just as she was rounding the front of the house, Liz turned back to Lawson and said, "You're right. It'd be stupid for both of us to go in there. You go. I'll watch your back."

"What?! You can't be serious."

"Okay, then I'll go and you watch my back."

"For fuck's sake, you're not giving me an out here, are you?"

"What's it gonna be, Chuck?"

She waited for his reply, studying his eyes to see if he was going to walk, or actually agree to her plan. It was quite the gambit, but it was all they had at that point. She didn't want to die, and didn't want to leave Freddy without a mother, but she was out of options and couldn't waste any more time.

Finally, after a minute of deep deliberation, Lawson said, "Fuck it, okay. I'll go in. Just please, don't let me fucking die."

"Well, then don't die." Giving him a wink to lighten the tension seizing her partner's body, she patted him on the back to usher him toward the front door.

Before he took a step though, he asked, "Wait, shouldn't you be monitoring things with some audio? I mean, if he takes me somewhere you can't see?"

He had a point, and she replied, "Well, it would have been nice if we had a wire, but your phone will have to do. Ford really didn't help us out here." She gave Lawson a call and when he answered it, she set his call to speaker and slid the phone into his pocket. "Whoa, what the hell? You set that to speaker and he's gonna wind up hearing you!"

"Not if I set this to mute, genius." Pulling out her earbuds, she plugged them into her phone and hit the mute button.

"Shit, how did I never notice that option?"

"Because you're not a very good detective," Liz answered with a grin.

Taking a deep breath, Lawson attempted to relax and said, "Okay, wish me luck."

"You don't need it, but good luck." With that, Liz slunk back into the bushes where she had a view of what was going on inside through her binoculars. Over her headphones, she could hear Lawson knocking on the door and then watched as Dalton made his way over to it. He seemed surprised to see Lawson there, but then Lawson showed him his badge and said, "Hi, I'm Detective Chuck Lawson. You're Philip Dalton, correct?"

Dalton nodded and said, "Yeah, what's this about?"

"Well, I'm investigating the deaths of Milton Humphreys and his girlfriend Jyll Masters. You were associated with him through *Black Berenice*, right?"

"Yeah, but I didn't know him that well. Marie did—you talk with her yet?"

"Marie LeBeau? Yeah, she's the one who thought we should come talk to you. You mind if I come inside? Feels a lot cooler in there."

It seemed Dalton was hesitating for a moment, and Liz worried they were about to be screwed out of their chance. But instead, he said, "Yeah, sure, come on in."

Dalton led Lawson inside his home. Unfortunately, the front door entered onto the second floor since the house was on a hill. If Liz was going to be able to help quickly, she hoped Lawson would request going down to the first floor. Thankfully, as Dalton moved into the living room to offer Lawson a drink, the detective pointed to the pool and said, "That's a nice setup back there. One of the biggest pools I've seen."

"Yeah, I swim a lot in my free time. Helps to have a bigger pool for doing laps."

"Must have cost a pretty penny."

"You want a closer look?"

Lawson shrugged. "I'd love to see the whole place if you're up to giving me a tour."

Once more, Dalton hesitated for some reason, but then smiled and said, "Sure, why not? I'll give you the tour and you can ask your questions as we go. Sound good?"

Lawson nodded and said, "That'd be great."

"Then it's settled. Well, since we're up here already, we can start with the living room. Would you like a drink?"

Lawson nodded and said, "Sure, I've been known to enjoy a good Scotch if you've got any."

"Only the best," Dalton said before quickly moving to serve one up for the detective.

Liz felt her stomach tighten at the thought that Dalton might be drugging her partner. It seemed like a very real possibility, and she couldn't believe Lawson would be stupid enough to drink anything that man poured for him. She just had to hope that he was faking his sips. Unfortunately, from his reaction, she wasn't sure that's what happened.

"Damn fine stuff," Lawson said.

"It ought to be. Cost me a pretty penny, as you said."

"Well, shall we move along with the tour?"

Dalton nodded and said, "Of course. You had some questions though, right? Or are you just a fan?"

"Guilty on both counts," Lawson laughed. "I thought you

were legit great in that other one you did with Marie, the erotic thriller."

"*Burning Passion.*"

"Yeah, that was quite a changeup from your earlier work."

"Well, it was my way of trying to be taken a bit more seriously. Seems it worked in your case." Dalton led them into the kitchen and said, "This is the kitchen."

"These granite countertops?" Lawson asked.

"That's right. Much easier cleanup."

"Right . . ." Liz wondered if Lawson was thinking the same thing as her and knew he was when he said, "That's quite the freezer."

However, seemed their hunches were wrong when Dalton opened it casually and said, "Got a lot of cuts in here, frozen for later use. Being single has its perks, but food spoilage is not one of them. So, I try to freeze as much as I can."

"Sorry," Lawson admitted. "I should get to my questions, not ask you about how you stay in such good shape."

Dalton laughed at this, "It's your time, Detective. I'm here to help in any way I can."

Dalton then led them into his bedroom and said, "This is the bedroom."

"Before we move on," Lawson said, "When was the last time you saw Milton Humphreys?"

"Would have been at San Diego Comic-Con with Marie. I'd wager that was the last time we both saw him."

"Well, technically she did see him once after. To discuss the details of the premiere for *Black Berenice.*"

"Hmm, news to me. Let's continue this downstairs."

"Lead the way."

Dalton led Lawson to the stairs and down to his first floor. There he had set up a game room for himself with a pool table and a few other fun little toys. "This is the game room—quite popular at my parties."

"Is that an invitation?" Lawson asked.

This got Dalton to laugh and say, "I don't think my friends would feel too comfortable with a cop at one of my parties." He then tapped his nose, which Liz took for a not-so-subtle indication those friends were doing blow at said parties.

"So you had last seen Milton at Comic-Con, but did you have any interaction with his girlfriend or know any of his business outside of *Black Berenice?*"

"That's a no and no. Frankly, detective, I'm surprised Marie sent you my way, but seeing how she normally treats me these days, I'd assume this was some kind of cruel joke of hers to waste my time."

"So you really weren't familiar enough with either victim to have an idea who'd want to kill them?"

"As I've said already, I was not. I don't think I can be much help to your case."

"Okay, that's disappointing to hear, but I guess we're done here. Do you mind if I take a look at the pool before I go?"

"Sure."

Dammit, Liz thought. She knew that Lawson needed to do something bold. If they couldn't get Dalton to reveal his true nature before he led Lawson off his property, they were screwed. It was too much to expect he'd try to kill Lawson right out in the open if he didn't think he was in danger of being exposed by the detective.

As the patio lights sprang to life, the two men stepped outside. Lawson approached the pool, with Dalton following closely, and pointed toward the bottom. "It looks like you got a little buildup down there. How often do you clean it?"

Dalton seemed surprised by this and moved closer to the

pool to check. "That's nothing, pretty standard to—" Before Dalton could finish speaking, Lawson shoved him into the pool.

"You son of a bitch!" Dalton spat as he surfaced. "You get the fuck off my property or I'll have someone *drag* you out! You're lucky you're a cop, or I'd kick your ass for this. You have any idea how expensive these shoes are?"

Moving to the edge Dalton pulled himself onto the cement and Lawson said, "I'm sorry, I was just messing around, but I guess I shoved too hard. Didn't think you'd actually go in."

"I don't fucking care! Just get the fuck out of here."

Lawson held up his hands in surrender and said, "Okay, okay, I'm gone."

As Lawson began to make his way around the house, Liz saw that Dalton was stripping down next to the pool. Clearly, he wasn't about to head back into his home in sopping wet clothes. First his shoes came off. Then his shirt, and finally his pants. Through her binoculars it was hard to spot them in the fading sunlight, but the lights around his pool gave just enough illumination for her to notice the two distinct red marks on his inner left thigh. Same as Milton, same as Jyll. If that killer was watching, they were sure to strike, and when that happened, Liz would move in.

Thankfully, she didn't have to wait long to find out.

As Dalton laid out his wet clothes over some chairs, he made his way to the door and a ninja-like figure clad in black crept quickly across the back patio toward him. Their sword was drawn without a sound and they were mere feet away when Dalton must have spotted their reflection in the windows he was facing. Apparently, the killer didn't notice because they weren't able to respond fast enough to what came next.

Dalton whirled around like lightning taking the ninja by the throat. He must have been squeezing hard because a scream was let out and then cut short. The sword dropped from their fingers, and Liz knew she had mere seconds to act.

Charging from the bushes, Liz drew her sidearm in a smooth motion and aimed it at Dalton's head. "Let them go!" she shouted. Dalton hissed at her, baring his fangs for the first time. Something had changed in his face, like all compassion had fled and in its place was a soulless shadow of a man. A creature that only cared about survival.

"I'm not fucking kidding. You drop them or you're dead."

"Shoooot," the ninja wheezed.

Dalton smiled and began to slowly approach Liz while still holding the ninja up in the air with one hand, as if they weighed next to nothing. In seconds, he'd be close enough to strike at Liz. She couldn't wait any longer and did the only thing she could think to do.

She took the shot.

The bullet found its mark, sending Dalton's brains spraying onto the patio behind him. His grip on the ninja ceased and he fell back onto the ground. Massaging their throat, the ninja said, "Thanks."

"I don't know who you are, but I think we're on the same side. I'm LAPD Detective Liz Gutiérrez, and I need your help."

"Well, you got it. You saved my life." The ninja's voice sounded feminine, which surprised Liz, who up to that moment had assumed they were male. But now that she analyzed the ninja's lithe frame, it seemed to make sense. Moving back over to her sword—which was a few feet away on the ground—the ninja picked it up.

Liz, meanwhile, was trying to check the corpse. She wasn't sure a bullet to the brain would kill a vampire, even if Dalton looked dead. So she approached cautiously, but when she was almost at the body, she heard Lawson's voice say, "Shit! You got him?"

When Liz looked up at her partner, she saw the ninja also looking in his direction. "It's okay. This is my partner, Chuck Lawson."

"Please to meet you, uh, ninja guy."

"The name's Elena. Now if you and your—" Elena turned to Liz as she spoke and immediately changed her tone to a shout. "Move!"

Liz didn't even have time to react before a vice-like grip encircled her ankle and squeezed with so much force she thought her bone might snap. This knocked her off balance and she found her body falling to the concrete. Philip Dalton leaped up to his feet, his snarling face looking ready to drain her dry. Before that could happen though, the actor found his end at the edge of Elena's blade. It sliced through his neck like butter and the detective watched in horror and fascination as it rolled across the ground and into the pool.

"Jesus Christ!" Lawson gasped.

"We need to get out of here. Somebody had to have seen this." Elena said, holding out her hand to help Liz up.

Once she was on her feet, Liz said, "Thanks. I guess that makes us even. We can drive you out of here, if you'll come with us."

"I have my own car. I've been following you guys most of the day, but wasn't sure what you knew. Now . . . I think we should find somewhere safe to talk."

YOU KEEP ME HANGIN' ON

1

Elena Dillinger had been tracking her prey for a total of six years at that point, including the time she'd spent with her father, Franco. Much of what she'd been told about the elusive vampire queen had been passed down by him. Franco's father had told him the legend, and his father before him. As the last in a long line of vampire hunters, Elena had been raised on stories about this force of nature who uprooted herself every three to four decades. Wherever she went, the elite would be turned, allowing them to spread their influence down the ranks until vampires silently ruled every facet of the location they resided in. When things turned sour, or she had stayed in one place long enough for her immortally youthful appearance to raise questions, she moved on. And those she had turned spread out to other places in hopes of growing new vampire communities.

From what Franco had told her, tales of the great French beauty known only as Adrienne first surfaced in the mid-eighteenth century. Although only known to the hunter community at the time, she had silently decimated the French aristocracy. Through her influence behind the scenes, she slowly managed to turn every important figurehead in the county into a vampire. But if enough change happens too quickly, the inevitable downfall will follow. So in the late 1700s, a revolution came for all of their heads. The vampires could have fought back, but against a big enough mob, even they were powerless. For the true secret of a vampire's strength resided in darkness. Though they could move about freely in the daylight, their strength, speed, and reflexes were reduced to mere mortal status. Thus they could be killed just as easily as anyone else. Adrienne, however, must have seen the writing on the wall.

The hunters at the time believed the vampire queen had been killed with the rest of the powerful, but sure enough, rumors began to swirl that she had fled to England. In the mid-nineteenth century, there were tales told of a great French beauty causing quite a stir amongst the upper class. These tales eventually spread to the ears of a hunter in the area, Thomas Howard. He found his prey in London, but even he was powerless to defeat her. For not only was she a great beauty, but all men who came close to her seemed to fall under her spell. And that was the last anyone in the hunter community heard of Thomas Howard.

There were rumors that he had not been turned into a vampire, though, but half-turned into what was commonly referred to as a familiar. The term had many different connotations over the years, but to those who knew the vampires that actually existed in the real world, familiars were more than mere human servants. Gifted with an extremely long life, they possessed the strength and the speed to protect their masters. The tradeoff was a rather a pitiful existence. It was a life of servitude, controlled by the every whim of their master. They were more like a husk of something human.

When Adrienne fled London, she next took root in New York at the turn of the twentieth century. She had managed to make a good life for herself there, with some powerful allies, but the stock market crash of 1929 once more caused her to abandon her new family and return to Europe. Which was where Elena's great-grandfather had found her during the Second World War.

It would surprise few to learn how many Nazis were secretly vampires, but it would surprise far more to learn just how many were not. That those unspeakable atrocities could have been committed only by demons in human form seemed far simpler to explain. But they were there nonetheless, hiding in the ranks, working the war to their advantage, with Adrienne behind the scenes.

Helmut Dillinger was the most notable vampire killer of his age, slaying well over a hundred of the undead—some in battle, others in their own homes. His actions naturally had branded him a traitor to his country, and he was forced to operate in the shadows. But when he found the vampire queen within the heart of the Nazi elite in 1945, his chance to slay her was disrupted by the Allied forces. The Nazis had been crushed in one battle after another and some of the vampires among them saw the writing on the wall, fleeing as far as they could travel. In Adrienne's case, escaping to Argentina.

Helmut soon followed, taking with his young son Heinrich, and his wife Elsa. They settled in Buenos Aires, and he continued his hunt. But even the best hunters can fall prey to their own egos. Not bothering to contact any other hunters to assist—as so many had died or become impossible to locate in the midst of the war— Helmut attempted to take the queen down all on his own. But she was not alone in Buenos Aires, and her minions had set a trap for the poor arrogant hunter. The next day, Elsa tried to identify his body for the police, but even she was unable to after how badly it had been mutilated.

Heinrich grew up in South America, never forgetting his father, or the demon responsible for his death. He had vengeance in his heart, fueling him forward to train harder and refine his tactics when it came to hunting the undead. Soon he was feared by every vampire south of the equator. But he never had his chance at revenge, as Adrienne had once more disappeared into the ether. So all his successes, his knowledge, experience, and his lust for revenge were laid at the feet of his son, Franco.

Elena's father was a very smart man, much more accomplished than his own father, who struggled since being uprooted from his home in Germany. Franco, though, studied hard and soon was accepted to NYU on a full scholarship. His move to America was not just a chance for a fresh start, but the chance to make his father proud by tracking down the monster who'd murdered his grandfather. There were rumors she'd fled north, but Heinrich never figured out where. So it was up to Franco to do right by his father, not just by becoming the first college graduate in the family, but by avenging Heinrich's death.

While in college, he quickly became enthralled by the many American beauties he found himself surrounded by. None more so than Kimberly Campbell, the young sociology major who'd won his heart with a single look. He didn't struggle to win her over either, as his accent seemed to make every girl in the school swoon. But their passionate love affair naturally led to Kim becoming pregnant. Unable to support herself and the child, she planned to drop out of school to raise the baby. However, her parents insisted that Franco marry her first, which he was more than happy to do. Unfortunately, only a few months later as she prepared to give birth to their first child, she died in labor.

Suddenly, Franco was the one having to drop out of school, in an attempt to raise his newborn daughter on the harsh streets of New York City. When he attempted to contact his parents in hopes of possibly moving back to Buenos Aires, he found himself unable to reach anyone. After some investigating, he was saddened to learn that they had both been found dead under mysterious circumstances. His father's rage possessed him, as he knew that deep down there was no real mystery to their deaths. It had to have been vampires—the only constant in their lives.

So Franco threw himself into the family business, taking all the training he'd been given by his father and doubling it for his daughter. She studied every form of martial arts available to them in New York. Soon enough, she was even able to take down her old man in a one-on-one fight. It was only natural that they started partnering up to hunt down the undead. Six years ago, they heard rumors of a vampire queen somewhere up north, whose followers had slowly trickled down to New York and beyond. As Elena's father moved them to Quebec to find what he hoped was the long sought-after vampire queen, she unfortunately found them first.

Elena wasn't sure how she'd located them, but one morning after going out to fetch her father breakfast, she'd returned back to their home to find him dead. This sent Elena on a bender that took almost five years to emerge from. When she finally had enough clarity to sober up, it was due to the presence of a new mayor of Montreal who seemed more sinister than those who came before. She smelled something wrong, and as part of the usual tactics employed by her father, she pursued her prey for confirmation he was one of the undead. She only hoped that he might have some information on the whereabouts of the one who turned him.

2

Mayor Cedric Perreault had arrived home around 8 p.m. that evening in late June. It was just like any other night, except for one small difference—Elena Dillinger was watching. She had found a good hiding spot at the edge of his property. It was far enough to be out of view, but also close enough that her binoculars could easily spot the evidence she needed. When it came to vampire hunting, things weren't as easy as they had been back in the day. There was once a time where the only way vampires could feed was luring their prey home or taking to the streets. This made their activities easy to track, and killing them much simpler. But with the changing times came changing tactics. With easier access to blood, whether through hospital connections, or familiars who'd capture prey for them, they could find ways of keeping their activities well under wraps. Which made it harder than ever to identify them.

The easiest way Elena found to recognize a vampire was to spot their turning mark. This mark was like a birthmark that all vampires possessed. Once turned, the bite they were given by their sire was permanent. As they were undead, the marks from when they were human remained and that meant those two puncture marks remained little red identifiers for all vampire hunters. Naturally, like all other means of throwing a hunter off their scent, the location of these changed with the times. As once they might have been found on the neck, now they were usually found somewhere more hidden—the inner thigh being the calling card of the vampire queen. This meant spotting a mark required the vampire to strip down before she could identify them.

The mayor was a smart one. Whatever means Cedric Perreault was feeding by, they were well hidden. Elena wasn't an expert at disabling security systems, so she couldn't get inside to check his fridge, but he never drank from clear glasses. Nothing that could let anyone snooping through a window see what he was having with his dinner. That was the other tricky thing about vampires. They could eat regular food. The taste was pretty foul to them, but the smart ones learned to adapt, to make others think they still enjoyed it. Often times having rare meat or using a special sauce on their food would help it go down easier. But again, nothing she could see made it clear the mayor was one of the undead.

It wasn't until he retired to his room to take a shower that she was finally able to get the evidence she needed. Mayor Perreault was careful, but not careful enough. While his bathroom was hidden from view, he didn't seem to mind stepping out into his bedroom in the nude. Why should he worry about voyeurs? After all, his floor-to-ceiling windows faced the St. Lawrence River. Unless paparazzi were in a boat with a telescopic lens, they wouldn't be able to see much. But luckily for Elena, and unfortunately for Mayor Perreault, she was able to see from her vantage point just fine. And the red marks on his inner thigh were clear as day under the bright yellow glow of his bedroom lights.

With all the evidence she needed, Elena made her way back to her car and waited for her time to strike. While it was true vampires preferred to operate at night when they were strongest, those who wanted to keep their secrets concealed chose to sleep when most humans would have done so. It was hard for a vampire to sleep at night, much like for a human during the day, and so most of these fakers would only get about an hour or two of sleep each night. Which was all they needed. As long as they continued to feed, they'd maintain their strength. So while it would seem the opportune moment to attack was when the vampire slept, that was actually when they were at their most dangerous.

No, what Elena found to be the best method was to simply catch them off guard. Whether at night or during the day, if they didn't see it coming, she could strike them down without having to worry about an attack that could take her head off. With Mayor Perreault, she figured the best time to strike was in the morning, when he was preparing to leave for work. Most targets never saw an attack coming when all of their focus was on the day ahead.

Elena didn't just want the mayor dead, though—her primary objective was some kind of clue as to where the queen might have gone, or what her current alias was. The simplest way to accomplish this seemed to be killing the mayor before he set his alarm. The problem with that was that she couldn't get to him easily before he left the house. So, after the mayor prepared for his day with what she could only assume was a blood breakfast, she managed to sneak past the cameras he had out front of his house and hide behind a bush with a perfect view of the window next to his front door—where the security keypad just happened to reside. As Perrault prepared to leave, he stopped at the keypad, ready to punch in his code. The eagle eyes of Elena Dillinger were focused and alert as he punched in the four numbers to set his alarm. Then he made his way to the door as she kept hidden.

When Perreault stepped outside, he carefully locked his front door and began the walk to his car. Unfortunately for him, Elena was well-trained at concealing her presence. She crept behind him so quietly, not even a creature of the night with acute hearing could have noticed her. As he popped open his trunk, she struck his neck with a single swift slice of her katana. Instead of his briefcase ending up in the trunk, his severed head found its way inside. Elena watched the now lifeless body of Cedric Perreault flop down onto the driveway and she flipped out her sword to let the blood splatter on the cement. Carefully sheathing the blade once more behind her back, Elena lifted the mayor's body into the truck and sealed it inside along with his head. She had made sure to swipe his keys and leisurely strolled back to his front door. The cameras would have picked her up by then, but luckily for her, it got nothing other than a figure clad all in black. Ninjas might have been a cliché concept, but they kept her identity a secret, and that was all she needed.

Once she was inside the mayor's home, she was quick to deactivate his alarm and kept an eye out for anything that might be a hint to the whereabouts of the vampire queen. Elena spent an hour turning over every inch of the place for clues, but kept coming up empty. Apart from the stash of blood that was hidden in his fridge, she couldn't believe there was nothing linking the mayor to Adrienne. Perhaps she had been wrong and he was turned by someone else. But the turning mark . . . it had Adrienne written all over it. Elena knew that spending more than an hour there was an invitation for the police to come snooping, so she had to wrap things up. Mayors didn't just disappear without anyone coming to look. And he was surely expected at his office some time ago.

Elena prepared to leave, making her way through the kitchen toward the front door. That was when her eyes caught the stack of mail on his kitchen counter. She felt like an idiot in that moment for having overlooked it when she first came in. But mail was not the first thing most people would check for clues. She assumed it was mostly bills or local government stuff. But hidden amongst those things was also an invitation. Its return address was the office of the Humphreys Brothers, a production company in Los Angeles. Elena wasn't familiar with them, but frankly didn't see a lot of movies, so that was no surprise. When she removed the contents of the envelope, she saw two tickets inside and a letter inviting the dear old friend of Marie LeBeau to the premiere of her latest film, *Black Berenice*.

Whoever this woman was in LA, she was somebody important in Hollywood, with a big new film opening. From the title, Elena assumed Marie was an actress, and then suddenly she remembered hearing something about the up-and-coming star. She didn't really pay attention to the goings-on in Hollywood, but some stories were hard to miss and this was one. The French-Canadian actress had emerged from obscurity to take Hollywood by storm the past few years. Suddenly it was like the last piece of a puzzle fell into place. Adrienne had changed her name and found a new home, a new place to colonize.

Hollywood.

There was no telling how many she'd already turned in the several years she had been rising to her current place in the film industry. Elena knew that if she didn't stop "Marie" soon, the power under the vampire queen's thumb would be immeasurable. After all, what better way to amass power and influence around the world than showbiz? And with enough powerful vampires around the world, their influence might be too much for even the hunters spread thin around it.

3

After selling everything she couldn't fit in a suitcase, Elena boarded a plane for Los Angeles. Of course, she didn't want to have to deal with her sword going through customs and mailed it to a P.O. Box she'd set up online. She just hoped it wasn't lost in the mail.

In the meantime, Elena wasn't about to walk around completely defenseless. Her first stop after arriving in LA was a Home Depot. She bought the biggest machete they carried and then tried to find a cheap place to stay. The most affordable she could find near Hollywood was one just north of the 10 freeway called Seaway Motel. It was under a $100 a night and clean—that was all she cared about. She had no idea how long she'd need to be in LA, but wasn't about to go apartment-hunting. Regardless, she did need a way around town.

Elena wasn't familiar with LA and perhaps that was her first mistake. Her second was thinking she could get around using public transportation. She quickly discovered that public transportation in LA was a joke, so she then had to figure out if it was more worthwhile to rent a car or buy a cheap used one. She opted for the latter. It was easier and she was able to pay cash, leaving less of a paper trail.

After taking care of all those matters, she finally began her hunt for Marie LeBeau. Her first clue was an envelope containing the movie tickets she'd swiped from the late mayor of Montreal. It had a return address of a production company in LA called the Humphreys Brothers. She thought it would be easy to find by plugging the address into her phone, but unfortunately, she didn't realize what a mess the freeways were and had to find her way on the side streets. Thankfully, she eventually found her way to their building and then begrudgingly paid for parking, since nowhere in LA had free parking near businesses.

Elena felt overwhelmed by the city, the immense size of it that seemed to just endlessly stretch off into the distance. Her phone was an invaluable tool to help her navigate that urban sprawl, and she made sure it was charged at all times. Her father would have laughed at this. In his day, he'd have used a map.

She thanked God she wasn't back in those days.

The next step after locating the Humphreys Brothers building was to find their latest leading lady, Marie LeBeau. Unfortunately, that information would not be easy to come by. Elena was no fool; she knew that anybody as important as an actor would have their location kept a carefully guarded secret. That meant her best bets were to either fake her way inside to try and get Marie's address (which she knew was destined to fail), or wait and hope that eventually Marie would stop by.

Elena knew what the vampire queen looked like thanks to Google, but it still would be a tricky stakeout. She'd have to remain close by and hope that Marie entered through the front door. She didn't see any other access points into the building, so she hoped that would be enough. After spotting her prey, it would just be a simple act of following her to her car and then following her home. Elena had done this before. Had she had the resources or been tech-savvy, perhaps she could have planted some kind of a bug on Marie's car, but that was not currently an option.

After some careful consideration, Elena decided to set up her stakeout outside the Humphreys Brothers building. She couldn't leave her car parked nearby as she would have to keep paying for it, so she did something a little sneaky. She drove it to an apartment building around the block and parked in front of that, as it was the only free area available. It was possible if she left it there too long somebody might have asked questions, but her hope was that she'd just be seen as any old tenant. The tricky part would be getting back to her car if she spotted Marie LeBeau. Her plan was that once she saw the actress enter the building, she would quickly retrieve her car and park it in one of the paid spots across the street. She just had to hope one was available. If they weren't, things could get trickier.

It took almost a week, but eventually, Elena's faith was rewarded as she spotted the very distinctive actress strutting her way toward the entrance of the Humphreys Brothers building. She thought for a moment about just taking her down right then and there, but it was too risky, and she still didn't have her sword. Damn postal service was apparently taking their time. So instead, Elena quickly made it back to her car and attempted to move it into the last available parking spot across from the building. However, as she approached that spot, she saw it being taken! It had been available a minute ago, yet someone had already snatched it up. Elena frantically tried to figure out what to do next. She didn't know exactly where Marie had parked, and couldn't just drive around trying to seek her vehicle out. She could keep circling the block, but that could also mean she'd miss Marie upon exiting the building. Unfortunately, there weren't a lot of options available and she circled around the block a few times.

On the third loop, she thankfully found a spot not too far from the Humphreys Brothers building. But the location concerned her. She was exposed. When Marie left, if she had the ability to sniff out a hunter—as some vampires supposedly could—then Elena wouldn't have any luck tracking her further. But she was unfortunately out of options and just had to hope things worked out, otherwise she'd have to try again at some point in the future. So as she spent the next two hours waiting in her car, she started to think she'd messed up, that Marie had somehow left already and she'd missed it. She had to refill the meter several times just to make sure she wasn't towed and this got to her even more. She wasn't made of money and really didn't like being stuck in this position.

But after those two hours were up, when she was desperately close to calling it quits, Marie finally emerged from the entrance and Elena caught her first close-up glimpse of the actress. Photos did not do her justice. Elena was usually attracted to the opposite sex, and even she felt an irresistible pull toward Marie. Part of her felt compelled to step out of her car and worship her, to bow at the feet of her magnificence. The only thing that snapped her out of this trance was a crazy fan that ran up to Marie begging for a picture, which the actress was all too happy to provide.

Elena then used this chance to quickly pull out of her spot and make a U-turn to get her car heading in the same direction as Marie. But Marie was taking her time walking down the street and Elena panicked that the cars behind her were going to run her off the road in frustration. Thankfully, Marie turned a corner and Elena followed. It seemed Marie had a Rolls Royce parked out of view on a side street with a driver still behind the wheel waiting for her. Elena didn't want to arouse any suspicion and drove right past Marie's car into an alley. There she managed to flip her car around and keep her eyes on the Rolls as it began to drive off.

This wasn't Elena's first time following someone by car. She had gotten pretty successful at keeping her distance while also never losing sight of her prey. Unfortunately, the streets of LA really tested her. She was constantly on the verge of losing Marie's car and on several occasions, was saved either by right turns on a red light, or what she came to find was the common practice of making left turns on a red.

Eventually though, Elena had made her way up into the Hollywood Hills and lost sight of Marie's car as it pulled behind a gate leading up a private road to what could only be her home. She took note of the location on her phone and marked it so she wouldn't lose it. Elena had a pretty great sense of direction, but in a place like the Hollywood Hills, even she needed help. Most of the city was broken up into an easily navigable grid system. But the Hills were a winding mess of roads complicated by numerous dead ends. Anyone unfortunate enough to get lost there would almost always need some assistance to find their way out.

The important thing, though, was that now Elena knew where her prey went to rest. She could watch and wait for the opportune time to strike and then, she would finally be free of the burden passed down through generations of her family. Sure, there would always be other queens that popped up, but Marie was a big shot, big enough to cause a whole mess of trouble for the vampire community. That was the kind of thing Elena lived for, to disrupt whatever order they had gained over the years, sending them back into hiding, fearing the light and what came with it.

4

After going back to her motel to rest for a few hours, Elena made her way back to the home of Marie LeBeau. She planned to stakeout the house from the rear—as it was too hard to see anything through the trees surrounding the property in the front. Unfortunately, she got hit with the shock of how cool the night air was in the Hollywood Hills. Even though she hadn't taken a jacket, she did have a blanket which she planned to place in her stakeout spot. Instead, she wrapped it around herself.

There wasn't the greatest vantage point from the street below Marie's home where Elena had parked her car. She could see parts of the interior, but as she was looking up at the property, much of it was obscured. She needed to climb the hill and with her blanket and bag of supplies, she made her way up. The dirt was dry and littered with small stones that almost caused her to lose her footing a few times. Thankfully, she had good enough balance to stay on her feet even if she lost some progress to sliding backwards.

Once Elena was high enough to have a view of the backside of the property, she made herself a home behind several bushes. She'd be exposed from the street below, but anyone down there would need to have a keen pair of eyes to spot her at night—especially with her dressed all in black. But Elena wasn't planning to stay there all night. She was running reconnaissance, getting an idea of the layout around the property and inside the mansion. Yes, that's right—Marie LeBeau lived in a mansion, or as close as Elena had ever seen to one. The house was massive to her minimum-wage eyes. She'd never seen something so decadent, so lavish and grand in scale.

It made her want to vomit.

Marie didn't take long to make her presence known as she flittered about her home in what looked like a silk negligee of some kind. It was halfway between a robe and a dress and looked quite comfortable. But Elena wasn't there to admire the clothes of her intended target. She was trying to get a sense of security. There was plenty of it, from what she could see through her binoculars. There appeared to be multiple security cameras, though she could only make out the ones illuminated by the numerous lights surrounding the back of the property. Then there was Marie's personal security detail. Elena had spotted at least four or five people. She wasn't entirely sure because they all looked similar—large builds, close cropped hair, and suits. If they were wearing sunglasses she'd almost suspect they were agents from that movie *The Matrix*, which she loved watching with her dad as a kid.

Aside from the cameras and security guards, there was no clear sign of any other security, but Elena would not have been surprised to find there was an alarm system set up with motion sensors. That sort of thing was pretty common in homes of wealthy people. If set off, it was sure to draw the cops there like bears to honey. She would have a hell of time trying to sneak in while Marie slept, so her only chance was drawing her outside in the day. Even then it was tricky, though. She doubted Marie would ever take an unsupervised dip into her pool, and those guards would probably follow her almost everywhere. Yet she didn't see them earlier that day when Marie went to the Humphreys

Brothers' office. It was possible she could take her out on the way there somehow, but she had to be careful. She didn't want to be spotted. A ninja outfit only got you so far when it came to hunting vampires. If you took it out in the open, you'd draw far too much attention, and attention meant cops. And her skill set did not include outrunning police officers.

It seemed that hunting Marie meant being in this for the long haul, following the vampire queen like a hawk until an opportunity presented itself. In the meantime, though, Elena thought it might be advantageous to track the vampire's movements in case it led her to any people who'd already been turned. The downside of this was that others could be turned while she was waiting for her chance to strike. That thought gnawed at her conscience, but she had to leave it be. She knew that killing a queen was far more important for the vast number of innocents it could save once accomplished. It wasn't worth blowing her chance just to save a single soul and let Marie escape to kill or turn hundreds or even thousands of others.

For the time being, Elena did what she thought was best and hung back, watching Marie every chance she had. This went on for days and eventually weeks. There were a few times she thought she might be able to strike at Marie, but something would eventually get in the way. Either she'd spot a nearby cop, or there'd be nobody around, only for a crowd to appear. That was the main issue with tracking a celebrity—they just drew crowds wherever they went. And if one had the pull of a vampire queen, those crowds could quickly get out of control.

A few notable events also happened that drew Elena's attention. One was a nighttime visit that Marie paid to producer Milton Humphreys and his girlfriend Jyll Masters—Elena was able to deduce their identities through Google. There was alcohol, music, dancing, and even a birthday cake—as it appeared Milton was turning a year older that day. Eventually, the three retired to the bedroom and faded from view. Milton seemed to have his bedroom purposely shielded from prying eyes of the paparazzi. It didn't take a genius to figure out what was going on in there, but one thing was clear to Elena from all her years hunting vampires. Those two would not leave that bedroom the same. They would either die in there, or they would be turned.

When she eventually did see them emerge, Elena knew the truth of the matter. But in her business, she couldn't act on hunches, no matter how much she knew them to be right. At some point, she'd have to stake them out and confirm her suspicions. This would take time away from Marie and that was further cause for alarm. If she missed an opportunity to strike, it could cost her in the long run—especially if taking out the other two potential new recruits raised alarms and Marie skipped town. The only thing that kept Elena confident the vampire queen might avoid running was she had something too good going on in LA— and a premiere to boot. If she skipped town after the producer was murdered, she'd likely be the prime suspect.

For the time being, Elena decided to keep her focus on Marie just a little longer. She was thankful that she did when it became apparent that Marie was leaving town for a few days. San Diego Comic-Con was advertising the fact all over the place. *Black Berenice* would be having a panel there with all the major stars present. This seemed like the first real shot Elena had since discovering Marie in LA. There would surely be security, but putting Marie up in a hotel exposed her much more than in her own home. This was something she could use to her advantage. Elena wasn't quite sure how she'd do it, but she had to try.

5

Marie LeBeau had been quite easy to track during her time at the San Diego Comic-Con. The hard part was getting close to her. The actress' movements during the event were closely guarded, from her hotel suite at the Hilton San Diego Bayfront to the convention center itself. Marie's security detail was *always* present, looking more alert than ever as they attempted to safeguard her from any potentially psychotic fan. Most of the people Elena witnessed at the convention seemed positively harmless, though. A few creeps tried to hit on her at one point, but that was about as dangerous as they got.

It wasn't until Elena learned of a special screening with an after-party that she believed she had an in. The screening itself would likely be a waste of time and she had no desire to be hypnotized by a film starring a vampire queen. But the after-party was a different story. There would be security for sure, but they couldn't be around Marie the entire time. She'd want some distance so she could mingle and they'd likely keep the majority of their focus on the areas where someone could attempt to crash the party. This meant it wouldn't be easy for Elena to sneak in, but she was no ordinary fan who needed the common entry points.

After trailing a few unsuspecting fans exiting the screening, she learned the after-party was at the rooftop bar of the Hard

Rock Hotel. To someone with her skills, it seemed the best way to crash a rooftop party was from below. Unfortunately, this rooftop wasn't technically the roof of the hotel; it was the roof of a set of shops along Fifth Avenue. But what that meant is where the roof ended, she could find a way to scale it away from prying eyes. And she found just the spot through an access point between buildings where there was a set of stairs. It seemed this set of stairs was more of an exit for those leaving the rooftop and naturally sealed off to those on the street—but Elena was craftier than that. She managed to work her way up to the roof of the Old Spaghetti Factory and then changed discreetly into her ninja garb, having kept it in a duffel bag with her sword—which thankfully arrived in LA before she left.

After quietly approaching the rooftop of the next building over, she watched as the party began. People started filling in the massive rooftop, which had been outfitted with a stage blocking part of her view. The pool and bar area were thankfully still visible from her vantage point. It was only a matter of time before Marie made her presence known. That radiance she carried with her that seemed to make her a shining beacon among the other poor souls surrounding her. It was like a guiding light, or a target for a hunter such as Elena. That target just so happened to settle near the edge of the roof—and away from her security detail—as she mingled with fans.

Working her way off the rooftop of the Old Spaghetti Factory, Elena carefully kept herself out of view from the street as she used her climbing claws to scale the side of the next building over. Anyone leaving the party through the back stairwell between the buildings would have spotted her easily if they were to look up, but thankfully nobody did—especially with a band playing that drew everyone's attention.

When Elena carefully peered over the edge of the roof, she

saw that Marie was still in her same spot by the edge. And now the fans who surrounded her moments ago had dispersed, likely to watch the band play. There was only one man near Marie—he was facing Elena, but from his nervous stance, she doubted he would give her much trouble. The more important thing was that Marie's back was turned. She wouldn't have time to dodge the attack and if Elena was quiet enough—she might not even hear it coming. The only possibility was that this man might alert Marie of Elena's presence first, but she felt capable of dealing with that. She just needed to be fast. Just like her father had taught her for all those years.

Climbing over the edge of the roof, Elena slid down the short wall that surrounded the pool area. Her feet landed silently on her toes and her hand moved to her back, ready to draw her sword. Before she could do this though, the man moved in with an incredible quickness that caught even someone as well-trained as her off guard. The force of his body tackled her to the ground and she felt the wind go out of her. Anyone else might have been down for the count, but Elena wasn't any ordinary person. And she damn sure wasn't going to let this guy catch her off guard a second time.

Kicking him off of herself with the full strength of her legs, Elena watched as he fell back hard into the ground. Marie gasped, which might have made Elena laugh under different circumstances. She knew the whole thing was an act, a façade to keep suspicion away. Marie then ran off to alert her security team and others who could stop Elena with a few bullets. She felt herself involuntarily say "shit" without a second thought.

Flipping up onto her feet, Elena knew she needed to get out of there quickly; Marie was out of range and she wasn't about to tangle with armed guards—not with only her sword to protect her. Before she could turn to escape, though, the man had already launched himself up into a sweeping kick, which she easily jumped over. Elena then followed with a kick at Marie's would-be defender, but it was surprisingly deflected and she saw him attempt to counter with an elbow strike. But her quickness wouldn't allow this and she blocked it, countering with a punch toward his midsection. Once more she was surprised that it was blocked. The guy was good, almost as good as she was—and part of her might have been impressed if she wasn't suddenly fighting for her life. There was no question she could beat this guy if given enough time, but she knew that there would be mere seconds before those guards were on her.

After trading a few more blows, the guards had made their way over and the man was distracted by this for just long enough that Elena landed a single punch to his face, which sent him tumbling to the ground. The guards had already gone to draw their guns, but they weren't fast enough. Elena hopped back over the wall she'd come from and found herself landing onto the stairs below. She rolled down them to break her fall, which killed her back and would leave her bruised the next day, but at least she was clear.

Then it was a matter of swiftly shedding a layer and blending into the crowd on the street. Her sword sheath was safely tucked under her arm to lessen its visibility. Nobody noticed her, but she was unable to hide her shame. She had finally gained one solid chance to take out her prey and it had been thwarted by some random guy she'd never seen with Marie before that night. He didn't appear to be one of the undead, and certainly didn't possess their strength, but he was damn good. Part of her hoped she might meet him again under better circumstances.

6

Elena made her way back to LA with her tail between her legs. She'd failed at the one chance she'd had since finding Marie LeBeau. Now she needed to weigh her options moving forward. She could stay on Marie's tail—perhaps gain the identity of the guy who protected her so fiercely at the party—or she could begin to follow the movements of the two people she was sure Marie had recently turned. She'd need clear evidence though, which meant watching them like a hawk until they either revealed their turning marks, or sought out prey. Thankfully, newborn vampires could be foolish in their attempts to feed, either leaving bodies out in the open, or exposing themselves to attacks. Their close contact to Marie meant it was possible she'd take them under her wing. Unfortunately for them, Marie would likely be hiding deeper than ever. She knew a hunter was on her trail now, for perhaps the first time in years. She wasn't about to do anything else foolish.

If Elena was a betting woman, she'd guess Marie probably wouldn't be caught around any large crowds again until the premiere of her film. Which meant Elena needed to keep a close eye on her tickets so she didn't lose them. There would still be a lot of security guards at the premiere, but they couldn't protect Marie every second. There could be a chance. For the time being though, she had to keep her focus on the opportunities currently available to her.

After arriving back in LA, her first stop was the office of the

Humphreys Brothers. Strangely though, she didn't see Milton arrive at all that morning. She stayed for several hours, trying to figure out if she missed him. It wasn't until she saw Milton's girlfriend, Jyll Masters, arrive and leave abruptly that she realized Milton must not have been there.

Following the actress back to the home of her boyfriend, Elena parked a good distance past his property in order to not draw any suspicion to her vehicle. She then made her way around the back to get a better view of things. There she saw Milton drinking out by his pool. He looked a little pale and under the weather, but this didn't seem to slow down his drinking as he worked on a laptop and talked with people over the phone. She didn't pay much attention to the conversations as they clearly related to the movie business. But she did watch his butler, who seemed very attentive to his boss, bringing out a new glass of alcohol as soon as Milton finished each one.

When the butler moved inside with the latest glass, he stayed gone for a long moment before returning with Jyll, who Milton didn't seem too pleased to see. Perhaps it was due to his sickly-looking condition or perhaps he was upset about something. Whatever the case, it was clear that Jyll did not seem to share the same illness afflicting her boyfriend. This caused Elena to wonder if perhaps she'd been wrong about the two of them. It was possible Milton had simply gotten sick from his time at Comic-Con—as a gathering that large could result in anyone catching something. Jyll not having gone was evidence in the camp of them not being vampires after all. However, Elena knew all too well how slow the transformation could take from human to vampire.

The process to turn someone was always the same; they were slightly drained, while the vampire also fed them some of their own blood. However, the transformation tended to vary by how much of the human's blood was taken. If most of it was taken, the transformation could take hours, sometimes even minutes. But if a small drink was taken, the transformation could take days, even weeks. She wasn't sure if it had to do with their immune system or what, but in Milton's case, it could be that his age and weight meant he was turning faster than his youthful girlfriend. Elena would just have to keep watching to confirm her suspicions.

And she didn't have to wait long.

The first evidence toward Milton being one of the undead was his distaste for the lunch his girlfriend had prepared. She seemed a bit disappointed by him only taking a few small bites before shoving it aside. He moved close to her in an attempt to kiss her and perhaps do a bit more, but she seemed just as put off at the prospect of kissing a sick man as he was by his food. It wasn't long before Jyll left and Milton returned back outside.

While Milton continued his work at the pool that afternoon, at one point he adjusted himself in his lounge chair to get more comfortable, and as he shifted up, it exposed the two red marks she'd been waiting to see on his inner thigh. She then made her way quickly around his property in her ninja garb, hoping nobody saw her—as it was still light out. Thankfully, the butler had left the sliding glass door in the back unlocked. That same door led inside where she found him with his back to her at the bar preparing a drink. Sneaking up behind him, Elena carefully knocked him out with the butt of her katana. The butler collapsed onto the floor like a sack of potatoes and the bottle he was pouring shattered on the ground next to him. Elena then found a good place to hide while she waited for her target to come back inside. She'd seen the rate he pounded back his drinks, and if the butler didn't show soon, he'd wonder why. That would be her time to strike.

From outside she heard Milton scream, "Juan! Where the fuck are you?!" And not soon after, the sliding glass door slid open so Milton could enter the darkened room inside his home. He seemed aware of the broken bottle right away, as its contents were drifting across the floor toward the door. Then he noticed the feet of his butler sticking out from behind the bar and approached him cautiously. As he made he his way over there, Elena also crept silently behind him. He crouched down to check the butler's pulse, but just as soon as he'd done so, Elena had drawn up her sword and took a single swift slice toward Milton's neck. She watched his head separate from his body and tumble away. Milton was left there for his butler to find when he woke, but by that time, Elena would be long gone, moving her attention to her next target—Milton's girlfriend. There was a very high probability Jyll Masters was one of the undead as well, but Elena still needed proof first.

7

Jyll Masters' home in Sherman Oaks was easier to find than Elena had initially thought. It helped that before she'd left Milton's house the previous evening, she'd spotted his phone still sitting outside by his lounge chair. His head might have been separated from his body, but at least it still worked to unlock his phone. Inside that small device was a veritable gold mine of information on celebrities Milton had been associated with: names, phone numbers, and addresses. Elena snapped photos with her own phone to make sure she had all of this information handy before leaving Milton's phone back outside where she found it.

The next morning, Jyll Masters left early before Elena even had a chance to get to her house. She wasn't prepared for what a nightmare traffic it would be trying to get to Sherman Oaks from her motel. There were only a few freeways that seemed to lead into the valley and she wasn't about to get lost in the hills again trying to get there. So she took the 405 north and eventually got to Jyll's house after about an hour. Thankfully, with Jyll away, she could at least scope out the place and find the right spot for her stakeout.

There was a large stone fence around the property that was hopped easily enough. Elena kept her eyes peeled for security cameras, but tried not to sweat them since she was masked. She doubted somebody like Jyll Masters would have or require the same kind of security that someone like Marie LeBeau did. Still, it never hurt to be careful.

Eventually, Elena found a tree in the backyard to nestle into the branches of and saw it gave her the perfect view of all the windows on the south side of the home without leaving her too exposed. However, she wasn't about to sit up in it all day, especially with Jyll out. She peeked through the windows for anything out of the ordinary, but came up short. There was even a cat moving about.

Her experience had taught her that often pets were the first things to go when a human transitioned into a vampire. So the cat was actually a good sign. There were also no signs of discarded or wasted food around the place, no evidence of blood or bandages, or excessive cleaning products. Either Jyll was more careful than most newly turned vampires, or Elena was in fact barking up the wrong tree.

Taking a break from snooping around Jyll's home that morning, Elena decided to kill some time wandering around the valley. She got lunch at a place called In-N-Out Burger, which she'd heard many people rave about. The food was quite good, except she was never much a fan of burgers, so she didn't think she'd be back. Surprisingly though, she found she wasn't hit after by the usual gut bomb that accompanied most meals at fast food places. She took that as one reason people might have recommended it to her.

It was unclear how long a typical day shoot would be for a TV series, but Elena could see from the billboards scattered around the valley that Jyll's show was quite popular. According to one, *You Go, Girl!* was airing on CBS, and a quick Google search told her that those shows filmed at CBS Studio Center. She thought about stopping by there, but knew she wouldn't get very far with all the security. It seemed better to wait things out, so she drove to Jyll Master's house once more, camping out in her car until it got dark. Elena hoped nobody spotted her inside, so she kept herself low in the back, trying to catch a few hours of sleep before Jyll got home.

When Elena woke, it was already dark and she cursed herself for sleeping too long. But she supposed she hadn't been getting much sleep lately with all the work she'd put into staking out these celebrities. As she got out and approached Jyll Masters' driveway, she climbed the wall the same way she had earlier and snuck around the back. This time, lights were on inside and she watched carefully for anything interesting.

Jyll seemed to be frantically pacing around her house. There were a bunch of items on the kitchen counter that looked like they belonged in the fridge. Milk, eggs, orange juice—it had all been removed to make space for something else. That wasn't good. In fact, Jyll's pacing now made sense in the context of the changes a human would go through on their way to vampirism. The first thing you notice is that you're always hungry, but no food or drink will satisfy you—you might even find their taste unappealing. Then comes the thirst. It can be gradual for many, but the closer you are to fresh blood, the more you crave it. And Jyll had a cat. A cat that no longer seemed to be prancing around the house.

It was probably enough evidence for Elena to act, but she decided to wait a little longer. After disappearing for a few minutes, Jyll reappeared with her normally blonde hair now a dark brown—clearly, she was wearing a wig. Elena didn't have to be a genius to understand why. When Jyll scooped up her car keys and made her way to the garage, Elena knew she had to move fast. Sprinting out of the backyard, she leaped over the stone wall surrounding the property and quickly entered her car a few houses up. Jyll's car was nowhere to be found, though, and Elena worried she somehow had moved too slow. But that didn't make sense to her. The gate alone would have held up the car a good amount of time. Those things were always slow to open.

Sure enough, after a few more minutes, the gate finally opened and Jyll's car left her property. It wasn't immediately clear what had taken the actress so long in leaving, but had she stayed a little longer perched up in her tree, Elena would have seen Jyll moving back and forth between the kitchen and the garage, taking rolls of plastic wrap with her. To any normal person this would have seemed odd, but to an experienced hunter like Elena, this would have been time to act. Instead, she found herself pursuing the actress to the freeway and then to Hollywood Boulevard—to one of the seedier areas along it, to be precise. She spotted all sorts of unsavory characters on the sidewalk and decided to check her locks while keeping the car moving as much as possible.

Eventually, Jyll's car stopped near some scantily-clad women that Elena took for prostitutes. And she'd have been right in that assumption as she witnessed one climb into Jyll's car. She needed to act now more than ever, but Jyll was bound to stop the car before feeding. Elena watched as the car pulled into an alley a few blocks up and drove a good distance down it. She watched as it passed an assortment of makeshift shelters among the dumpsters that created a shanty town for the homeless.

Jyll's car soon stopped in a darker portion of the alley away from the few lights present down it. Elena couldn't wait any longer and immediately stopped her own car, climbing out and oblivious to the fact that she left the keys inside. At least she took her sword and as she was still in full ninja garb apart from her face, she got some surprised and confused looks from the homeless she passed. Whether it was her sword or how she was dressed drawing the looks she didn't care, as she was sure to get a whole lot more in a few moments. She had to hope that nobody there would care enough to ID her.

A scream was uttered from inside Jyll's car and Elena charged for the driver side door. She could see through the back window that the prostitute was struggling to break free from a death grip Jyll seemed to have on her, attempting to pull her close enough to feed. Before she could, though, Elena was at the driver-side door and shattered the window with the scabbard of her sword. Jyll whipped her head around, flashing her fangs and hissing at Elena. The prostitute didn't waste a moment, opening the passenger door and running away screaming.

Jyll leaped straight through the open window at the vampire hunter, knocking her back into a dumpster. Her sword clattered away on the ground, still in its scabbard. This was a fatal mistake as she knew better than the try and kill a vampire at night, especially without a weapon. She hadn't even thought to bring with the machete—which would have been a good backup. Instead, she found herself pushed to the ground, Jyll's hands coming around her throat and beginning to squeeze. Elena could feel the blood trapped in her head, swelling, and the pressure on her throat cutting off her airflow. Jyll opened her mouth wide and let her drool fall onto Elena's face as she slowly moved in to make the vampire hunter her next meal.

But Elena wasn't about to let that happen.

Jyll might have had her in a death grip, but she wasn't unable to move the rest of her body. She twisted sideways with her arms and legs, throwing Jyll into the side of the dumpster. It likely didn't hurt the vampire, but it shocked her enough that she lost her grip on Elena. It also caused the wig to topple off her head before flopping under the dumpster. Scurrying forward, Elena quickly snatched up the handle of the katana and used her other hand to unsheathe the blade.

A bloodcurdling scream sounded behind her and Elena knew the next move coming from Jyll. She'd seen it all before. Young vampires loved to charge their prey like a wild beast. They were functioning almost entirely on instinct, letting the thirst take over for their higher brain function. Spinning around in one smooth swift motion, Elena sliced the air in a horizontal arc, letting the edge of her blade find the side of Jyll's soft white neck. It sliced through her skin and bone like warm butter. Jyll's body fell lifelessly to the pavement. Her head bounced off the ground and began to roll right under the dumpster. Elena didn't feel any need to retrieve it.

Looking around as she sheathed her sword, Elena noticed that several bums had witnessed what had transpired. She couldn't tell under the dirt covering their faces if they were scared or merely surprised by the event. Perhaps both. But she wasn't about to stick around to find out which. So she calmly made her way back to her car and got inside, backing out of the alley. She was grateful nobody had stolen it.

8

The next day, Elena watched the news and was thankful they didn't show a police sketch of her face. It seemed she'd gotten away with both killings the past two days and that made her breathe a sigh of relief. Now she could keep her focus back on Marie where it belonged. Unfortunately, things had gotten a bit more complicated since she left the vampire queen in San Diego.

Scoping out Marie's home from her previous location at the backside of the house, Elena was confused by what she was seeing. The man who she fought in San Diego appeared to be now working for Marie, unless he just enjoyed walking around in very expensive-looking suits in his downtime. When she saw him at the party, the guy had been dressed in a nice shirt, but it looked cheap by her estimation. She figured he was some random fan or something. But the way he was constantly following Marie around her home like a watchful guard dog made her think the vampire had added her savior to the security detail always around her property.

While the complication of having to face down that guy again was a risk Elena would have preferred not to deal with, part of her was a little excited to spar with her most capable human opponent yet. That is, unless he was packing the same firepower as the rest of Marie's guards. Then her skills wouldn't matter. But she had to put those thoughts out of her head. The more important thing now was trying to get Marie separated from her security team—new and old.

She was only staking out the house for a few hours before she was surprised to see two guests arrive who did not look like friends of Marie. In fact, they looked like cops. This complicated things even further. It was possible they were just following up with her after Milton's death, but if they got too close to the truth, they would be two more innocents Elena would have on her conscience.

As she watched the detectives talk with Marie, she noticed something odd. At a certain point Marie appeared to snap at her new security guard and take the guy out of the room to chew him out a bit further. He then seemed to storm off in a huff and Marie put back on her best face to deal with the cops. Thankfully, if she was planning to kill them, it wasn't right then and there. But Elena was shocked to hear someone moving through the pool area of the property, where she had been safely nestled in a bush.

As she pulled the binoculars away from her face, Elena realized it was the guy she fought in San Diego—he was apparently trying to sneak around the backside of the house toward the front. This was very odd, as it meant he was either trying to sneak away from his master—which she couldn't believe—or he was trying to perform some kind of a sneak attack on the detectives. She felt compelled to act, but didn't want to make her presence known, so she slowly crept out of the bushes, keeping clear of the more visible parts of the pool area from the windows.

Once Elena had made it around to the front of the house, she realized she had lost sight of where that guy had gone and suddenly grew very nervous he had set a trap for her. Not wanting to fall into it, she moved behind another set of bushes near the garden. Keeping her eyes peeled for another minute or two, Elena waited for anything bad to happen. But as the front doors opened and the two detectives stepped out, she started to wonder if she'd gotten all worked up for nothing.

Then she saw the security guard approaching them from behind.

Pulling up her sword, Elena unsheathed it and prepared to charge. Before she could, the guy said, "Detectives, can I have a quick word?"

The female cop turned to the guy before looking at her partner, who shrugged and said, "Sure."

The guy then said, "Marie would likely fire me if she knew I was telling you this, but I think she's stubborn and has some kind of bad blood when it comes to the LAPD. The thing is, I'm worried that her stalker is connected to Milton Humphreys' death."

This piece of information came as a shock to Elena, who up to this point had assumed this guy was entrenched with Marie, possibly a familiar. But as she heard him talk about theories to which he had no certainties of, it was clear he was just some chump duped by a vampire queen into working for her. If the stalker he was referring to was supposed to be Elena, it meant Marie fed this guy some line about a stalker to keep him from asking too many questions about the attack.

The male cop asked, "What are you talking about?"

"That incident in San Diego. It wasn't a stalker, it was . . . well, like a ninja. I know that sounds crazy, before you say anything, but Marie confessed the whole mess to me afterward." *Confessed a whole lot of bullshit*, Elena thought. The guy continued, "How she had a bad break-up with this guy in Japan who was connected, and she thinks he's trying to kill her, that he, like, sent people here to do what he couldn't do himself." The guy was even more gullible than she realized, and it was only then when she noticed just how young he looked. The young were always so easily deceived.

The cop said, "Look . . . Chris, right? That first bit didn't sound nearly as crazy as everything that came after it. It's no wonder somebody as young as you is working for her— she's clearly got you wrapped around her finger. I don't know what the truth of the matter is, but trust me, that person who attacked her can't be connected to Milton Humphrey's death."

Elena wondered in that moment if perhaps the cops didn't know as much as she hoped they did. If they had all the facts, they'd know Elena was behind both attacks, yet they seemed to believe someone else was responsible for the murders. She listened on intently for what came next, but was surprised when the female cop looked at her partner and said, "Don't, Lawson."

It seemed Lawson got the message and didn't continue any further, but Chris was now more curious than ever and asked, "What? How can you know it wasn't connected? Do you know who did it?"

"Do what you want, Liz." Lawson said before climbing into their car.

The detective paused before answering, but then continued with her voice a bit lower as she moved closer to Chris. Elena had to make her way around the bushes, a little closer to try and make out what was being said. Missing the first bit, she heard Liz say, "The person who killed Milton? It looked like they also killed his girlfriend. She was found dead this morning. We think they were tied up in something bad—I highly doubt it had anything to do with this attack on Miss LeBeau."

"But do you know for sure?"

"How long have you been working for her?"

"Two days," Chris said. "Is it that obvious?"

Liz seemed to find this amusing and said, "You stuck out like a sore thumb." Elena couldn't disagree with that. From the back of the property, he looked like any other guard, but seeing him up closer, the suit didn't fit him quite as well as she thought before. He seemed visibly nervous and out of place.

"To be honest, I wonder at times why she hired me."

"She said you saved her in San Diego. I just assumed that you were working for her at the time."

Shaking his head, Chris said, "No, I was just a fan at a party. Right place, wrong time . . . or right time, I guess. When that ninja popped out, I thought I was going to die, but all my years taking martial arts, I guess they paid off. Next thing I know, security is charging in and this attacker jumps off the roof. Craziest thing I ever saw. Guess I'm just lucky they didn't pull the sword on their back."

Something about this information seemed to startle Liz and Elena wondered for a moment if she was finally putting the pieces together. "Sword?"

"Yeah, I said they were dressed like a ninja. Figured you got the full picture, but I guess not."

Elena became startled herself as Liz took Chris fiercely by the shoulders and said in an even quieter voice something that Elena could no longer make out.

Chris said, "What? I don't understand."

"I can help you understand, but you have to trust me."

"How can I trust you if you won't tell me why?"

Releasing his shoulders, Liz said, "I will, but it's not safe here, please just come with us right now."

"If I say no, are you going to force me?"

"Yes. It's that important. Now get in the car."

Elena knew she was going to have to follow them and didn't wait to see if Chris got in the car. She quietly took off at full speed through the trees surrounding the property. Moving quickly to the wall around the place, she hopped over it and didn't even care if the cameras picked her up this time. She landed quietly on the street below and sprinted for her car without even bothering to remove her mask. She'd left her bag back in the bushes that had the remainder of her stakeout supplies, but she didn't have time to go back for it. This was too important. At least she still had her sword, which she made sure to conceal under her seat before she started up her car.

Watching the front of Marie's property, Elena caught the gate opening and the detectives driving out with Chris sitting in the back seat. He was talking to them about something and looked pretty nervous. Elena wished she could hear what they were saying, but she'd just have to keep pace and hope all this got sorted out once they stopped.

She found her curiosity escalating when she saw the detectives stop at the morgue and get out with Chris. Seemed they planned to show him something there, and she deduced that if they did know about Jyll and or Milton being vampires, it was from their corpses. Elena wasn't any kind of science wiz, but even she knew vampires never showed up normal when bloodwork was done, and closer examination could reveal other things to make it apparent what their true nature was. Unfortunately, most vamps were smart enough to have inside people remove these bodies before the news could get out. She assumed Marie would have someone taking care of that here as well, but perhaps she had other things to deal with currently. Whatever the case, the detectives and Chris soon exited the building and the young guy looked a little green around the gills. Most likely he'd puked at the corpse they showed him.

They then took Chris to another location, a small house in Santa Monica. It was here that Elena thought very hard about approaching the three and offering assistance. But she still didn't have all the facts herself, and having some crazy woman in ninja garb approach could just as easily get her arrested. Her previous encounters with police told her to err on the side of caution. After a few minutes, the detectives left the house without Chris and got back in their car before driving off. Elena very much wanted to approach the house and speak to Chris, but at the same time, she knew where he was located now and didn't want to lose the cops without figuring out where they were headed next, so she chose to follow them instead.

Their destination was apparently a police station, but after some time, they departed—thankfully not before Elena was able to eat a sandwich she'd kept in her car. Then it was off again, and she really hoped the detectives hadn't noticed her car following them. It was old, but not so old that it stuck out, plus she'd had enough experience following people that they'd have to be really astute to notice her.

Soon enough, the detectives stopped at another home in the Hollywood Hills that she was unfamiliar with. This made Elena extra cautious. They could have been following up on a lead from an unrelated case, but something told her this was related to Marie—especially when she saw them sneak around the back of the house. Elena soon found herself pursuing them and hiding in her own bush in the back. She couldn't see where they'd hidden— if that's what they had done—but hopefully they didn't notice her.

It seemed to Elena as she watched the house that the detectives were starting to think like her, staking out a target until they had something to go off of. She just wasn't sure if they knew what they were looking for. And after the sun began to set, it appeared that perhaps they didn't.

Liz stepped out of the bush the two were hiding behind and her partner stopped her in her tracks. Elena couldn't hear what was being said, but it seemed they came to some kind of an agreement as she headed back behind the bush and Lawson snuck around the property toward the front of the house, keeping to the shadows. Elena wasn't exactly sure what he was doing until she saw the guy they were watching approach his front door to find Lawson standing there.

The guy seemed to be playing the generous host as he invited Lawson inside and began to give him a tour of the place. This left Elena rather confused. If he was a vampire, she couldn't figure out why this guy was entertaining the cop—and if Lawson suspected him of being a vampire, she wasn't sure what he was trying to do to gather the evidence he needed. But Elena didn't need to wait long for an answer as the two exited out the back of the house. Heading toward the pool, she heard Lawson point and say, "It looks like you have a little buildup down there. How often do you clean it?"

The owner of the house didn't seem to understand what was being pointed at and looked at the pool closer to confirm said buildup. "That's nothing, pretty standard to—" Elena almost gasped as she watched Lawson casually shove the man from behind.

The guy belly flopped into the pool and quickly emerged from the water screaming, "You son of a bitch! You get the fuck off my property or I'll have someone *drag* you out! You're lucky you're a cop or I'd kick your ass. You have any idea how expensive these shoes are?"

The guy swam to the edge and pulled himself up onto the cement. Looking down with a grin, Lawson said, "I'm sorry, I was trying to just mess around, but I guess I shoved too hard. Didn't think you'd actually go in."

"I don't fucking care!" the guy spat as he got to his feet, "Just get the fuck out of here."

"Okay, okay, I'm gone," Lawson said.

The owner then began to strip off his clothes as Lawson made his way toward the front of the house around the side. Elena couldn't believe the gambit had worked. This clever detective had figured out a way to get this guy to strip down to reveal the same turning marks she would have been looking for. Soon enough he was down to his skivvies and Elena took note of the turning marks on his inner left thigh, meaning he was another of Marie's converts.

Elena wasn't sure what the detective in the bushes was going to do, but she wasn't going to wait for her to do something stupid like try and shoot a vampire. That would be as useless as trying to arrest him. So instead, she crept out of her own spot in the bushes as the vampire made his way back toward his house. Unsheathing her katana, Elena found herself right behind him as he approached the sliding glass door, but she hadn't anticipated the reflection she'd leave in the glass from the lights he'd turned on around the pool.

Spinning around with all the reflexes of an experienced vampire, the guy took Elena by the throat and she knew that he could kill her in a matter of seconds. This wasn't like her fight with Jyll the previous night; this guy knew what he was doing. Whenever Marie turned him, it must have been some time ago. She felt the sword drop from her fingers and then heard some rustling behind her.

"Let them go!" Liz shouted. The vampire merely hissed at the detective, showing off his pearly white fangs. "I'm not fucking kidding," she asserted, "You drop them or you're dead."

"Shooooot," Elena tried to say through the pressure around her throat. She knew the bullets wouldn't hurt a vampire, but they might slow this one down enough for her to get away.

Smiling as he kept Elena elevated off the ground like she

weighed nothing, the vampire approached Liz calmly. But it seemed she wasn't fazed by this and fired her gun a single time. The bullet tore into the vampire's head and brain matter splattered onto the patio below.

Elena slowly stroked her throat to try and bring the blood flow back. "Thanks," she wheezed.

"I don't know who you are, but I think we're on the same side. I'm LAPD Detective Liz Gutiérrez, and I need your help."

"Well, you got it. You saved my life." Elena was relieved to know that she wouldn't be going to jail, and furthermore wouldn't have much explaining to do. When she moved to pick up her sword, she heard Liz approaching in her direction.

"Shit! You got him?" Elena heard Lawson say as he approached their location.

"It's okay," Liz assured her. "This is my partner, Chuck Lawson."

"Please to meet you, uh, ninja guy." Elena realized with her mask on, this detective still thought she was a man.

"The name's Elena," she clarified. "Now if you and your—" Elena turned back to Liz, realizing the detective had gotten dangerously close to where the vampire was lying on the ground. Even worse, his eyes snapped open just as she began to shout, "Move!"

Unfortunately, Liz wasn't fast enough to realize she needed to move and the vampire snatched her ankle in his death grip. This sent Liz off her feet and down to the concrete. Elena wasn't going to waste another second responding, and as the vampire leaped to his feet, she struck at his neck with her katana. The head separated from his body and rolled across the ground into the pool. His headless corpse then collapsed, blood spilling out from his open neck to paint the patio crimson.

"Jesus Christ!" Lawson shrieked.

"We need to get out of here." Elena said. "Somebody had to have seen this." She then held out her hand and pulled Liz to her feet.

The detective said, "Thanks. I guess that makes us even. We can drive you out of here, if you'll come with us."

"I have my own car. I've been following you guys most of the day, but wasn't sure what you knew. Now . . . I think we should find somewhere safe to talk."

"We have a place. If you can follow us, we'll lead you there."

Shaking her head, Elena said, "You guys follow me first. I need a change of clothes and something to eat . . . if that's okay with you?"

Liz and Lawson looked at each other. Then he said, "I *am* pretty hungry, Liz."

"You're always hungry," she scoffed.

9

fter stopping at her motel, Elena had a change of clothes and retrieved her machete. She handed it Liz, saying, "Better if somebody has this. As you've seen, your guns won't do much against vampires. I'd recommend picking up another one of these before too long."

"A machete?" Lawson asked as he watched Liz unsheathe it to check out the blade.

"They're not that hard to come by. I got this at Home Depot."

Sheathing the blade, Liz said, "Yeah, except you can't just walk around with one of these on the street. Or your sword, for that matter."

"And yet I've been getting around fine the past month," Elena said.

"Okay, so you got your stuff. You said you also wanted something to eat?"

"Can you recommend anything?"

Lawson perked up at this and said, "There's a Roscoe's not too far away on Pico."

"What's that?" Elena asked, sincerely having no idea what a Roscoe's was.

"You've never heard of Roscoe's Chicken 'N Waffles?!" Lawson turned to Liz in disbelief and continued, "We gotta take her there, Gutiérrez. It's fucking *Roscoe's.*"

His partner didn't seem quite as into the idea as he was, but she relented, probably knowing he wouldn't let it go. "All right, fine. I hope you're hungry."

And hungry was exactly what Elena was—starving, in fact. Which was perfect, as the meal she was served at Roscoe's was one of the biggest and most filling she'd ever had. She was worried she'd go into a food coma after and Lawson even joked she'd get something called the 'itis,' whatever that was. Still, she couldn't deny that the food was delicious and she never would have expected fried chicken and waffles to go so well together, but it seemed Roscoe's had proved her wrong.

Through the red neon haze inside the restaurant, she could also see that Liz was itching to get a move on. She clearly wanted to discuss more about the vampires and didn't feel comfortable doing so out in the open, which Elena would have agreed was not the wisest thing. But once they had arrived at the location the detectives believed was safe, she planned to share everything she knew and find out everything they knew as well.

After leaving Roscoe's, Elena followed the detectives toward the place they had initially intended for them to talk. For a good portion of the trip, she wasn't sure where the detectives were leading her, and this mostly came down to her lack of familiarity with Los Angeles—despite driving around quite a lot of it in the past month. Once they got to Santa Monica though, she had a pretty good idea where they were headed. And sure enough, they finally stopped their car in front of the same house they had dropped off Chris at hours earlier.

Parking behind the detectives' car, Elena exited her vehicle and approached them before they could lead her inside. "You dropped that guy Chris off here earlier. You said we were going somewhere safe. If Marie knows he's here, we're all in danger."

Holding up her hands in assurance, Liz said, "Relax, Elena.

You said you'd been following us earlier, so it seems you already know that Chris works—worked—for Marie. That's done with now. He wants to help us."

Elena shook her head. "I already heard most of what he was talking to you guys about and while he seems innocent enough, you've never seen someone under the influence of a vampire—especially a queen like Marie. Do you know if he drank her blood?"

Lawson perked up at this and asked, "Why would he drink her blood?"

"Has he?" Elena asked with urgency.

The detectives glanced at each other and then shrugged. "Not that we're aware of," Liz said.

"Look, if he drank her blood, without letting her drink him, he wouldn't turn into a vampire. He'd become her familiar. You saw that guy with her? The old butler?"

They nodded.

"Well, he's almost certainly a familiar, and possibly some or all of her security team is too. It basically will keep someone devoted to their vampire lord. Extended life and greater strength are just some of the perks, but if they're separated from the vampire too long, they can grow unpredictable—violent even. Picture him like a drug addict—which I'm sure you've dealt with in your line of work. He'll go into withdrawals, depression, an uncontrollable urge to rejoin her. That could make Chris a real danger to be around."

"Then should we ask him if he's had anything unusual to drink?" Lawson asked.

Elena nodded. "Not a bad idea. But he might avoid telling you the truth out of fear, or might not even know if he had. Some vampires are pretty sneaky about stuff like that."

"Shit," Liz said, putting her hands on her hips and clearly

mulling this over. "Well, what do you suppose we should do, then? Go somewhere else and leave him here? He said Marie doesn't know of this place, so he should be safe."

Shaking her head, Elena said, "He might feel compelled to call her or just drive back to her place. He's a liability, no matter how innocent you may feel he is in all this."

Liz and Lawson exchanged a look, waiting to see what the other might say. Finally, Liz said, "Look, he might be a liability, but he at least deserves an explanation. The guy just had his whole world turned upside down. I think whatever you know should at least be shared with him, and if you wanna ditch him after that it's your business. But as police officers, it's our duty to keep him safe."

"Speak for yourself, Liz," Lawson said. "If she's right about the kid, it's probably better to cut and run. He doesn't know where we live, even if Marie might be able to find out. I'd rather just disappear without the guy, to be honest."

Liz sighed and said, "Whatever . . . can we discuss all this inside? I'd at least like to speak more to Elena about all this."

Elena didn't like where things were going, but she needed some allies at this point. The deck was stacked against her too much when it came to Marie, and perhaps having an insider with the vampire queen might not be the worst thing in the world. She'd naturally have to keep a close eye on him, but it would be a change in tactics, and change was not always a bad thing. Finally, Elena acquiesced. "Okay, let's head inside."

Waving the two detectives onward, she followed them up to the front door and Liz knocked firmly three times. When the door opened, it wasn't Chris standing there, as she expected—it was an Asian guy about Chris' age, who didn't look as fit as him, and honestly quite a bit nerdier. "Um, hi. Who are you?" he asked.

"We're here for Chris," Liz said. "Can we come in?"

"Wait a minute, are you guys cops? Whatever Chris did, I didn't have anything to do with it, okay?"

Lawson laughed at this. "I take it Chris didn't tell you why he came here?"

"He said he was in some trouble, something to do with Marie LeBeau, but he didn't mention anything about the cops. Just that some people would be coming around later."

"Well," Lawson said, "We're those people. Can we come in now?"

"Who's she?" Nick asked, pointing to Elena. "She doesn't look like a cop. And . . . is that a *katana* in her hand?"

It's true Elena had been holding her sword, but she wasn't about to leave it back in her car. Not under current circumstances. So she said, "Yeah, I keep it for protection."

"From what? Psychotic Ren Faire fanatics?"

This got a chuckle out of Lawson, but Liz was not amused. "Just let us in, please."

A toilet could be heard flushing from the nearby bathroom and soon after, Chris finally appeared behind his friend asking, "Who's at the door?" Noticing the cops, he said, "Why are you guys just standing out there?"

"Where the hell have you been?!" Lawson asked, "Your buddy here is trying to pretend he's the Black Knight from *Monty Python and the Holy Grail*."

Nick laughed at this and said, "I love that movie. Okay, Chris clearly knows you guys, so you can come inside."

"About time," Liz huffed.

Once they were in the house, Chris noticed Elena—who he hadn't met—and asked Liz, "Is she your daughter?"

At the same time, Liz and Elena spoke, the cop saying, "Do I look that old?" and Elena saying, "Do I look that young?"

Nick laughed again and said, "You guys are a regular comedy

act here. I gotta use the bathroom, but you're welcome to help yourself to food or beverages if you want." Moving toward the open bathroom door, he waved his hand in front of his face and said, "Aw Chris, what the fuck did you *do* in here?"

10

Over the next hour, Elena explained her history as a vampire hunter to her new companions. Nick was probably the most shocked by all this, as he was the only one who hadn't been previously let in on the whole secret society of vampires lurking around LA. Naturally, nobody gave him a hard time when he started accusing them of playing some kind of prank on him, which prompted him to search his place for cameras. Once he'd calmed down and realized they were serious, he naturally got nervous, but Elena did a good job of keeping her cool and making it very clear to everyone there that she was fully capable of handling things.

"I understand if you're scared, nervous, worried for your loved ones and yourselves, but you have to trust me. I've been doing this my whole life. I know what I'm doing. If you want to bail, I get it and I'm not stopping you."

Chris shook his head, "If you're so sure you can stop Marie, then why haven't you yet? Even I wouldn't have been able to stop you much longer at that party had you kept it up or pulled your sword."

"I can't get close to her because of that damn security team. That party was one of my only chances and I blew it. Fighting a single human hand-to-hand is one thing—hell, fighting a single vampire can be managed with a bit of caution—but more than one vampire? A bunch of guys with guns, let alone potential *familiars* with guns? I can't deal with that alone. I'm not a one-woman army."

"Wait, you said familiar?" Nick asked. "Like the guys who are like . . . servants of vampires?"

"I take it you've seen some movies," Elena said.

"Yeah, Chris and I are pretty big horror buffs."

"Well, it's best if you forget everything you know about vampires. Crosses, holy water, garlic, and stakes don't work. But they do have a problem with silver, and can't survive a decapitation. No head, nothing to control the body. Also, sunlight won't burn them. No creature in nature just spontaneously combusts like that. However, sunlight does weaken them, but not the way you might think.

"At night, vampires are stronger than the greatest bodybuilder to ever live. But during the day, they're only about as strong as your average human. It can help level the playing field, which is why most vampires wouldn't be out as much during the day. Ones like Marie, though? Queens? They play the long game. She wouldn't worry about having to defend herself when she's got others to protect her. And having familiars around only makes things that much more complicated."

Nick looked annoyed and said, "You still didn't fully explain the familiars. If the movies aren't right, what's so special about them?"

"Imagine a human who's almost a vampire, but not quite. A familiar is someone who's devoted themselves to their vampire lord, by drinking their blood, but not having their own drained. They gain increased strength and reflexes, but at the cost of their free will. They will find an irresistible pull toward their master at all times and find it impossible not to protect them. They don't have the thirst of a vampire, but are slaves in all but name."

"Thomas," Chris said, pondering something.

Elena wasn't sure who exactly he was talking about and waited for Chris to clarify.

"Marie's butler. He does almost everything for her. He must be her familiar, right?"

"The old man in the suit?"

"Yeah, you saw him then when you were watching the house?"

"Yes, but I didn't know his name. I'm afraid to say he may be the lost hunter from almost two-hundred years ago. My father told me about him, Thomas Howard. He was famous for being the only hunter to successfully cross paths with Marie, but was never seen or heard from again. Everyone had assumed he was killed, but it seems she had a fate worse than death in store for him."

"Wait," Nick said, "Hold up, you're telling me this guy working for Marie—sorry, her familiar—is *two hundred* years old? How is that possible?"

"Familiars aren't immortal like vampires, but they do have unnaturally long lives, as part of the gift given to their body from the blood. My guess is from how old Thomas looked, his time is almost up. Which could explain why she brought you into her company, Chris."

All eyes turned on Chris and he suddenly became very nervous.

"Did you drink any of her blood?" Liz asked quite seriously. She was visibly concerned and Elena worried he might lie to alleviate any fears from the group he had willingly done so. But she didn't believe he would have, he was too innocent.

"Why would I drink *anyone's* blood?" he asked.

"Elena said she could have tricked you somehow."

"Like in *The Lost Boys!*" Nick exclaimed gleefully, as if his movie knowledge had somehow answered a big question on a test.

"What happened in that?" Liz asked, looking confused.

Lawson surprisingly spoke up, apparently aware of the film in question. "The vampires gave this guy a bottle of wine that was really blood."

"Wine . . ." Chris said in shock, as he made a horrible discovery in that moment. "She gave me wine the first night I was with her. I thought it tasted a little . . . different. But she assured me it was a special kind she was personally making in Napa Valley. I don't know much about wine, so I just thought—"

"Jesus Christ," Lawson said as he ran his fingers through his hair.

"Wait," Nick said, "That doesn't mean anything for certain, right? I mean, isn't there some way to be sure?"

Elena gave this some thought. She'd never heard that someone could drink a vampire's blood and not become a familiar, but at the same time, she'd honestly never looked into the science of it. Any familiar that crossed her path in the past, she disposed of as quickly as she could, otherwise they could be a major hassle. "Let's step outside."

As Elena walked to the front door, she heard everyone's footsteps behind her. She opened the door and stepped outside, pointing to Nick's car that was parked in the driveway. "I doubt you could normally lift that. Right, Chris?"

"Definitely not, that's a fucking car."

"Well, try it now. Get a good grip and see what you can do."

"That's crazy," Chris said, "I could seriously hurt myself."

"Then don't strain yourself, just see what you can do. I hope to hell I'm wrong and that car doesn't budge an inch, but if you've made the change, this thing shouldn't be too hard to lift."

Chris sighed as his friend and the cops watched in fear and curiosity from the doorway. Stepping up to the front of the car, he crouched down low like he was ready to do some squats and got a good grip under the front bumper. Then he lifted . . . and couldn't believe what happened next.

The car rose several feet off the ground as he stood up fully without much of a hassle. "Holy shit!" he exclaimed and quickly dropped the car back down to the ground where it bounced on its front tires.

"My car, man!" Nick cried.

Chris was in shock at the events that had just occurred, and didn't even acknowledge his friend's worry for his vehicle. Instead, he just made his way back toward the house with his head hung low, staring at the ground. Elena wanted to say something to the poor guy, something that might offer a small measure of comfort to ease his troubled mind. Instead, she let him walk past, and so did everyone else. Entering the house, Chris proceeded into the living room where he plopped down on a chair, the air hissing out of the cushion from the force of his body. "I need a drink," he sighed, looking at Nick. His friend had fear in his eyes before Chris rolled his own. "Alcohol, not blood, Nick."

Nick sighed in relief. "Of course. I got some vodka in the freezer."

"I told you already he won't have the thirst," Elena clarified once more. Moving closer to Chris, she took a seat next to him. "Look, you need to understand, your life is not over, Chris. This connection the familiar has to their master, it only lasts as long as the master lives. The hold their blood has over you dies with them."

"Great, so then I just have to hope you guys can actually pull this off, right?"

Elena looked to the cops, hoping one of them might have their own words of encouragement, but they seemed to be waiting for the vampire hunter to speak. Nick thankfully returned from the kitchen with a cold glass of straight vodka that he handed to

Chris. He gulped the whole thing down like it was plain water and handed it back to his friend.

"Thanks," Chris said, "I needed that." Looking to Elena, still waiting for a response, he asked, "So what's the plan? I assume you have one, or had one already?"

"Honestly . . . no."

Throwing up his arms, Chris said, "That makes me feel a *lot* better, then!"

"Look, Chris," Liz said firmly, "We can try and take care of this, but in the meantime, it's probably best you stay here with your friend, so he can watch over you."

"What the hell does that mean?"

"It means you could be liability to all of us," Elena said. "The longer you stay away from Marie, the more dangerous you could become. Especially knowing we intend her harm."

"But that's crazy, why would I do that?"

"How have you been feeling since you've been away from her so far?"

Shaking his head, he said, "I mean, I miss her, yeah, but I just. . . I cared for her, you know? Before I knew she was a vampire. I can't just wipe those feelings away."

"Have you spent any other time away from her previously? A longer period of time, perhaps?"

"Yeah, she sent me to watch this other actor she knew, Philip Dalton, the one the detectives went after 'cause we thought he was a vampire. I take it we were right, and that's how you guys ran into each other?"

"Yeah, he's been taken care of," Elena clarified. "But you were watching him for how long?"

"About a day . . . I spent the night there. I have to admit— now that you're asking about it—I felt like shit the next morning. Like waking up after a night of hard drinking."

Elena sighed. "That's the pull. Trust me, it'll only get worse."

"Then what the hell do I do?"

"Honestly? I don't know. We could tie you up, but you'd likely break free. Your friend Nick isn't going to be able to stop you either, if you want to leave."

"What if I tried to fight it?" Chris asked.

"I don't know, I mean, I've never worked with a familiar before. I don't even know if that's possible."

"You said familiars are like junkies, right?" Lawson asked. "I had an informant once, a junkie I couldn't trust to go a block without scoring some smack if he had cash on him. But he provided me with plenty of valuable intel on the local gangs and I didn't want to lose him, so I helped him get clean. It was hell, let me tell you. Watching what that guy went through. But it *can* be done. And if he can do it, I don't see why Chris can't too. It's just another drug, right?"

"It's still a risk," Elena said. "How are we supposed to keep him contained?"

"If vampires are weaker in the day," Liz said. "What about familiars?"

"I haven't run into enough to really know for sure, but they could be."

"If you don't know, that means something. If vampires get weaker in the day, it stands to reason anyone with some of their blood inside them would also have their powers diminished. If that's true then we should at least be able to keep him restrained during the day. That gives us some time to try and take care of Marie."

"And what if we can't take care of her by tomorrow night, and Chris breaks free?" Lawson asked.

Elena nodded. "Like I said, it's a risk."

"What's the alternative?" Chris asked. "You kill me? Or

maybe just let me head back to Marie. I'm still me, maybe I could find some way to help you guys. Something that doesn't directly put her in danger so I won't have to fight against it."

"It might not matter—all Marie has to do is ask where you've been and you'd be forced to tell her. We'd be screwed before we even got inside. At least right now, we have one advantage—she doesn't know we're working together."

"There's something else you guys haven't mentioned," Nick said. "What about a distraction? I'd say Chris presents a pretty large one, am I right? He's important to Marie. Can't you use that to your advantage, strategize some kind of attack that uses him as the bait?"

Chris looked at his friend and said, "Thanks, Nick. Glad you think so highly of me to make me the bait."

"Sorry, man. I'm just telling it like it is. And if it's the best chance we have of stopping this vampire and returning you to normal, isn't that worth the risk?"

Elena tried to think about Nick's suggestion. It was a risky maneuver, but probably still a better idea than just keeping Chris tied up. Both scenarios wouldn't give them much time, but one could at least put them in a more advantageous position. Leaving Chris behind meant they still had to deal with Marie's whole security team and Thomas—if he still had some fight left in him. But if they sent Chris out there, possibly to meet with Marie, she might just come alone. It was a big risk, but one worth taking. Chris wouldn't be in any danger either way, but his presence could put them in danger if they failed to stop Marie before Chris lost all control. It would take some careful planning no matter what, an airtight scheme, and a careful selection of where to strike.

11

The plan was conceived, broken down, detailed out, and set in motion.

Chris would call Marie early in the morning, about sunrise, to tell her he managed to get away from the police—who kidnapped him—and needed help. He'd ask that she help him since he didn't have money for a ride and or his car. He would pretend to be worried how long he'd last before they found him.

Marie would likely ask what they wanted and he'd have to tell her the truth, that they knew her true nature and wanted to stop her. Of course, this wouldn't likely be news to her at that point. By that time, she'd have had both bodies removed from the morgue, attempting to clean things up. Which would mean her focus would be on finding the cops. The last thing Marie LeBeau would expect was her new familiar betraying her. After all, she'd get the truth out of him as soon as he returned.

That's what made Chris the most nervous; if she chose to question him at the pick-up location, before the detectives and Elena could act, then they'd likely all die. Marie was weaker in the daylight, but she wasn't any less intelligent, and Elena expected that she wouldn't move anywhere without her security detail anymore. Which meant they would at the very least be keeping an eye out for an attack. Whatever moves Elena and the detectives made, they'd need the element of surprise to pull it all off.

Nick would be staying behind. He was never truly involved in things and Chris didn't see a reason to involve him any further than using his house as a base of operations. Of course, Nick was mostly fine with this. He didn't want to tussle with any vampires if they didn't know about him. But what Nick *wasn't* fine with was if the vampires *did* know about him. Nobody seemed to believe they'd been followed, but he wasn't convinced. If he was going to stay behind, it would be with his *Kill Bill* replica katana. It wasn't Hattori Hanzo steel, but it was still damn sharp and he hoped it was enough against a vampire.

There was one more complication about their meeting the next morning. It was only a matter of time before the decapitated body of Philip Dalton was discovered. And when it was, the police would start asking questions like why the two detectives who'd been staking out the actor's home had disappeared around the same time as the murder. It didn't help that a slug from Liz's Glock would likely be discovered, as she never saw where it landed after tearing through Dalton's skull. She was sure at the very least they'd be asking questions about him being shot in the head before being decapitated. But she couldn't worry about that at the moment, it was more important to focus on the task at hand. Once that was accomplished, the body of Marie LeBeau along with Philip Dalton would be evidence enough, if they could convince Hank to play ball. She just had to hope the vampire queen didn't have any friends on the force, or Liz would never see her son again.

Elena thought the plan was thin and could very likely fail, but she still felt it was better odds than a full-frontal assault on the home of Marie LeBeau. That was practically suicide, and frankly she didn't see any other choice between the two due to their time constraint of attempting to help Chris. Part of her wanted to just cut him loose, to not let his presence alter her plans, but there wasn't just him anymore. Those two detectives had their lives on the line and wouldn't live another day without her help. There was a big difference between helping a familiar—which to her was a lost cause—and helping humans. These were detectives who worked a job to bring criminals to justice; they were supposed to be helping people and her letting them die would make things that much worse for so many others. She couldn't live with that, and just hoped that they would be capable enough to help her succeed.

All they needed was to take out Marie. The guards that should be with her were all armed. Currently only the detectives had guns, two pistols, and a shotgun stored in their car. Elena did know how to fire a shotgun—despite not liking guns—but Liz was not okay with her using a police shotgun, so she stuck with her sword. She just hoped continuing to use her ninja costume was enough to keep her identity safe. If the cops showed up during the whole ordeal, everyone could end up in jail—or dead.

The pick-up was arranged in the parking garage of the Santa Monica shopping mall. Chris told Marie that he needed her to pick him up somewhere secluded since he was afraid of the cops spotting him. It was the best option he could think of where she could drive right in and pick him up quickly. Thankfully, Marie agreed to this. The question remained if she'd arrive alone.

The detectives would stay parked on the roof, keeping a lookout for Marie's approaching car. Once they saw her, they could communicate this to Elena and Chris to get ready. Chris would just have to wait there and make sure she didn't hightail it out of the garage before greeting him.

Elena's part was more complicated, though—she would need to be dropped off in the parking garage earlier. There are not many places to hide that early in the morning, as the parking garage was mostly empty, but that still left a few spots. She'd need to get nestled in some out-of-the-way nook and wait for the detectives' signal.

Then it would be time to act.

12

The parking lot was nearly empty. The weather was cool, with a gentle sea breeze blowing into the structure. Elena had found a decent spot to hide behind one of the only cars on the second level where Chris would be waiting. This car gave her the ability to at least change her cover depending on the spot Marie was at. As for the choice of the second-level, it was far enough in that it would be difficult for Marie to escape quickly, but not so far toward the top that she might become suspicious. It was more important that she believe Chris just wanted to avoid a view from the street where police might spot him.

Speaking of police, Detectives Gutiérrez and Lawson were camped on the roof with their car—since it was a vehicle Marie could recognize. They needed the car to pursue, if necessary, but putting it any lower could tip her off. At the time of the actress' arrival, they would have to make their way down several levels on foot. Thankfully, it wasn't too difficult with the nearby stairwell, but it could still present a problem if things didn't go as planned with Elena.

The hope was that the vampire hunter could take out Marie before she or her security team noticed. Once they had, the detectives would provide covering fire for Elena to hightail it with Chris to the stairwell, where hopefully they could make it back to the detectives' vehicle safely. But Elena knew there were a million ways this could go wrong and just had to do her part to not screw up.

After Chris' call from his mobile phone, everyone was waiting with heavy anticipation for the arrival of Marie LeBeau. Elena had listened to his conversation and Chris had done his part well. It seemed Marie wondered how he still had his phone on him, but at least his story made sense. The cops had taken him hostage, wanting to use him to get Marie out of hiding, but he'd escaped, managing to snag his stuff on the way out in the middle of the night. She wondered how he pulled that off, but he explained how he had a trick to escape handcuffs he learned from a magic book years ago. Finally, she agreed to meet him at the parking garage and he thanked her for everything.

After almost an hour, the detectives alerted Elena via her phone that Marie was coming inside and she flashed the signal to Chris to get ready. As the black Rolls Royce pulled into the concrete structure, it slowly made its way up to the second floor. Elena adjusted herself from the front of her car to the side as the Marie's vehicle rounded the corner to approach Chris.

He must have felt a rush of excitement at the presence of his queen. His eyes lit up at the sight of the car and Elena's concern that he'd betray them moved that much closer to reality. But as the window drew down, and Chris leaned inside, she heard him say, "Marie, I've missed you so much. I was so scared."

The sniffles he got from crying might have been real, or an act. Elena didn't much care because it seemed to work. Marie stepped out of her car, exposing herself for the first time and Elena thought very hard about charging her right then and there. However, part of her was preoccupied with where the security detail was located. Marie had driven herself, which was odd since Elena had seen a chauffeur before. Clearly though, she wasn't the only one thinking this was strange.

Chris moved in to hug Marie as she approached, his puffy face visible to Elena. She knew she needed to move in now. This was the moment, the time Marie would be most distracted as she comforted her new familiar. So as Chris spoke, Elena began to quickly and quietly approach from behind the car.

"I'm glad you're okay, Chris," Marie said. "I've missed you too."

"I'm just glad you got here before the police could find me. I was so scared, I couldn't believe what they did. I don't care if they were right about you Marie, I love you." He looked up to see Elena almost there and began to break from the hug, attempting to keep the focus on himself. "I thought you'd have your security with you, though. These cops are no joke."

"Well, who needs a few overpaid security guards when you have the LAPD on your side? They were very displeased to hear what two of their detectives had done." The news of what Marie had done shocked Elena to her core, but she hadn't heard any sirens and wasn't about to waste her chance—even if it would land her in jail.

Swinging her sword straight at the neck of the vampire queen, Elena saw the blade cut through the air in its usual silent approach. But right before it found its mark, Marie ducked. Elena was so caught off guard, she didn't even have time to counter Marie's next move. The actress' leg kicked out and knocked the vampire hunter back across the hard concrete, scraping her body badly against the rough surface.

Elena caught her bearings, but saw Marie was already helping Chris back into the Rolls. He wasn't putting up any resistance. Perhaps he was too scared, or he was already completely under her spell. Regardless, they would be gone in a matter of seconds and she hoped the detectives were right behind her to strike. Sure enough they were, opening fire on the actress' vehicle as it backed up to turn around quickly. The bullets seemed to harmlessly bounce off the glass and metal exterior. Elena wasn't sure if the car had been bulletproofed, but it didn't matter. She'd be getting away and their plan had utterly failed.

To make things worse, though, as Marie pulled her car down to the first floor, police sirens erupted from all around and several patrol vehicles could be heard making their way up the ramp past Marie.

"What the fuck?!" Lawson cried.

Elena groaned from the ground, trying to get to her feet. "She went to the cops, told them what Chris said about you two kidnapping him. We can't talk our way out of this. We need to go, now!"

Liz fumed and turned to Elena, picking up the hunter's fallen sword and handing it back to her. "You get out of here. They don't know about you. We'll cover you."

"But they could kill you!"

"If we gotta go to jail, then so be it. You can still see this through."

"No! They might be in her pocket for all you know. You can't throw your lives away!"

Before anybody had time to react further, the cops were on them. Even more cars drove up the ramp and the two in front turned to block their exit. As the officers exited their vehicles, they didn't even stop to offer a warning, they just opened fire. Instinctively, Lawson drew his own sidearm and met their fire, but as he had no cover, he was quickly riddled with bullets and Liz only had time to cry, "No!" before Elena grabbed her wrist and pulled her toward the stairwell. Bullets ping-ponged off the walls around them, sending small pieces of concrete soaring through the air.

As they burst through into the stairwell, bullets collided with the metal door, playing a song of death. Boots pounded their way up the stairs from below and Elena knew there would be no going down. Instead, she pulled Liz up the stairs with her. They exited onto the roof, where it was clear there would be only one way for Elena to escape. There was a lower roof just to the south where a bunch of solar panels were placed. She could make the jump, but the distance to run would leave her completely exposed before hopping down to the top floor of the open-air mall.

Liz must have known this because she turned to Elena and said, "You need to go. You won't make it without my help. I knew what I was getting into when we started this. I'll still try and get away if I can, but the most important thing is that you make it away safely. If you can't stop Marie, nobody will. Now go!"

Elena knew arguing with the detective was pointless, so she simply said, "Thank you, Liz. I hope you make it."

Liz nodded and then prepared herself to fire at the first cops out the stairwell. She probably wasn't comfortable firing at other officers whether or not they were ultimately in the pocket of a vampire queen. But she had made it her mission to give Elena enough time to escape. And that was all that mattered.

Hopping down to the lower roof, Elena landed in a roll to prevent any bones from breaking. She then sprinted forward, hearing gunfire erupt behind her. She didn't know what happened to Liz, but she wouldn't be able to check. All she could do was wait and watch the news for any reports. If she heard nothing, it just might be possible the detective somehow got away. But having the entire police force after her would not make things any easier, and some sinister part of Elena thought maybe it was better if the detective didn't make it.

After hopping down to the top floor of the mall, Elena drew a lot of strange looks, but didn't let it slow her down. She avoided the escalators and elevators and ran forward trying to decide where to head next. That's when she noticed the massive Nordstrom building and charged for the entrance. Pushing through the doors, she dove behind the nearest rack where she removed her mask and top, to reveal a black tank top underneath. It wasn't clear if the police saw her enter or not, but she wasn't about to go and check. She then grabbed several outfits off the rack to conceal her sword and made her way rather casually toward the fitting rooms.

Moving into the first open room, she changed her clothes, knowing the security tags were going to be a problem. Thankfully, she always kept cash on her while in her ninja suit just in case she ran into trouble. The new clothes didn't fit the best, but at least she could look somewhat normal and conceal her sword in her bundle of ninja clothes. Making her way back into the store proper, Elena found the nearest cashier to ring her up. Thankfully she didn't need to swap her shoes as she wore pretty plain-looking black Onitsuka Tigers. The cashier was nice enough to understand her desire to wear her new clothes out of the store and removed the security tags. Elena then asked for the biggest bag the cashier had and placed her old clothes and sword in it.

Walking out the front of the store on the street level, Elena spotted cops all over the place trying to locate her. It almost brought a smile to her face that they hadn't realized she was right in front of them—and not looking too bad in her new threads, either. An ambulance had shown up to take at least one body— which she suspected was Lawson—but she couldn't see any evidence as to whether or not Liz got away. And it wasn't worth the risk to hang around there any longer to find out. Too much was on the line.

KILLER QUEEN

1

Nick had been anxiously waiting for an hour after the group had left that morning. He'd already called in sick to work—which he was now regretting, as that might have at least distracted him from the waiting game of death. Considering the short distance the group had traveled, and the time Marie was expected to arrive there, he should have heard something from someone.

But he hadn't.

Something had to have gone wrong. And when a firm knock hit his door around fifteen minutes later, Nick was surprised to see who was standing in his doorway.

It was Dan Lopez.

Dan hadn't known about the vampires as far as Nick knew—it seemed Chris had chosen to keep him out of danger, but Chris also hadn't bothered to tell Nick what happened to Dan. He wasn't sure if Dan skipped town or stayed at their apartment, because frankly it hadn't occurred to Nick to ask Chris about any of this.

So when Dan arrived all smiles at his door, Nick chose his words carefully. He wasn't sure what Dan actually knew. He might have been wondering where Chris was—or what was going on—and Nick didn't think it was his right to tell Dan anything that could have come from Chris. But being as nervous as he was, a familiar face helped ease the tension a little. He figured until he heard from the others, letting his friend keep him company wasn't the worst idea in the world.

"Hey Nick, glad you're home . . . I was wondering if you've seen Chris? I haven't heard from him in a few days. He said he'd been staying with that actress as part of his job, but I don't know where she lives. I tried calling him a few times and haven't gotten a hold of him. You don't think he's ghosting me, do you? Our rent's due, so I thought I'd use my day off to make sure I got his half."

Nick realized it was now August, so Dan's fear was warranted. But still he didn't feel comfortable telling him where Chris was. He also thought it was odd that Dan drove all the way over there without calling first to ask. "You know you could have called instead of coming over here."

Dan sighed and laughed. "I know, I know. I just happened to be in the neighborhood, so you know, it made sense. You're not sick, are you? I guess I probably should have asked that, right?"

"No, not sick. Just . . . needed a day off."

"I get it, but . . . have you seen or heard from Chris?" Dan waited for an answer, seemingly studying Nick for his response.

Nick didn't want to get caught in an outright lie, but his experience had taught him that bending the truth usually worked. Since Chris was expected to return at some point, he said, "Chris did call last night, he wanted to borrow some movies I had this morning. To show Marie, I guess. Don't know what time he'll be by though."

"Oh really? Can I come in and wait then? I mean, you're not doing anything, I'm not doing anything. We could hang out for a bit if that's cool. Just really would like to get that rent money."

Nick realized he was starting to look like a jerk, so he finally said, "Sure, come on in."

Dan nodded in thanks and entered the house. Nick stepped

out of the way so his friend could enter and then closed the door behind him. Dan was looking around when Nick approached him. He asked, "You move some stuff around in here, Nick?"

"Yeah, I wanted to make some room for those new bookshelves I got over there." Nick pointed to the bookshelves he recently bought for his ever-expanding collection of films. Dan seemed satisfied and went to sit down on the couch. "You want anything to eat or drink?"

Dan shook his head. "Not hungry at the moment."

Nick was surprised by this answer. Dan was quite a bit heavier than Nick and never seemed to turn down free food. Perhaps he'd just eaten. Except . . . he hadn't said that exactly. A chilling thought then went through Nick's mind. He'd seen enough horror films to realize that it was possible he had made a very serious mistake. He hadn't seen Dan since Comic-Con and if Marie knew where his friend was, it stood to reason she might have turned him into a vampire to use against Chris. But it was just as likely that Nick was being paranoid. Dan had asked to enter, but Elena didn't make any mention of real-life vampires needing to ask permission. So, Dan could have just been trying to be polite. He was also out in the daytime, which had made Nick not even suspect anything at first, but remembering what Elena had told him, Dan could be one of the undead. Except she'd mentioned vampires lost their strength in the daytime, which would give Nick a fighting chance. All he needed was something to defend himself with. Unfortunately, he'd left his sword in the living room, right next to the couch Dan was sitting on.

Thinking for a way to get himself closer to a weapon and further away from Dan, Nick made up an excuse. "I think I'm going to make myself a drink."

"Isn't it a little early?"

"Not on my day off," Nick chuckled, trying to mask his fear.

Moving into the kitchen, he asked, "You sure you don't want a drink?"

"Maybe later." These words sent a chill down Nick's spine. He was almost certain his friend was a vampire, but how could he learn the truth without being attacked? He didn't want to just cut and run if Dan was still human, but if his friend was there to drain his blood, he needed to do something fast. Sunlight wouldn't expose him, nor garlic, or crosses. He wondered for a moment how the hell Elena hunted the damn things without constantly killing humans by mistake.

As Nick prepared himself a margarita in the blender, he pulled a lime from his fridge to chop with a knife. He planned to pocket the knife while Dan wasn't looking, but as he glanced over the counter separating the kitchen from the living room, he felt his blood go cold.

Dan was no longer on the couch.

Spinning around holding the knife in pure panic, he found himself face-to-fang with Dan, who smiled back at him, exposing inch-long canines. He moved alarmingly fast and the only thing that stopped him was Nick instinctively stabbing forward with the knife.

Dan was stopped in his tracks, his hands frozen in mid-grab as he abruptly turned his head down to see the knife stuck in his gut. He then looked up at Nick and grinned. He was not even hurt by this action, and it became immediately clear if Nick was going to stop him, he needed his katana.

Shoving Dan away, Nick leaped over the kitchen counter toward the living room. Before he could clear the counter though, something grabbed his foot with such force he thought his bones might break. Dan was anything but fit before, yet now, even without super-strength, the guy had a grip that would put a seasoned bodybuilder to shame. As that grip attempted to pull

Nick back over the counter, he grabbed firmly onto the edge and tried to pulled himself forward. But even with both hands, it seemed he didn't have the strength to stop Dan. So, Nick started shaking his leg violently to get Dan to let go and when that didn't work, he kicked back at the guy.

Unfortunately, Nick was no martial arts expert.

He might have loved kung fu movies, but Nick only took one year of Wing Chun in his youth before quitting. So when he kicked out at Dan, it was not with proper technique or even the full strength of his body. It was more like a flailing limb that didn't break the hold Dan had on him. Now his own grip was slipping from the counter's edge.

Nick watched helplessly as his fingers slowly lost a hold on the counter one at a time. His body flew back into Dan and the two collapsed onto the ground. Dan quickly shoved Nick off and leaped onto him with a quickness.

Flashing his fangs once more, Dan said, "I've actually been *dying* for a drink, Nick. Thank you for not making this too difficult." He lunged in for the kill and Nick closed his eyes in anticipation of death.

But that death didn't come.

There was a *whooshing* sound, followed by a *thud* on the floor near Nick and he felt warm liquid leaking all over him. When he opened his eyes in confusion, he saw that liquid was blood pouring freely from the stump that used to be Dan's neck. Standing over him was Elena, brandishing her katana and looking none too pleased. When Nick looked to his left and saw Dan's severed head, still flashing those pointy white fangs, he gasped.

Holding out her hand, Elena said, "You want help up, or do you wanna lay under this guy's corpse the rest of the day?"

It took a moment for Nick to react, but then he held out his hand and she pulled him to his feet. Dan's body slid lifelessly to the floor. "Jesus," Nick said, "I thought I was good as dead."

"You came close," she said, wiping off her blade with a kitchen towel. Clearly, she didn't think Nick would mind after she'd just saved his life.

"I just can't believe Dan was . . . a vampire."

"So I take it you knew this guy?" Elena asked before sheathing her sword.

"You think I'd have let him in if I didn't?"

"We should clean this mess up. It's not safe for you to stay here, but we don't want anybody finding his body."

Nick felt strong emotions bubbling up from within and suddenly found himself shouting, "He's not just *some guy*, dammit!" Elena seemed taken aback by his outburst, and Nick tried to calm himself down, but couldn't do much. "This is Dan Lopez, Chris' roommate . . . my friend. He was . . . looking for Chris." Suddenly realizing his other friend was nowhere in sight, he asked, "Where *is* Chris?"

Turning from him, either in shame or trying to focus on something else, Elena said, "He's with Marie." She then moved to a closet in the hallway and asked, "Is this where you keep your cleaning products?"

"Yeah, but wait, what about the detectives? Did they make it?"

Opening the closet, Elena pulled out some rubber gloves, floor cleaner, a bucket, and a mop. "I think they're both dead, but even if they're alive they'll be in jail and of no help to us." Moving the bucket to the sink, she began filling it with water. "Marie got the cops involved and they weren't the least bit interested in hearing our side of the story. If I had to guess, I'd say some or most of them are in her pocket." Turning off the water, she poured in some of the cleaning solution and set the bucket on the floor. Then she slipped on the gloves and said, "Wouldn't surprise me with it being LA, but at the very least she's turned one cop with a lot of pull in the department." Putting the mop in the bucket, she let it soak up the solution.

"Could she do that?" Nick asked, finding it crazy that this vampire could turn any police who could further her plans, whatever those might be.

"We need to move the body. Do you have trash bags?"

Nick wasn't sure if she was dodging his question or just more focused on the task at hand, but he did as she asked and got some trash bags. He then noticed she'd removed Dan's car keys from his pocket and grabbed her sword.

"Okay, I need you to hold up the body. And you might want to turn your face away—this is about to get *very* messy." Nick looked away as she sliced off Dan's arms and legs. He wondered why she didn't take the body to the tub, but seeing how much blood was already all over his kitchen floor, it seemed pretty apparent why. He almost threw up several times, but managed to keep it down.

As Elena began collecting the body parts in trash bags, Nick attempted to distract himself. "How can Marie get to the cops like you said she did? I mean, people in the industry I get, but some high-ranking police officer?"

"This is what she does, Nick. I've been tracking her for years. She moves to one city, turns the most powerful people in the area, and when things get too hot for her, she moves on." Finishing up her last bag, Elena tied it off and said, "That's it for the pieces. Once it gets dark, I can put these in your friend's car. Then I'll dispose of that and the bags, but for now I'm gonna put them in your tub."

"I'd prefer if you didn't."

"Just be glad I didn't start all this in there. Now if you can begin with the mop, that would be a big help."

Nick looked at the mop, then at the bloody mess that used to be his kitchen and wondered how the hell this would be enough to clean everything up. There was blood splattered on the cupboards, even droplets on the blinds on the window. Knowing it was pointless to argue with Elena, he begrudgingly picked up the mop and started to work on soaking up the blood.

When Elena came back into the kitchen, she picked up a roll of paper towels, a bottle of cleaning spray and began to work on the cupboards. She didn't miss a beat and seemed solely focused on the task at hand, but Nick still had a million thoughts rattled around in his brain. Eventually, he asked, "So if Marie knows you're after her, why is she still hanging around LA?"

Elena shook her head. "She's got a good thing here. She's not about to give it all up because she thinks I'm getting close. Now, if I had her backed into a corner without support, that'd be a different story. But it isn't right now. Our team is down several key players. I'm not even sure I can take her on by myself. Especially not now."

"But we gotta do something, right? I mean, you can't just leave Chris in her clutches. He's my friend."

Stopping her work, she turned to Nick and said, "Look, if I'm being honest, I *want* to cut and run. This whole situation is fucked, much more so than any I've faced in the past."

"Then why don't you?"

Elena sighed. "Because I swore an oath, same as my father, and his father before him, to protect humanity from these things. Marie has her claws deep in LA, but if I can stop her . . . well, as history has shown, when a queen falls, it's the same as if she fled the area. Her brood will scatter. It won't magically fix LA, but it'll be a hell of a lot better off than if she stayed. We might even be able to take a few others with influence along the way, that'll cut further into her stranglehold on the city."

"So then what's next? What's the plan?"

"You got any fighting experience?"

Nick shook his head.

"Any weapons training?"

"I fired a gun once or twice at the range."

"Guns won't do shit against the undead, I thought that was already clear. I meant with swords, stuff like that."

"No, sorry."

"Shit, well that makes things a bit harder. I can't exactly go around recruiting. Not to mention, Marie's security will be tighter than ever and your place isn't safe for us anymore."

"Then what do we do?"

Elena looked like she was thinking for a moment and then said, "We can head back to my place, but we aren't ready to strike yet."

"Then when will we be?"

"Soon."

2

Chris still couldn't believe it. He'd gone back to Marie, betrayed those he'd vowed to help and possibly led to their deaths. He had no idea what happened to Elena and the two detectives when he got in Marie's car and drove off, and part of him simply didn't want to know their ultimate fates. All that seemed to matter to him in that moment was Marie. The pull of her aura was real, just like Elena had told him. His love for her was still there, but something stronger had overwhelmed his free will. Whatever he felt toward her as a person didn't matter anymore; she was his master, someone to worship and do the bidding of. He knew it was pointless to fight that feeling of devotion. Yet somewhere in the back of his mind was his old self shouting to fight, to break free from her emotional shackles.

Staying silent during the drive back to Marie's house, Chris was left to stew in his thoughts, to think about things that would never be. As her familiar, he would likely have no reciprocation of his love, only gratitude for his willingness to fulfill her every wish. The part of him that loved her somewhat broke in the face of this realization. Yet some small piece of him clung desperately to the belief that she felt the same way about him, that maybe, just maybe, there could be some kind of happily ever after for the two.

Once they arrived back at Marie's home, she finally turned and smiled at Chris. "Let's go inside. I'd like to talk about . . . well, everything. I'm sure you have many questions for me. Sorry for the silent treatment on the ride back, but it was easier this way."

Chris fought for some way to speak his true feelings toward her in that moment—the anger at his powerlessness to truly do anything—but instead he simply nodded. Marie then stepped out of her parked Rolls Royce and walked around to the passenger side door. Opening it for Chris, she held out her hand and he took it willingly, allowing her to lead him inside her home. Thomas was there to hold the door for them, still a slave to his queen. Chris wondered for a moment if that would be his own fate, or Marie's vision for him in the not-too-distant future.

Once they had entered the living room, Marie sat on her long couch and patted the seat next to her for Chris to join. As he obediently sat down, he took in the wonderful view of the valley from her extravagant floor-to-ceiling windows. He thought how blissfully ignorant everyone down there must be about what was really going on in the world around them. And how not so long ago, Chris was one of those poor souls.

Reaching toward Chris, Marie let her fingers worm their way through his hair to caress his scalp. He found the sensation to be pure ecstasy, that tingly delight that instantly put him at ease, no matter his current situation. When he turned to look at Marie, he could see that she seemed sympathetic to how he felt, as if she could read his mind. "I know you're concerned, Chris. Worried about the ones you were trying to help, for your friends, for your future. But you don't need to be worried about any of that. Not anymore."

"Because you need a new familiar? A new slave?"

Ceasing her massage, Marie threw back her head in laughter and attempted to stop the sudden outburst. "Oh Chris. I'm sorry, I shouldn't have laughed, but it's just . . . is that *really* what you think I wanted for you?"

"It's what Elena told me. It's what vampires do, if they're not trying to kill or turn a human. You had me drink your blood, right? In that wine?"

"Elena, Elena, Elena. The elusive vampire hunter, correct?" She didn't wait for a response, but could see in Chris' eyes she was right. "Yes, she's been following me for quite some time it seems—her whole family, in fact. I had the pleasure of meeting her father in Montreal, but not Elena. I had hoped she might lose interest in me, but humans have such a hard time letting go of a grudge. Us vampires are not so petty."

"Yet you have no problem killing people."

Shaking her head, Marie explained, "I kill when I need to, for survival, but don't assume just because I am, as they say, 'a creature of the night,' that I don't feel anything." Putting her hand to Chris' face to stroke his cheek, she continued, "I do care for you, Chris. I don't love easily. It becomes hard when you've lived as long as I have, but I wanted you close, so I could be sure before I gave you the choice to turn."

"Choice? What choice? You took that from me when you fed me your blood."

"I'm sorry for the deception, Chris, but I had to make sure you didn't try to leave me. I may be a vampire, but I can still be wounded quite easily—emotionally, at least. I was planning to present you with the choice before you left. I'm just glad I was able to reclaim you from those fools."

"Those fools are trying to protect people, Marie."

"From who? From me?"

"From all vampires."

Marie shook her head. "Like I said, they're fools. We vampire are legion; it would be no easier to wipe us out than an entire race of people. Genocide might be possible in a confined area, but not when spread across the globe, as we are. Idealists have their place, but not here, not now—especially not in *this* city."

Chris found himself frustrated, but wanting to know more, so he asked, "What do you mean?"

Standing up, Marie moved her hand through the air, motioning to the valley beyond her windows. "This place is *vile*. The people your associates are so intent on protecting? I have to wonder why they truly wish to? Especially if they know most of them the way I do. Hollywood is full of users and abusers, people less interested in helping each other than using their so-called friends for steps in a human stairway. Their only interest is in climbing their way to the top. Milton alone was someone I knew to be abusing women on a weekly basis. Most of his meetings were just excuses to get them alone. His girlfriend, Jyll? She was merely another one of these girls before he got his claws in her. Then after a while, she seemed to want in on the fun. Even Philip Dalton was nothing more than a sociopathic piece of filth. But everyone I turn, I change for the better."

"How? They have to kill to survive."

Marie looked disappointed in Chris and said, "We need blood to survive, true, but that doesn't mean we have to *kill* to get it. The thirst is powerful and it can, in the worst cases, drive a vampire to kill. But if they train themselves to master the thirst, it's simply a matter of finding ways to acquire blood that don't raise alarms. Philip knew this, and had I had more time with Milton and Jyll when the change took hold, they would have learned too, as my other acolytes throughout this city have."

"I still don't understand what you're trying to do here. How is this helping?"

Marie took a seat next to Chris and took his hand in hers. "I'm trying to help you understand, dear. Once the transition to a vampire completes, the person they were fades away, and in their place is someone new, someone more enlightened. And, more importantly, unable to act against my wishes."

"That still sounds akin to slavery."

Shaking her head, Marie clarified, "It's not like a familiar, Chris. A vampire still has autonomy, but my guiding hand is unquestionable. This means no one can cross me if they get out of line. I only wish for us to thrive, in secret and without drawing attention the way a vampire driven by their thirst might. My desire is to lead all vampires toward a better life, for themselves, and for others. Can't you see? This city is a cesspool, but with my guidance, I can turn it into a true City of Angels. Things here, the films made in Hollywood . . . they have a ripple effect across the globe. They provide entertainment, but also insights, ideas, things that can influence people for generations to come. Imagine what could be accomplished if the person overseeing all of that could move everyone toward a better path."

"You make it sound like you want to control the whole world."

"Not control, only improve."

"That's what every leader says they want. More often than not their definition of improvement is focused squarely on their own lives."

Without replying, Marie moved Chris' hand slowly up to her soft, warm cheek. He wondered for the first time how that was possible if a vampire was undead. Looking directly into his eyes, Marie said tenderly, "Do you believe me? Do you *trust* me?"

Chris knew that he was being pulled toward the desire to say what she wanted to hear, but even then, he knew deep down that he truly did have faith in her. Somehow, he felt that no matter what she said or did, she would never hurt him. "I do."

Smiling back at Chris, Marie lowered his hand and released it. "Then I think it's time."

"For what?" he asked as she stood up.

Holding her hand out to him, Marie said, "To give you a choice."

Chris took her hand and she helped him to his feet. "Is this where you offer to turn me?"

"That's right, Chris. My blood runs through your veins, but until I drink *your* blood, you won't begin the change. The more I drink, the faster that change will come. It can be a frightening experience, but if you give yourself over to me completely, you will see how freeing it truly is."

"And if I refuse?"

"Is that what you wish?" Chris hesitated, unsure if he could even say no to this, but she continued before he could say anything. "I could kill you to be sure you didn't speak to anyone else about me, but I wouldn't do that—not to you."

"What about the blood I drank? I can't just walk away."

"How much did Elena tell you about familiars?"

"Just that anyone who drinks a vampire's blood becomes their slave, they live longer than normal humans, have super-strength, and can't leave their master without inevitably returning."

"Those are the basics, yes, except she left out one key detail. You drank my blood, but it doesn't stay in your system forever. Like a drug you've taken, eventually it works its way out unless I give you more. It's not difficult, as such, to keep a familiar. But if a vampire *truly* wanted to let them leave, they could. Given enough time, you could walk out my door and never have to see me again. But something tells me you won't do that."

Chris knew why, he just couldn't bring himself to say it, not in that moment. He'd already said it before, but it seemed like saying it again would only weaken him. Instead, Marie said it for him.

"You love me, Chris. I know this for a fact, as you said it when I came to get you. I don't think you had said it before, but I could always tell. From the moment we met, there was some connection between us, something I couldn't explain. But we both felt it. And I don't think you'll turn away from it so easily. I've told you what I am, what you can expect for yourself, and what I plan for this city. Now, will you join me?"

Staring back into Marie's sapphire blue eyes, he found himself falling in love with her all over again. Part of him was afraid of the life awaiting him on the other side of humanity, but with her there by his side, supporting and loving him back, he was ready to take that leap. "Okay," he said, "I'll join you."

And with that, Marie leaned in slowly, moving to Chris' lips and kissing them tenderly. She then led him back to the couch, reclining him against the plush leather surface and moving down to his belt. She carefully undid the buckle, popped the button at the top of his pants and lowered the zipper, before sliding them off. Moving to his inner thigh, she kissed the area lightly, feeling the gooseflesh that stood at attention to her touch. He closed his eyes and gasped, anticipating the bite to come.

But after a few seconds, Chris wondered why it hadn't.

Opening his eyes, he glanced down at Marie to find she was carefully studying his face, waiting for him to calm himself before she acted. With a simple nod, he gave her his approval and she let her fangs sink deep into his flesh. The immediate sensation was a sharp pain, followed by a wave of euphoria that swept through his body like the strongest orgasm he'd ever experienced. When the overwhelming effect had subsided just enough for him to remain aware of what was happening, he moved his hand to the back of Marie's head, urging her to continue.

3

After Elena had showered and changed into fresh clothes that Nick was kind enough to provide, she left him alone while she disposed of the dismembered corpse of Dan Lopez. She didn't tell Nick where she was going, nor how she would accomplish this, but the less he knew the better. Once that was done, she took an Uber back to Nick's house, got him into her car, and drove back to her motel. It was there that she presented her idea for when to attack Marie, with two tickets to the premiere of *Black Berenice* that coming Tuesday.

"A movie premiere?" Nick asked in disbelief.

"What? You don't think they'll let us in?"

"No, that should get us in. They expect friends, family, anyone who was given tickets outside of those involved in the production. You won't walk the red carpet, but they also won't interrogate you where you got the tickets—unless you try to walk inside with your sword."

"Well, I'm gonna need that."

"Then I suggest we find a way to sneak it in. Still, that won't help us against Marie's security if they have guns."

Elena shook her head. "I don't think they'll be there. This is her movie, right? Her *big* night. She's not going to want to look weak or afraid. Chris will be with her, I'm sure of that, but I think he's all the security she'll want."

"How are we supposed to deal with Chris then?"

"I don't know. I'll need some time to formulate a plan. And to get you ready."

"I told you I don't know how to fight."

"Then you'll learn."

And Nick *would* learn, but Elena had her work cut out for her.

They had five days until the premiere.

Five days to plan, to prepare, and to try and prevent Nick from being a completely useless sack of meat.

It turned out Nick had taken about a year of Wing Chun when he was a kid, but didn't like it. He said he didn't have the patience for it and thought there'd be more kicking. The good thing was at least he knew how to throw a punch and take a firm enough stance that he didn't topple over from a single blow. But she really put him through his paces over the next five days. After running out to buy some pads and protective equipment from the local Big 5 Sporting Goods—as well as some sports tape to protect his wrists—they went to work.

Nick wasn't in the best shape, but he wasn't in the worst shape, either. He had a decent amount of flexibility that she tried to improve by stretching him to the point of breaking. Five days was not much time to improve flexibility, but it was still something. Lots of ice was needed, and plenty of water.

At the end of their grueling training sessions every day, they worked on the plan. The first step that Friday evening was to take a trip to Grauman's Chinese Theatre in Hollywood. That was where the premiere was supposed to take place, according to the tickets. Elena reviewed the interior, scoping out exits, and the best places to corner Marie away from any security. By her estimation, the best place was the women's lounge. The problem was there was no easy exit.

The lounge, which connected to the bathroom, was located

at the bottom of a set of stairs. Being underground meant there were no windows, which was good for cornering Marie, but bad for Elena if security was alerted. And with Chris being the only expected security, he'd likely be at the top of the stairs waiting on Marie.

Which was the other problem.

While Marie didn't know Elena or Nick's faces, Chris Hart certainly did. If he was fully in Marie's grip at that point, he'd be a major roadblock in any plan of attack. Once Marie was dealt with, it would hopefully free Chris from her clutches and he might actually assist them, but while she was still alive, he remained a slave. A slave with superior strength.

The only ways they could get past Chris would be to either distract him, or knock him out. The latter would be very difficult, as Elena could not deal with Marie and Chris on her own without causing a major situation that would draw more eyes. The only way the plan could work was if Nick and Elena were in sync, coordinating their efforts to distract Chris and then move in for the kill.

So, the best thing Elena could figure to do was have Nick cause a scene, something that would draw Chris and the others' attention. Then he'd have to find a way to sneak out of there and join Elena, who would have already been hiding in the bathroom. Nick could block Marie's exit and distract her at the same time. Hopefully, this would allow Elena the opportunity she needed to kill the vampire queen. Of course, it was just as likely they could end up in jail or dead. About a million things could go wrong, but as far as Elena saw it, this was still their best hope of taking her out without any more people dying.

4

When Chris awoke, it was nighttime. He was staring up at the radiant face of Marie LeBeau. She smiled sweetly down at him as she caressed his cheek.

"How do you feel, Chris?"

He wasn't about to lie, he felt, "Great." Looking around, he then asked, "How long was I out?"

"It's Friday night—you were out an entire day. But that was as expected. I drained you almost completely. It makes the change come faster, but your body needed time to recover. We are creatures of the night, even if we can still move around in the light."

"So . . . then I'm a vampire now?"

"Yes, now you can see what my world is like."

And could he ever.

Colors were vibrant, all sensations deeper—he could practically taste the air as he breathed it in and then wondered whether or not he needed to actually breathe.

Holding out her hand, Marie waited for him to take it and said, "Let me show you all the things you've been missing." Guiding Chris out of her bed, she led him to her balcony and opened the glass door to it. As soon as she had, his senses were assaulted by a cacophony of sounds, smells, and sights.

What sights they were.

Every light in the city was alive, dancing and flitting about through the cool night air.

Turning back to Marie, he said, "It's like the whole city is a part of me."

"Don't worry, it's always overwhelming the first time. You'll get used to it, be able to tune things out with practice."

Sighing he said, "That's good."

Realizing how dry his throat felt, he said, "You have anything to drink?"

She grinned. "Of course, silly." Marie turned and headed back inside.

Chris followed her closely, letting his hunger drive him. Part of him was nervous, scared even, to find out what she was leading him toward. Did she have some secret dungeon where she kept people to drain them? Were there bodies in cold storage somewhere? So many awful thoughts swirled around in his brain, it felt like they just might be enough to turn him around. But that thirst . . . it was unstoppable. He needed a drink so bad he felt his stomach rumble in frustration. He'd had attacks before from low blood sugar where it felt like he was going to pass out if he didn't eat anything. But this was far worse. It was like he would just about *kill* to get something to quench his thirst.

Marie moved to the large fridge in her kitchen, which he'd been to before and knew was only filled with standard food and drinks. Confused, he said, "I never saw any blood in there, Marie."

Giggling at this, she said, "You didn't look very hard." Flipping a small switch hidden on the side, the fridge began to move outward, revealing a walk-in fridge behind it. Inside was what could only be described as a vampire wine cellar, except this wine had to stay cool. There must have been over a hundred bottles of what he assumed was blood in there. Stacked across the room, row on top of row, carefully held up by racks. All that blood looked like it was there to survive a major disaster—or perhaps the end of the world.

Pulling one bottle out, Marie looked at the label and said, "This was a good vintage. 1994. Bottled in Canada . . . Quebec, to be precise. I spent a number of years there. The climate didn't quite agree with me, but I can't tell you how nice it was to be speaking my native tongue after so long. I made many friends there . . . and a few enemies. But eventually, my journey led me here, to finally pursue my dream and to make it a reality."

Popping the cork out of the bottle with her fingernail, Marie handed it to Chris. "Drink." She then pulled it back before he could grab it and said, "Unless you'd rather have it warmed up first?"

Shaking his head, Chris knew he couldn't wait a moment longer. The second she popped that cork, his nose was assaulted with the fragrant salty odor of human blood. He quickly lunged at Marie and snatched the bottle from her grasp, knocking it back and chugging the whole bottle. It was like liquid ecstasy, filling every inch of his body with the most incredible pleasure he'd ever experienced. When he was done, he burped, a little blood trickling down his chin.

Marie moved up slowly, taking the sleeve of her sweater and wiping his mouth. "My thirsty boy. How do you feel now?"

Sighing, he said, "Satisfied."

5

The night before the premiere, things were almost ready. Elena gathered her supplies in a duffle bag and made sure to go over the plan with Nick one last time. "We need to head to the theater tonight so I can stash this in the women's bathroom. Since they use drop tiles in the ceiling, I should be able to safely store it above without anyone being the wiser. Thankfully, it doesn't weigh too much.

"Tomorrow, we'll show up to the premiere as expected and head inside. I'll make my way into the bathroom and get my bag. It'll be your job to alert me when Marie is heading toward it. You can text my phone—as long as nothing in there blocks the signal we should be good."

"And what if something does?"

"Has that ever happened to you there?"

"No."

"Then why are you worried?"

Nick shook his head. "I don't know, you just brought it up. I wanted to ask."

"Worst-case scenario, you can make a bunch of noise from the top of the stairs. Hopefully I'll hear it."

"And that's the scene you want me to cause, right?"

"Yes, but preferably not right at the top of the stairs to the lounge. Remember you want to lead Chris *away* from it. The

231

further the better. It's also best he doesn't see it's you causing the commotion . . . if he does, our cover is blown."

"So how do you know Marie will be alone in the bathroom? What if she goes in with a big group of actresses or something? Don't women like to go in groups?"

Elena stared at Nick like he was an idiot and said, "Marie isn't an ordinary woman."

"Right, of course. But I mean, wouldn't she be safer with other people?"

"No. Again, she's a vampire, remember? Do you think vampires need to use the bathroom like a normal person?"

Nick sighed, clearly feeling like an idiot and finally understanding what Elena was getting at. "Right, so she just wants to keep up appearances."

"Exactly. If other people are in there, she's going to want them out, for privacy, otherwise somebody could ask questions."

"So then how do you keep her from spotting you?"

"I don't. The idea is, to just get her to *think* I'm not there at first."

"How are you supposed to do that if you *are* there?"

"Oh ye of little faith. You should know by now I wouldn't be very good at my job if vampires could always detect me before an attack."

"Except, you said yourself, she's no ordinary vampire."

"Vampires are still flesh and blood like you and me. They are constrained by the same physical limitations as any other human. Their strength and senses are enhanced for sure, but if they can't see, smell or hear you, then you're all good."

"She won't smell you?"

Elena shook her head. "One of the tricks of the trade. I mask my scent with my ninja garb, which will be in this duffel bag." She patted the side of the bag as she spoke. "That'll be enough to throw her off, as well as the usual smells that tend to linger in a bathroom. She likely won't even really be in the bathroom. I imagine she'll hang around that lounge area, check her makeup, hair, and dress and then head back up. Remember she's just giving the illusion that she had to use the bathroom."

"So wait, how can she check herself in the mirror? I thought vampires, you know . . . don't cast a reflection."

"More bullshit from the stories, Nick. I told you, I know everything about them. If I haven't mentioned something, it's because it's not worth mentioning."

"Okay, so then while she's checking herself in a mirror, that's when you strike?"

"Exactly."

"But that lounge is surrounded by mirrors. She'll *definitely* see you coming in there." And this much was true from their time scouting the location on Saturday. The basement women's lounge was circular, with mirrors facing every direction. However, Elena had to trust in her abilities. Even if Marie spotted her, she still had backup.

"And that's where you'd come in. After your distraction, you're going to beeline for the women's lounge. Sneak down there and help me. If Marie spots you, all the better. It'll give me a chance to strike."

Nick sighed, taking in the whole plan. "Just seems like a *lot* could go wrong."

They'd discussed the broad strokes before, but as the premiere was quickly approaching, he seemed to be getting more and more anxious. Elena spotted his right heel rapidly tapping against the floor, as if he was trying to expend excess energy.

Not knowing what else to do, she placed a hand on his knee and said, "It'll be okay, Nick. The worst thing you can do is lose confidence. You just need to trust me, okay?" He looked back into her eyes, saw the unwavering confidence therein, and somehow this seemed to ease his tension. She felt the muscles in his leg begin to relax and smiled at him. "That's better."

Finishing her packing of the duffel bag, Elena zipped it up and slung it over her shoulder. "Let's head to the theater."

6

Marie had helped Chris dress to the nines for the premiere of *Black Berenice*. It was his first tux, and he was surprised how good he looked in it. Chris wasn't the type to typically wear suits, yet wore them well, and the tux was even a step up from that. But no matter how good he looked in a tux, it was nothing compared to the ethereal radiance of Marie in her elegant crimson dress. She looked like she'd stepped out of some classic work of art, some untouchable beauty unfit for mortal man. Thankfully for Chris, he was no longer mortal.

When the two left for the premiere, Thomas drove their limo. Chris assumed usually a limo service would have their own driver, but not for Marie, it seemed. Thomas was everywhere she needed him to be. To think Chris could have been convinced for even a moment that Marie would want him to replace Thomas was simply laughable. The guy wasn't there for protection. Maybe in another time, another place, that had been his function, but no longer.

The limo made its way down from the hills into Hollywood proper. They were entering a new world, a world of stars and neon lights, a place of fantasy and dreams. A place where vampires could rule without the average person being the wiser to it. This thought gave Chris some pleasure and a smile formed on his face.

"What are you thinking about?" Marie asked.

Turning back to her, Chris said, "I was just thinking about everything you've accomplished here. Would it be fair to say that you run this town now?"

This got a giggle out of Marie. "Run? I wouldn't go that far quite yet. I've got my influence in the places that matter, but I've still got a way to go before this town is changed for the better. Then we can start focusing on the world. I wish you could see that . . . I wish you could see my dream."

Putting his hand on hers, he said, "I'm sure you will show me in time. I'm just glad I'll be by your side to see it when it comes."

Marie smiled back sweetly and said, "I'm glad you stayed by my side, Chris. You had me worried for a while."

"It's okay, admittedly I had things I needed to work out. It's not every day you meet a vampire. But I'm here now, and I won't ever leave you."

Leaning in at the same time, the two kissed passionately, and Chris felt the world melt away. In that moment, it was just the two of them together, their essences combining into a magical cocktail that he would have gladly drunk forever. But then the kiss broke, and he was back in his body, staring at the woman he loved. He knew in that moment he would do whatever it took to keep her safe.

7

Nick and Elena had made their way to Hollywood early, first picking up the appropriate attire to attend the premiere. Nick was shocked at the wad of cash Elena apparently carried around everywhere and didn't bother to ask where she'd acquired it. He was still nervous on the ride to the theatre, but seeing the confidence exuded by Elena, it helped calm his nerves somewhat. Still, it was hard to remain calm knowing he would be facing another vampire—especially a queen. Elena had made Marie sound so deadly that he wasn't even sure if an experienced vampire killer could take her down.

And then there was Chris, who Nick had known for almost eight years at that point. The guy was like a brother to him, and the idea of having to fight his brother, was a truly terrible thought. He also knew that it was a fight he was never going to win. Chris had the experience, and now the strength, to put Nick and Elena in the ground if he so desired. And that was still an unknown to Nick that scared him more than anything. What exactly was it that Chris desired at that point? Was he truly and completely under Marie's spell? Was it something that he'd die for before letting his master be killed? Nick simply had to hope Marie would fall before Chris could come to harm.

When they arrived at the Chinese Theatre, there was some waiting, the usual song and dance you'd expect from a premiere, and Nick was no stranger to it, having seen a few premieres from the outside before. But this was the first time he had tickets belonging to a guest of someone involved in the production. He knew the organizers had no interest in sending guests down the red carpet, so once they were instructed where to go, they entered the building.

The lobby of the Chinese Theatre was different when it was packed with the Hollywood elite. There were so many faces Nick recognized, it put any party at Comic-Con to shame. Part of him was tempted to mingle, to shake the hands of every personal hero of his in attendance, but Elena was having none of that.

"Okay, I'm heading down to the bathroom. I haven't seen Marie yet, but keep your eyes peeled. We don't want Chris spotting you, so stay to the side. Talk to some people if you must to keep up appearances, but don't get distracted." She must have noticed that Nick was already getting distracted because she snapped her fingers in front of his face. "Hey, focus!" When he turned to Elena, she asked, "You got all that?"

Nick nodded and said, "Yeah, I'll just be waiting over in the corner there by the stairs to the men's restroom."

"Fine, just don't go down there. I can't have you messing this up. Once Marie heads down, don't forget to text me, okay?"

"Okay." Elena was about to turn away, when Nick added, "Good luck."

"Thanks," she said, "Same to you." Then she took off toward the stairs to the women's lounge.

After Elena disappeared, Nick was left with himself and a lobby full of celebrities. If it wasn't for all the famous faces he recognized, he might have been distracted by the lavish design of the walls, the intricately detailed lights on the ceiling, or the various movie costumes behind glass. Trying to stay focused on the task at hand, Nick made his way over to the stairs leading down to what was labeled as the men's lounge.

He then kept his back to the wall and his eyes focused on the entrance as other celebrities made their way inside. Nick assumed Marie would be one of the last, so she could take the full attention of the room. It's what he'd have done in her shoes. Before he could spot her, though, he was approached by an elderly woman who said, "Oh, I just loved you in that superhero movie. I wanted to say hi. I think you really kick butt."

Nick had an idea who she was mistaking him for, but also was mildly annoyed at the racist old woman who must have thought all Asians looked alike. Not wanting to cause a scene though, he just mumbled, "Thanks."

Coming up quickly behind the old woman was none other than the villain of *Black Berenice*, Martin Conroy. The classically trained British actor was a screen legend who Nick had grown up loving from his spy films. "I'm sorry about my mother, she gets very excited at these events," the actor said. His mother seemed mildly annoyed, but then wandered off to meet someone else.

Nick was in mild shock, meeting one of his idols, and quickly stammered, "N-no problem, Mr. Conroy."

"Oh," he said, surprised. "You know who I am?"

"Of course I do. I grew up on the Fairfield movies. You're a legend, man."

"Well, it's good to know someone here appreciates my earlier work. As time goes on, it seems people become more and more disconnected from the past. Especially at this sort of thing. All these young up-and-comers who don't know a damn thing about film history."

"Well, I do and I have to say, an actor of your caliber deserves respect."

Nodding, Martin said, "I appreciate it, my boy. You have my thanks and my respect. Hope you enjoy the rest of your evening. Now, I'm off to try and find my mother once more."

"Good luck," Nick said and then turned his attention back toward the front door.

It seemed Nick had become too distracted, even if only for a minute, as he spotted all eyes in the room on Marie LeBeau. She'd entered in one of the most stunning red dresses that he'd ever seen. By her side at all times was Chris. Trying to make sure his friend didn't spot him, Nick ducked behind some other guests and kept his attention focused on the actress. For the next several minutes, he saw her working the room, moving from person to person, greeting them all and making them feel like the most important person there. All this waiting was driving Nick crazy, and part of him worried Elena's plan wouldn't even have a chance to start if Marie never went down the stairs to the women's lounge.

Then, Marie finally started to move in that direction.

Before she got there, another woman had come up the stairs and greeted Marie with a smile and a hug. Nick recognized her instantly, as she was another important actress in Hollywood. She'd aged out of the kind of roles Marie was getting, but still could hold people's attention more than most. Marie stopped to talk with her for a bit and they were all smiles and laughing; Nick couldn't help but wonder if an actress of that acclaim and importance had any idea who she was really conversing with. Or worse, if that actress was *also* a creature of the night.

Marie ended the conversation and briefly spoke to Chris, clearly instructing him to wait for her there as she made her way down the stairs. Elena had told Nick that Marie would likely check the bathroom and lounge first to make sure it was clear before she felt comfortable—and before the vampire killer could strike. But he was still so nervous, Nick couldn't waste any more time waiting to act.

Pulling out his phone, Nick quickly texted Elena that Marie

was heading downstairs and his distraction would be imminent. Of course, he still needed to figure out what the distraction would be. And that's when he noticed an elderly man moving toward the top of the stairs to the men's lounge. Nick felt guilty about possibly seriously injuring the guy, but knew this was his best chance of drawing a crowd. As the man went to take his first step down the stairs, Nick shoved him from behind and ducked out of the way back into the crowd.

There were audible gasps and screams of pain as the man tumbled down the stairs. Nick heard several people shout, "Oh my god!" Another cried, "Somebody call an ambulance!" Then the crowd was surging, sweeping directly toward the stairs and Nick pushed his way through, like a salmon swimming upstream. He tried to look out for Chris, but he couldn't see much of anything with everyone pushing past him to get a look at the tragedy he manufactured. Nick made a mental note to at least check the guy was okay the next day, if it made the news—which he was sure it would. Accidents always seemed to, especially at important events.

Once Nick was free of the crowd and had a clear view of the stairs to the women's lounge, he was shocked to see that Chris had not completely cleared out. He'd moved ten or fifteen feet from the stairs, giving Nick enough space to possibly sneak by him, but if Chris turned at any time, Nick was screwed.

Keeping low and moving quickly and quietly, Nick snuck along the wall toward the opening that led to the stairs. He kept his eyes fixed at all times on Chris, and it seemed like his path was clear as his friend made no sign that he was aware of Nick's presence. Once Nick arrived at the stairs, he was shocked to see Chris suddenly spin around and face him. "So, you're helping *her* now?" he spat. For the first time, Nick saw a ferocity and anger in Chris' eyes that scared him. Somehow, he'd not only detected

Nick's silent approach, but knew exactly what he was there for. Then Chris did something that shook Nick to his core.

He flashed a pair of fangs from his open mouth.

Nick couldn't help but scream and tried to run for the stairs, but then felt himself struck in the back as Chris tackled him. The two men went tumbling down the flight of stairs together, Nick feeling every blow. Thankfully, his neck didn't snap like a twig when they landed hard at the bottom.

Chris was quickly on top of Nick, holding him down and flashing his fangs once more in a hiss. Nick looked across the floor toward the women's lounge and saw Marie staring at the pair in shock, her lipstick in one hand. Behind her, both men could clearly see the ninja-clad Elena sneaking up on her prey. Unfortunately, Marie was also aware, spinning around like lightening and catching the blade in her hand.

"You never learn," Marie said and snapped the blade in two.

Elena screamed, trying to strike with her broken sword, but Marie caught her arm and tossed the hunter like a ragdoll across the room. She collided into one of the many mirrors along the wall and the glass shattered. The mask Elena had been wearing tore free from her face, giving Marie a clear view of the woman who was so bent on killing her.

"I'm disappointed in you, Nick," Chris said from atop his friend. "Sorry it had to come to this."

"Me too," Nick said, and then kicked up into Chris' privates. His former friend might have been a vampire, but apparently, he could still feel pain down there and toppled off Nick.

Spotting the fire alarm on the wall near the stairs, Nick lunged at it. He then smashed off the protective covering before yanking the alarm. As a deafening siren sound filled the room and red lights flashed, Marie and Chris grasped their ears. Clearly Nick was witnessing the downside of supernatural hearing.

Elena scrambled to her feet and charged for Nick, grabbing his arm and pulling him toward the stairs. They ran up as fast as their feet would allow. Nick turned back briefly, but didn't see Chris or Marie chasing after them. At the top of the stairs, he could see most of the people in the lobby had already cleared out as everyone made their way to the exits. Elena led Nick out one of the exit doors and into the crowd of people waiting outside. From there it was a simple matter of sneaking away from the group to the parking garage where they'd left Elena's car.

The two had not only managed to blow their one big chance to stop the vampire queen, but there were other concerns now swirling around in Nick's head. Marie had finally seen both of their faces. That would be a problem if she had people looking for them. Then there was Elena's sword, which had been broken in two. That was her main weapon against vampires, and he wasn't sure what she still had at her motel they could even use. Who knew when their next opportunity would be? There were so many stressors at that point all bubbling up to the surface at once that Nick abruptly found himself puking as they made their way to her car.

Stopping briefly to check on Nick, Elena asked, "Are you okay?"

Wiping his mouth clean, he said, "Physically? Sure. Mentally, I'm a mess."

"I'm sorry. I really fucked that up."

"So did I. But let's just get back to the motel. I need to sit down and catch my breath."

8

Elena was furious with herself—and to a smaller degree with Nick. But she was the one who failed to strike the fatal blow. She should have known better. This wasn't the first time Marie had avoided a killing stroke. No other vampires could see it coming a mile away, but somehow Marie could. Elena's lack of experience fighting a queen was the thing that got to her the most. Everything her father had taught her all those years, it meant nothing. Not against Marie LeBeau.

They weren't back in the motel more than five minutes when Elena had changed clothes and told Nick, "I need a drink." They then left the motel after searching on the internet, where Elena had found a bar not too far away called Mandrake. It certainly fit the way she was feeling, with its red neon sign reading "Unhappy Hour" over the bar. She quickly ordered two shots of tequila and then looked at Nick before correcting her order to three.

After being handed one of the shot glasses, he asked, "Who's the third shot for?"

"For me," she said before pounding back both shots.

She'd left the lime wedges on the bar and Nick asked, "You didn't want a wedge of lime?"

"Fuck that. I'm here to get *drunk*."

"Are you sure that's a good idea after everything?"

"If I'm gonna die, it's not going to be sober, scared, and

hiding under my covers waiting for that bitch to find me."

"So you're just giving up?"

Shaking her head and motioning for another two shots, she clarified, "I never said that."

"Then what the fuck are we supposed to do next?"

"I thought that was clear. We are going to drink, and then I am going to pass out on that shitty motel bed. Tomorrow we can worry what to do about Marie."

"I don't know if I'm comfortable doing that." Nick said.

Elena looked over at the still frightened twentysomething and realized just how young he really was. Not in years, but in life experience. She'd been fighting for so long, she never had a chance to stop and live what might be considered a normal life. In that moment, she envied his life—before he was sucked into her mess. She could feel the tears welling up in her eyes and quickly pounded back her next shots.

"You know you never told me much about your life," Nick said, "I mean, I know you hunt vampires, but how did you fall into that?"

"Family business." She motioned for more shots. "You still haven't taken your next shot."

Nick took his next shot and used the offered lime wedge that time.

"You know, you really should do that first."

Nick looked at her, confused. "What do you mean?"

"The lime wedge. Take that with the sprinkle of salt first, then take the shot and swish it around in your mouth before swallowing. *So* much better."

"Really?" Nick asked, clearly not believing what she was telling him was the right way to take a shot of tequila. Then he requested another. Sprinkling salt on the lime wedge before sucking on it, he proceeded to pound back the shot of tequila and squished it around before swallowing. "Wow that *was* better! Like a little margarita in my mouth. Where'd you learn to do that?"

"From my father." A smiled formed on Elena's face as she felt a slight release of tension at helping Nick experience something she'd loved since the first time her father had shown her. It almost made her forget for a moment how she was really feeling inside.

"I'm ready for another," Nick exclaimed with a smile. He must have decided it was now okay to get drunk. If Elena was bent on getting sloppy, then so was he. She wasn't sure if he was still feeling apprehension toward their current situation, but she wasn't about to poke that hornet's nest until the next day. "So you and your father were pretty close?" he asked. The words stopped her dead in her tracks and Elena wasn't aware she'd frozen, until Nick continued, "You know, keeping up the family business. Killing vampires?"

Elena nodded, "Yeah, we were. He trained me since I could walk, took me everywhere with him, wherever we were needed. Then he . . . he died a few years back. Marie killed him. That's why I can't stop until she's dead."

"I'm sorry," he said with complete sincerity. "That must have been hard. I lost my mom . . . when I was eight. I know it doesn't compare exactly to what you've been through, but I just wanted you to know that I know what it's like to lose a parent."

"I never knew my mom," Elena admitted and realized in that moment, he was the first person she'd ever talked to about her mom—aside from her dad. "She died giving birth to me. Sometimes I wonder, you know, if maybe my life would have turned out different had she lived?"

"Who's to say?" Nick held up his shot glass and waited for Elena to join him. This time she took the lime before pounding back the shot. "So it's just been you out there all this time? How long?"

"About five years since I lost my father. His name was Franco."

"And you've just been . . . alone since then?"

Elena nodded her head, admitting, "It hasn't always been easy. For a while after he was gone, I wasn't exactly continuing his legacy. I had a few hard years. Found and lost love, sometimes with a person, other times with a bottle. In the past couple months, Marie helped to return my sense of clarity, helped me focus on what truly matters."

"Killing vampires?"

"Revenge."

"You can't honestly have that be the one thing that drives you. Like that old saying about digging two graves."

"Don't feed me that proverb bullshit. Marie is a scourge upon this planet. If you knew her history, you'd know what I'm talking about, and why she needs to die. If I don't do it . . . I don't know, somebody might eventually. Or they could be too late. Whatever she's planning here in LA, it's not good. It's bigger than anything she's done before."

"But how are we supposed to stop her?"

Shaking her head, Elena said, "I don't know. But it won't be tonight, so let's just drop it, all right? We can talk about this more tomorrow. Tonight, we drink." And drink they did. After a few more shots, they were both good and drunk, and Elena called them a ride back to the motel.

Nick tripped when they entered their room and fell onto the bed, before bouncing off and landing hard on the floor. Elena found herself uncontrollably laughing at his blunder. Waving her hand in front of her face, she said, "I'm sorry. Sorry! It was really funny."

Turning back toward her, he groaned, "Can you help me up at least?" Nick dangled his arms out toward her and she pulled him to his feet, before losing her own balance and falling back against the wall. Nick landed right on her, accidentally pinning her in place. Elena could smell the tequila and lime lingering on his breath as he apologized again. He looked like he was ready to push himself away from her, but instead of letting him go, she pulled his head close and kissed him. It wasn't exactly clear to Elena what made her kiss him in that moment, but she hadn't felt the touch of anyone in so long—not since she got clean. It could have been the alcohol that drove her into that crummy motel bed with Nick, giving him what had to be a highlight of his life up to that point, but Elena was only human. She was a prisoner of the same emotions that drove every human being on the planet. When she felt the most helpless, that was when she reached out for the support of others. She only hoped that Nick understood in the morning.

As the sun rose on the Seaway Motel, Elena's head felt several sizes too small and she quickly ran to the bathroom to puke out all the gunk that was making her feel so terrible. *Better out than in,* as her father used to say. Something about throwing up after a night of hard drinking was always infinitely better than letting that crap settle in your stomach for the following day. When she was lucky, the worst she'd have was a hangover, but this time she'd gone a little too hard on the tequila after years of sobriety. If she had ever been part of AA, she figured she'd be phoning her sponsor that morning, but she never had gone through that. Sheer force of will and the need for vengeance had fueled her change. She needed to hold onto the hope that one day soon she would have her revenge.

When Nick rose from the bed, he seemed confused and then asked, "Did we . . ."

"Yeah," Elena said as she pulled on her pants. "I would have thought that was obvious."

"I thought it was a dream." The guy laid back against his pillow and stared up at the ceiling with stars in his eyes. Elena knew she had to shut that shit right down.

Taking a seat on the bed beside him, she said, "Look, about last night . . ."

Nick sat up and stared at her, clearly aware of where this conversation was headed.

"I needed that, maybe you did too, but it doesn't mean . . . I mean you were just—"

"A guy when you needed one?"

Elena nodded, slightly ashamed of him calling her on it before she could admit it herself.

"I get it, believe me. I thought it was great. I mean, it's still pretty hazy, but if you want me to forget it happened, I understand."

"Good, because we still have work to do."

"So what are we supposed to do next? I mean, our plan got shot to shit last night. You said that was our best chance of getting Marie. So what now? We wait until there's another event where she's not under heavy security?"

"I don't know. I mean, we can't wait too long. Who knows what she ultimately has planned for this town. But I suppose there's no rush now."

"What do you mean?"

"I mean your friend, the one we were trying to save, has been fucking *turned*, Nick. There's no coming back from that, it's a whole different ball game from being a familiar."

"So what? You're just going to kill him too?"

"He's a vampire, that's what I do."

"But *why*? You don't know what he's like now. How do you know he's evil?"

"Because they *all* are. Despite what you may think, there are *zero* good vampires. They feed on people, there's nothing good about that. And before you tell me, 'well, they could get some blood without killing someone,' I've never known them to do that. They'll drain a human dry, dispose of their corpse and, at best, store some of the blood for later. But their way of life hinges upon human suffering."

"Please, he's still my friend. Can't you at least give him a chance?"

"If he gets in my way, I'm sorry, but he's going down same as Marie. If he chooses to run . . . well, maybe I could give him a head start. But I'm not in this business to leave loose ends. There's far too many for me to kill, and I'm not the only hunter out there. Might only be a matter of time before another finds him."

"That's the first time you've mentioned other hunters. Where are they? Who are they? Can't you get them here to help?"

"I wish. Despite what you may think, there's no secret hunter organization. Maybe at one time there was, but too many were killed or scattered over the years. As the vampires spread, so did we—or so my father told me. It's what led his grandfather from Germany to Argentina after the Second World War. It's what brought my father to New York some thirty-plus years ago. And it's how I eventually ended up here. We follow the trails where we find them, but this is a solitary business. Safety in numbers is just a pipe dream. I'm thankful for your help, I really am, but you have to understand hunters—we have a pretty short life expectancy."

"So then what do we do? After that attack, the police are bound to get involved, right? She broke your sword. If you used that on those others I saw in the news, they'll be all over Marie, waiting for you to strike again."

"That's right."

"So then we're fucked? I mean vampires are one thing, but we can't deal with the whole police force. She's already got them in her pocket, like you said."

"All of this is true."

"So then what? Do we cut and run?"

"You know I can't do that."

"There's no other way I can see. We can't get to her like this. Not with that kind of heat around her."

"Then we find a way to remove the heat," a familiar voice said behind Elena. She noticed Nick looking toward the doorway as light flooded the room. It only occurred to her then that she hadn't remembered to lock the door in the night . . .

Turning around, Elena saw a female figure, backlit by the morning sun pouring through the open doorway. The woman stepped into the room and closed the door behind her. A wave of shock and relief flooded through Elena's body as she found herself staring at the face of Detective Liz Gutiérrez.

"Liz? You're alive?"

"Yeah, and I need to get you two out of here."

"Why? Do they know we're here?" Nick asked anxiously.

"If they don't, they will soon." Grabbing the television remote, Liz clicked on the TV and made sure it was on the local news. It wasn't long before they saw a police sketch for Elena and a photo of Nick. They didn't have her name yet, but they sure as hell had his, which was a major problem.

"Jesus Christ!" Nick exclaimed. "How the hell could they have all this?"

Elena sighed. "Guess you can't trust that friend of yours after all, huh?"

Nick looked extremely saddened by the realization that Chris was now a common enemy. But he wasn't going to let this fact bring him down, and quickly moved to get dressed.

"I have somewhere we can go," Liz said. "It'll buy us some time. They're looking for me too if you didn't know—which judging by your faces when I entered, you clearly didn't."

Elena spent the next few minutes gathering up her stuff, getting it all into Liz's car—which wasn't one she'd seen before—and hurriedly paying for the room. Her own car was still at Mandrake, but she wasn't about to go retrieve it in broad daylight. Better to figure that out later if it hadn't been towed by then. After everything was taken care of, Liz drove them off toward her supposed safe house. Elena just hoped there wasn't anyone following her. The heat was far too close for comfort. If it was anyone other than Marie, she'd have just cut and run, but she knew fleeing was no longer an option.

9

Liz wasn't sure how she was alive at first. The last thing she remembered was firing at the first officers coming through the stairwell door of the parking garage. At least one was hit, but so was she. It was a clean shot through her right thigh that dropped her hard to the concrete. So hard in fact, that her head took the weight of the fall.

Then came the blackness.

When consciousness returned to the detective, she found herself in a hospital bed. Sunlight was leaking out around the edges of the curtains over the window. She tried to raise her right arm only to find it was cuffed to the side of the bed, along with her left. In a matter of minutes, a nurse had come to check on her. Not soon after she'd left, Captain Ford entered the room to talk with Liz. It didn't take a genius to understand why the nurses and doctors would allow this right after she'd woken from a coma. The nurse had told her she'd been out five days and the handcuffs keeping her on the bed told her she was heading to jail as soon as the hospital gave the all-clear.

Noticing the disappointment on her Captain's face, Liz had a horrible thought flash through her mind that he was in Marie's pocket. If he had helped turned the cops on Lawson and her so fast, it would explain the lack of concern about her condition. Ford might not have even been the *only* one on the force who was a secret underling to the vampire queen. Still, the question remained if he was a familiar or a vampire. Luckily for Liz, she wouldn't have long to wait before she found out. Unfortunately, though, that knowledge would come at a price.

"Goddammit, Gutiérrez. You just couldn't leave it alone, could you?"

"No honest cop could. You're working for her, aren't you?"

"Yeah, the pay is better than the department, and the benefits . . . well, I doubt you'd be able to understand."

"What I don't understand is why I'm still alive. Wouldn't it have been easier to just kill me like Lawson?"

"Under normal circumstances, yes, but you left us with a lot of loose ends to tie up. So for now, we need your help answering a few questions."

"Why should I help you? The second I tell you what you want, how do I know I'm not a dead woman?"

"Because I'm still a cop and if you give me a choice, I *will* send you to jail over giving you a lead shower. Before you question my sincerity, understand that we've already found the slug you put in Dalton . . . before your little ninja friend chopped his head off. So, the question is, how long of a sentence do you want? You could be looking at life in prison, or we could pull some strings, maybe get you out of there before your son reaches adulthood."

"Don't you *dare* use Freddy as a pawn in your sick game, you fuck."

This made Ford laugh. "You did that yourself the second you and Lawson decided to take the law into your own hands. Now, I don't really care what happens to you, or your son, but I also don't think it's worth killing anybody who could be used as a future asset. Just looking at you, I can tell those gears are already turning in that big brain of yours. You're wondering if maybe you could get out of here, spill what you know to the papers or whoever might listen. But you and I both know you don't have shit for evidence, so throw those thoughts right in the trash, because they're not going to get you out of this mess. You have just one road ahead of you, and I *highly* suggest you take it for your son's sake."

Liz felt like throwing up. She knew he was right about her lack of evidence. Jyll and Dalton had probably already been removed from the morgue. They might have even silenced Hank Morris, for all she knew. Whatever they could do to cover their tracks. If Elena was gone too, Liz only saw one path ahead of her. "Just tell me what you fucking want, Ford."

"We want to know where your ninja friend is. Chris Hart didn't know, but something tells me that you do." And just like that, Liz felt a rush of relief flood her body. If they didn't know where Elena was, or *who* she was, there just might still be a chance to stop Marie and her minions. But Liz needed to escape her handcuffs first. Luckily, she had some experience there.

"Okay, I'll tell you what you want to know. Just promise me that you'll leave Freddy alone."

Ford smiled and said, "Of course." There was something sinister in the smile, and Liz knew that he had no intention of leaving her son alive, but she didn't care, she was only stalling for time.

As Ford stepped around the left side of her bed, Liz asked, "Are you still human, Ford? Because if you are, maybe I can believe you." Her right hand was hidden from view, and she prepared to pop her thumb out of joint to slip out of the handcuff. She'd dislocated it about five years back and ever since could easily pop it out of place with some force. It meant being a bit more careful with her right hand, but in the case of handcuffs, it was an easy way to win a few bucks whenever fellow cops bet she couldn't escape them. If Ford was a little smarter, he might have seen this coming, but he was either too cocky or too focused on the question at hand.

Moving closer, Ford said, "I'm *more* than human now, and that has zero impact on my ability to lie. But you have my word."

Keeping the handcuff taut where it was attached to the right side of the bed, Liz pulled back hard against it as she said, "Well, I'm sorry to say your word ain't worth *shit* anymore." Her right thumb popped out of place the moment she cursed at Ford. She hoped that it helped to hide the sound of the pop, and from the anger causing Ford's face to go flush, she got her answer.

Pulling out a syringe, Ford furiously spat, "We could have done this the easy way, but since I can see you're going to be *difficult*, we'll do this the even *easier* way." Liz silently slid her right hand out of the handcuff as Ford removed a small vial from his pocket. Drawing the vial up, he inserted the needle in the top, extracting the contents into the syringe. "Something to loosen your tongue."

Liz knew she needed to act fast. The second he injected her with what she assumed was sodium pentothal, she would give up Elena's location at the motel. Even Freddy wasn't safe if Ford asked about him. Popping her right thumb back into place, Liz yanked the IV from her left arm and struck Ford in the carotid artery with it. He screamed in pain, grabbing for the open wound on his neck and dropping the syringe to the ground.

The remaining left handcuff would be easy enough for Liz to pick with the IV needle, but no sooner had she attempted this than Ford lunged at her, screaming like a madman. She instinctively drew back the needle and this time stabbed it into his eye. Screaming even further, Ford flailed around, and Liz knew she wasn't going to get out of the left cuff with him there. Gripping the left sideguard, she flung herself to the right, sending the bed down to the floor with her. The electrodes on her chest became disconnected and her vitals ceased on the monitor. Taking the IV needle still in her right hand, she finally managed to unlock the remaining handcuff.

Now that she was free, there was still the problem of Captain Ford, who was currently cursing her name as he thrashed about. Before she could try to deal with him, though, a nurse had opened the door. She'd been drawn to the room either from the noise or due to the disconnected electrodes. Regardless, she took one look at Ford and screamed. She then attempted to leave the room, but Ford's vampire thirst must have gotten the better of him. He lunged at the nurse, quickly tearing out her throat and gorging himself on her blood. Liz didn't know what else she could do, so she charged for the door and burst out of the room before he could reach her.

Taking off at full speed down the hall, Liz tried to make the elevator, but it seemed someone was trying to reach her floor. As the doors opened, another cop was revealed inside holding a cup of coffee. Seemed he must have taken a break from watching her room, and as soon as he spotted her, the cop dropped the coffee and went for his sidearm.

She wasn't about to let him reach it, though.

Tackling the cop back into the elevator, a few of the staff let out audible gasps before the doors closed behind her. Liz didn't want to hurt the cop, and went for the quickest way to render him unconscious. Taking him in a choke hold, she secured him with her legs. He flailed around briefly before going limp. Looking up, Liz saw the elevator was approaching the parking garage below the hospital. Somebody down there must have called it. So while other cops might have expected her at the lobby, she'd hopefully get off where they weren't looking. The real question was if she could still hotwire a car like she'd done in her youth.

As the elevator doors opened, a shocked elderly man gasped

and Liz pulled the cop's gun on him. "Into the elevator. Take it wherever you need to go. Just don't come back." She grabbed the cop's wallet before exiting the elevator as the man entered. The doors then closed between them.

Running through the parking garage, Liz looked for a vehicle a bit out of the way—and one old enough to not have a security system protecting it. When she found a car that fit her needs, she quickly broke the window with the butt of the pistol and unlocked the door. Wiping the broken glass from the front seat, she climbed in and began hotwiring the car. She was amazed she could still remember everything she needed to do. It really was just like riding a bike.

Liz could hear police sirens approaching and knew they had to be entering the garage. She had to get out of there, but had no parking ticket, nor any change of clothes other than the hospital gown. It seemed like the only way she was leaving was as fast as possible. Taking off like a bat out of hell, she took the car up the ramp and toward the exit, charging through the gate. Snapping off the stopper, it clattered uselessly on the pavement and she made a hard right onto the street, where several police cars were visible in her rearview mirror.

After losing the cops with a few sharp turns, Liz managed to stash the car in a nearby alley behind a clothing store. She then ran into the store and quickly grabbed a few garments that she could change into. Casually approaching the front, she paid for everything with cash from the cop's wallet. She also grabbed a hat and sunglasses as an impromptu disguise. Once she was outside, the cops who had swarmed the location didn't even stop to look at her as they ran into the store. It was then a simple matter of getting on a bus that had stopped on the street corner and riding it a few stops away.

Once Liz managed to get a burner phone with her remaining

money, she called Lydia and asked to be picked up. She had to lie about most of her current situation just to convince the babysitter and her family that she had done nothing wrong. Thankfully, they didn't need much convincing, and agreed to leave town for a while. Lydia was even kind enough to leave her car for Liz until she could get things sorted out. Freddy, meanwhile, was left in his mother's care, who couldn't think of anything better than to drive him all the way to her sister's home in Las Vegas. More excuses followed there and the next morning, Liz saw on the news what had gone down at the premiere. She then convinced her sister to watch Freddy for a few more days and drove back to LA.

"Which brings us to the present," Liz said, finishing her story in Lydia's car. Along for the ride were Nick and Elena. They seemed amazed at the string of luck the detective had, but this also drew a suspicious look from the vampire hunter. Knowing exactly what she was thinking, Liz said, "I'm not a vampire, Elena. You can check me if you don't believe me."

This apparently calmed the hunter down and she asked, "Where are you taking us?"

There was only one place Liz could take them—and it wasn't Lydia's house. It might draw too much suspicion for them to stay there, despite the owners currently being away. All it would take were a few looks from noisy neighbors for the cops to swarm them. So instead, Liz took them to her brother-in-law's, who lived out in Compton. She knew nobody would snitch on them over there. It wasn't the safest place under normal circumstances, but these *weren't* normal circumstances, and with the current people out to kill them, it actually *was* the safest place they could go.

When Hector Gutiérrez opened his door to find his late brother's wife standing there, he wasn't exactly thrilled to see her. "Where's my nephew?" he asked. Clearly, he was upset that Liz hadn't been by with her son since the death of her husband. "And who are these other two? Am I in trouble or something? 'Cause I didn't do it, whatever it was."

"I'm not here on police business, nor is this a social call. I need help, Hector, and you're the only one I can turn to."

Hector studied Liz for a moment, trying to decide whether or not he should let her in. But despite their history and disagreements had in the past, she was still family. So, he let her inside, along with her two mysterious companions.

Closing the door behind them, Liz took in the state of the place, which was just about exactly how she remembered it. Hector didn't have a lot of money, but what he did have seemed to go entirely to his entertainment setup in the living room. Everything else wasn't looking so hot. Still, she didn't want to make waves and said, "Place looks nice."

"I know you don't mean that shit." Hector moved toward the kitchen. "Can I get you or your friends a drink?"

"It's a little early for that, isn't it?"

"Not for me." He removed a beer from the fridge and popped the cap before returning to the living room. "You gonna tell me what you're doing here?"

"I take it you haven't seen the news?"

This grabbed Hector's attention and he asked, "Why? What's on it?"

"I am, and so are my friends. Cops are looking for us, and they're looking pretty damn hard, I'd imagine."

"But *you're* a cop, Liz. What the fuck are you talking about?"

Sighing, she took a seat on his couch and said, "We stumbled onto something big, something real fucking bad and now I don't know who to trust."

"Can you break it down for me, then? 'Cause I still have no fucking idea why you came to me if you're in trouble."

"You heard of vampires?" Elena asked, jumping into the

conversation. Liz really wished she hadn't, but didn't have much control anymore, so she just sat back and watched how things played out.

"Of course, I love that shit. That movie with the vampire bar in Mexico? One of my favorites."

"*From Dusk Till Dawn*," Nick said with a laugh. "I love it too."

Hector didn't seem to care and asked, "Who are you two again?"

"That's Nick, I'm Elena, and we didn't come here to talk movies," Elena stated, "We came here because Liz thought you might be able to help us. I know this is going to sound crazy, but I have to put all the cards on the table here. Vampires exist, I hunt them for a living, and your sister in-law found out about them. Once word got to her superiors, they've been trying their damnedest to kill her, and us."

Hector stared at Elena for a moment, and then burst out laughing. "That's a good one. But it's a little early for Halloween. Liz, you gonna tell me why you're *really* here?"

"It's just like she said," Liz admitted. "I knew you'd think it sounded nuts. I was ready to lie to your face if it got you to help us, but everything Elena said is true. I've seen it all myself. Hell, I'd show you the proof if it still existed, but by now the body that convinced me has likely disappeared from the morgue. The reason we're here, and the *only* reason, is we needed somewhere to plan our next move without worrying about anybody alerting the cops."

Hector admitted, "You definitely came to right place for that."

"Whether you believe Elena or me, we only need your place for a short time, just as somewhere to crash. You let us do that and I'd be infinitely grateful. I'm sorry I haven't been by since Óscar died, but I'd like to change that, *if* we make it out of this alive."

"You said the cops are after you . . . what about Freddy?"

"He's safe, with my sister in Vegas. I had to get him out of state. I don't think they expected me to leave LA. They know the only chance I have of clearing my name is to kill Marie LeBeau."

Hector had been taking another swig of his beer as he heard the name. The second he did, he spit it out all over himself. "The famous actress?!" He looked at the three faces around him for validation and they all nodded their heads. "You gotta be fucking kidding me. You're saying she's a *vampire?*"

"Not just any vampire," Elena added. "She's a queen. I've been tracking her for years. My whole family has. Once she's gotten her fangs in a city, she won't stop until something major forces her to flee. But her goal is always the same—turn those in power, until she has total control. From my estimation, she's already done that. All she needs to do now is use her status to spread that influence further than ever before."

Hector laughed. "Okay, now I know you're bullshitting me. I mean, she's been out in the sunlight, I've seen it myself. Don't vampires burn up in the sun?"

"Only in movies. I've explained it to these two, but most of what you've heard from books and movies, it's bullshit. Sunlight weakens them down to human levels of strength and speed, but at night they are *very* hard to kill. With Marie, though, she seems impossible to sneak up on even in the daytime. I've been killing vampires most of my life, and she puts them all to shame."

Hector shook his head in disbelief. "I'm sorry, but you have to admit how crazy this all sounds. You're saying Marie LeBeau, one of the hottest actresses currently working in Hollywood, is not *only* a vampire queen, but you've tried to kill her *several* times and failed? Well, that at least would explain why the cops are after you three. I just still don't understand why you haven't cut and run? That's what I'd do if I was in your shoes. Your situation sounds pretty fucked, to put it bluntly."

"We know," Nick said, "Elena killed one of my friends the other day because he tried to rip my throat out. My best friend has also been turned into a vampire. I have every reason to run away, but I can't give up, not now, not when I've already lost so much. Marie needs to be taken down. If what Elena told me is true, these other vampires, they'll scatter when their queen is gone. It leaves them exposed, unorganized . . . it's the only way we get our city back."

Hector finished off his beer and then stood up. "I think I need another beer."

He moved to the kitchen and Liz followed, asking, "Are you going to help us?"

Pulling another beer from the fridge, Hector said, "I know this shit sounds crazy, Liz. But lucky for you, I've seen plenty of crazy shit in my time on this Earth. And I don't think you'd lie to me. We've been at each other's throats a few times, but I've never seen you lie, not to me, not to Óscar. If this shit is really true . . . then you got one more soldier in the fight."

"Thank you," Liz said in relief. For the first time she truly felt like she could rely on her late husband's brother.

10

The group spent the rest of the morning hiding in Hector's home, out of sight from the law. Hector had moved Lydia's car into his garage and took out his own to go on a run for supplies. Liz knew that Hector was friends with all the wrong people, but under the current circumstances, it happened to be all the *right* people. He returned after a few hours with a duffel bag full of guns and another full of edged weapons that Elena had requested. It was enough to satisfy a small army, and since they'd be up against one, they sure needed the weapons to deal with that kind of force.

Scratching his head, Hector said, "I didn't know what you guys needed, so I got a bit of everything here."

"Jesus," Nick gasped, staring down the massive haul. "How much did all this stuff cost?"

"Don't worry about that, I called in a few favors."

"Then I take it none of this was legally obtained?"

"Even if it was, you'd still be going to jail for using any of them, as Liz well knows."

Liz nodded, though not necessarily in approval. The guns were all untraceable, but this didn't really matter—they were already wanted by the law. And she wasn't about to make her case any better by running into the lion's den where the LAPD could be waiting.

That's what caused her the most concern.

Marie's guards were one thing, they'd all sworn to protect her. Whether or not they knew the truth, they'd made their bed. But if there were cops guarding her? Liz didn't know where any of them stood. They could be dirty just as much as they could be completely ignorant of the situation. Captain Ford was the only one she knew had knowledge of the truth. And he was a vampire to boot, which made taking him out an easy choice. But she hated the idea of killing anybody she didn't have to—especially fellow officers. There was no way for her to justify acting against them, unless they really were as corrupt as Ford. Unfortunately, the situation was too dire to try and take out whoever was there non-lethally. She just had to hope that she wouldn't be the one pulling the trigger. It was easier to turn a blind eye than face the truth head-on.

Currently, her main focus was on what kind of firepower everyone there was packing. Hopefully, they could handle it with the weapons Hector had procured. From a quick glance at the contents of the bag, it looked like there were a variety of pistols, a few shotguns, and even a MAC-10—which Liz shouldn't have been too surprised to see. Those were, after all, very popular in drive-bys. Whatever the case, she was glad there were no assault rifles, as they'd need to be traveling as light as possible.

"You got ammo for all these?" Nick asked, as he examined the MAC-10.

"Yeah, I gotta unload that next. You ever fired a gun before?"

Taking aim down the sight, Nick said, "A few times at a range."

"Ever shot anyone?" Hector asked. Nick suddenly looked embarrassed and Hector snatched the MAC-10 away. Looking at Liz and Elena, he said, "Maybe one of you two should handle this."

Liz nodded in agreement and took the gun. She figured she'd be having to do most of the shooting, anyway. Wondering how close their group could even get before being spotted, she asked, "You got anything long-range here?"

"Yeah, my hunting rifle. But nobody is using that but me."

"I'm not here to argue that point, but it's something we're lacking at the moment. We still don't know what kind of firepower we're up against."

"Then we run reconnaissance next."

"After dark. We can't afford to go there in the day, we'll be too exposed."

"But daylight is our only chance to stop Marie," Elena stated. "I already had a hell of a time fighting her during the day. At night and with her guards and the police around her? She'll be too powerful. There's also Chris to consider. We're gonna need every advantage we can get."

"Speaking of which," Hector said, "I got another surprise to bring in with the ammo." And a pleasant surprise it was. Setting down the two remaining duffel bags, Hector unzipped them to reveal one filled with ammo as promised, while the other had suppressors fitting a variety of guns. "This should help us get close."

"Now *this* is a surprise," Liz said as she examined one. "Where'd you get these?"

"Don't ask and I won't have to lie. I promised to help and I'm doing that, but don't make me snitch on my friends."

And so, Liz kept her mouth shut as they sorted everything out. Once that was taken care of—and everyone got a bite to eat—the group made their way to the Hollywood Hills in Hector's car. Any sort of reconnaissance required a bit of creeping around, so Hector and Liz volunteered to take care of that. Elena and Nick stayed in the car, keeping a lookout for any cops or onlookers.

Hector also had picked up a few radios and headsets for them to use and keep in contact while they scoped out the property from below.

From what Liz could see there were at least two security cameras and four guys patrolling the back of the property. She didn't recognize them as cops or Marie's personal guards, but they looked like private security, which made her feel a sense of relief that she wouldn't be going up against her brothers in blue. As for the location of Marie's guards, Liz assumed Marie was keeping them close along with Chris, but currently none of them could be seen from her vantage point.

Hector, meanwhile, had crept around a neighboring property to get a peek over the wall surrounding the front of the mansion. From what he said over the radio, it sounded like at least two more cameras in front, plus half a dozen more private security guys. Almost a dozen guards for one celebrity, along with another half-dozen she already had on staff. Which meant the odds were definitely stacked against them. If they expected to make it to her alive, and leave the same way, they'd need to play things *very* smart.

After making their way back down the hill to the car, Nick seemed pretty on edge, while Elena just looked mildly bored or depressed—perhaps a bit of both. Liz didn't have to guess why, and hopefully they could finally resolve the whole ugly mess the next day. She wanted her life back, and desperately wanted to see her son again. With all this looming over her head, there was no way she'd survive the week. The most important thing though, was evidence. She knew there were vampires in all the right places, but with the right kind of proof, hopefully, at the very least, she could clear her name—as well as Nick and Elena's.

11

Chris stared out into the night, watching the lights of the city dance around in the darkness. The ebb and flow of traffic presented a magical rainbow of colors. He'd slept most of the day, not because he was exhausted from his encounter the previous night with Elena and Nick, but because he needed time to process what had happened . . . and what to do next.

When Marie slid up behind him, wrapping her hands around his midsection and resting her head on his broad shoulders, she asked, "What are you doing?"

"Thinking."

"About your friend?"

Shocked she could know where his mind was focused, Chris turned around, meeting Marie's gaze. "How did you know?"

"Wasn't hard to figure out. We didn't really talk much last night, and then you went to sleep. Couldn't even wake you this morning and believe me, I tried a few methods that should have done the trick. So, do you want to tell me about it?"

"I've been best friends with Nick since college. I never thought in a million years he'd try to kill you."

"You know it wasn't his idea, right? It was that hunter."

"Elena."

"Whatever. Her name doesn't really matter, does it? She's just another in an endless line of killers."

"She might say the same thing about you."

"We've been over this, Chris. And you've been around me a little while now. Do I look like a killer to you? Have you actually *seen* me kill anyone?"

Chris knew she was right about this. It did cross his mind that she likely had others willing to kill *for* her, but part of him had to put his trust in her—for survival more than anything else. They were linked now—for an eternity he supposed, or until they grew tired of each other. Whatever the case, he knew Marie better than Elena and what little he did know of the hunter, he knew she only had one goal in life—killing vampires. Sure, there were probably losses on both sides, but who could honestly know at this point who started the war? All Chris knew was he had to pick a side, and that choice was easier than ever considering his current condition. Elena likely wouldn't let him live, even if Nick felt he should be given a chance. Marie had just as much stake in survival as Chris did, so why shouldn't he put his full trust in her?

"I don't want to argue with you, Marie," Chris admitted. "Whatever you might have been at one point, if ever, you don't strike me as a killer now. Elena, though, I know she won't stop until you're dead. Nick, I don't know, *maybe* he could come around if I had a chance to talk with him, but not with Elena there. We have to do something, stop her before she does any more damage."

"I couldn't agree more. That's why I already sent a few of my brethren after them."

"You know where they are? How?"

"I'm not a fool. I knew they'd come back here at some point, which they did before you woke. Nothing happens around here without my knowledge."

"So what's going to happen then? You're just going to kill them?"

"Is that such a bad thing? They wanted to kill us."

"I told you, Nick is my friend. I don't think he needs to die."

Marie made a pouty face that was clearly intended to be playful, but under the circumstances, Chris wasn't amused. "You wanted to turn him, huh?"

"I don't know, I just thought I could talk sense into him. That's all. Isn't there a way to stop this attack?"

"Not now."

"They don't have cell phones or anything?"

Shaking her head, Marie said, "It's a stealth attack. It's what we do best. I told them to go dark until it is done." Feeling disgusted at the thought of his friend being torn apart by vampires, Chris pushed Marie away. She seemed hurt by this and asked, "Was it something I said?"

"It's what you did, Marie. I love you, and I know you love me, but we're in this together now. You couldn't be bothered to talk to me about this first?"

"I did this for *us*, Chris. For our survival. I know you care about your friend, but he's human. Sooner or later, you'll have to realize it's us versus them. It'll always be us versus them until I can change the world for the better, like I'm trying to do. But we need a chance, and this helps to ensure we get that chance. I can't afford to take any more risks. They've gotten too close."

Marie tried to move to Chris in an attempt to console him, but as she reached for his face, he pushed her hand away. "I . . . I'm sorry, Marie. I think I need some time alone. To think." And with that, he took his leave of the woman he loved, the woman he swore to protect at all costs, and marched out of her home, past the guards, and off the property. He had no idea where he was going, but at the moment, he didn't care.

12

The night air coming through the open window was cool and quiet. While everyone else slept, Elena stayed awake. Her nerves were almost shot, but something about their current situation rubbed her the wrong way. The scouting of Marie's house seemed too easy. She knew they were coming and whether or not Liz knew this, the ease with which Hector and her cased the place was all kinds of wrong. Elena would have said something after they were on the way back to Hector's home, but part of her wanted to be wrong. Perhaps they'd just gotten lucky, or Marie had grown too confident in her ability to deal with approaching threats. Whatever the case, Elena kept quiet, and her dark thoughts kept her awake.

As she sat there in the dark of the living room, with only the faint glow of the lights outside to keep her company, Elena found herself in a fairly meditative state. She listened to the stray sounds emanating from the street—a car horn, tires screeching, a dog barking. Perhaps she might have heard a gunshot or two. But she wasn't focused on any of that. She knew the signs of a vampire attack, that quick shuffling they seemed to make as they crept into a domicile, or the eagerly approaching mouth as it opened to take the first bite of its prey. She'd almost been a victim herself on occasion, but her father taught her to be prepared, to keep her senses attuned for the warning signs. The bars outside the windows should have kept them safe from any intruder, but a vampire with super strength could make short work of those bars quite easily.

Elena thought she heard a sound from the kitchen, a sound like the abrupt rending of metal, but she needed to investigate it to be sure. Drawing up one of the machetes procured by Hector, she slowly and carefully approached the kitchen. If any vampire decided to slide through an open window head first, they would be losing that head shortly. Elena rounded the corner and spotted an open window—a window without any bars to protect it. Something had torn them free with ease, and she knew exactly who—or what—had done it. The question was whether the vampire had also managed to enter undetected, or if it was waiting outside for her to poke her head out in curiosity. Adrenaline coursed through her veins like liquid lightening. Her grip tightened on the machete and she waited for an attack.

Moving closer to the window in the kitchen, Elena scanned the area high and low, looking for the intruder. But as she came up empty, a horrible thought flashed through her mind that perhaps this had been done to trick her, not as bait for the kill, but to keep her occupied while the others were attacked. In panic, she did the only thing she could think of. "Wake up! Everybody, wake up! They're here!"

A hiss could be heard from outside and before Elena could even react, a dark figure was leaping straight through the window and slammed her back into the kitchen counter. The force of her body knocked everything on the counter to the floor, as well as the machete which fell from her grip. The vampire lifted her up by the neck, keeping her pinned to the cupboards above and her legs kicked out uselessly. There were screams and some shuffling from the other rooms, but she couldn't help, couldn't see what carnage was ensuing without her aid. Flashing his fangs in disdain, the vampire said, "You must be the hunter. Of course you'd go and spoil our surprise. It was Marie's idea to lure you out. She knew you'd take the bait. Now that you have, you'll be just as dead as your friends."

His grip tightened as he prepared to strangle her, but unfortunately, he'd spent too long talking and Elena had already figured out what to do. Grabbing his arm, she supported her body as her legs bent up to press against him and her head slammed back. The cheap wood making up the cupboard door snapped apart and the vampire found himself stumbling forward. Using this as leverage, Elena kicked him off of her and his grip released from her throat. She then watched him topple to the ground as she landed butt-first on the counter. Next to her was a set of kitchen knives that she'd knocked over and her hand went straight for the biggest one.

As the vampire stood to lunge at her once more, Elena stabbed out with the knife and nailed him straight in the eyeball. He screamed in pain, attempting to wrench it out, but Elena was already down on the floor. Her hand shot out for the fallen machete and in one smooth motion, she stood, turned, and sliced. The vampire's head was separated from his shoulders and toppled uselessly to the ground, an expression of pain and frustration frozen on his face.

The noise from the other rooms continued, a sign that her comrades were still alive. Charging for the first bedroom, she smashed through the door to find Liz struggling with a female vampire who'd pinned her to the bed and was attempting to tear out her throat. Liz was using all her strength to hold her off and it appeared she'd managed to stab the vampire through the midsection with a machete. Unfortunately, it hadn't accomplished much other than angering her.

Running up fast, Elena went to chop off her head, but the

vampire released Liz and lunged for Elena. She sidestepped the creature, who went slamming into the wall, while Elena spun around and sliced through her neck. When the head plopped against the soft carpet, Elena looked at Liz, who shouted, "Hector!" She almost charged out of the room, when Elena stopped her and handed the cop a machete. Liz took off and Elena retrieved the other one still stuck in the decapitated vampire's torso.

Bursting into the master bedroom where Hector and Nick were, Elena saw that Liz was already furiously hacking at the male vampire who'd been attacking Hector. She'd managing to hit everything except his neck. First went the hands, then the forearms and finally, with no arms left to defend himself, Liz took off his head. Elena had meanwhile gone straight for the female vampire on top of Nick. The creature was cackling and appeared to be toying with him on the ground, making small cuts on his face and body with her long nails. She'd been tasting some of his blood when Elena had lopped off her head.

Nick looked up from the ground, finally opening his eyes. He'd shut them in fear as if that might somehow help him escape the pain he'd been enduring. But as blood splashed down on him from the headless corpse above, he cried out in panic and shoved the body off. "Jesus Christ!" Panting from terror and exhaustion, he slid back across the ground toward the bed, as if some distance from the corpse might relieve him from the panic he was experiencing. It didn't seem to help though, and Elena knelt down so she could meet him eye to eye.

"You're okay. She's dead now, they're all dead."

His breathing was still rapid, but sense began to return as he asked, "Are you sure?"

Looking up, Elena spotted Hector and Liz, but no other sign of intruders in the home. She then returned her gaze to Nick and nodded. "Let me take a look at those cuts." Holding out her hand, she waited for Nick to take it and then pulled him to his feet.

Hector and Liz approached, ready for more action, but relieved that things seemed to have ended for the time being. Liz looked around and asked, "That's all of them, right? How'd they find us?"

"How do you think?" Elena said. "Marie sent them here. She let us scope out her house earlier so she could track us back here."

"Jesus Christ," Hector sighed. "You guys weren't kidding about the mess you're in. So what do we do now?"

"Pack up everything and hit the road," Liz said. "We can't stay here."

"Then where do we go?" Nick asked.

"I still have Lydia's car—Freddy's babysitter. Her family left town at my insistence and though it would have been stupid to try and stay there before, if we're just doing it for the night, I doubt anyone will notice us. It's too late for people in that neighborhood to be out and about. We can head to Marie's in the morning, since she'll be too strong right now. But we need to strike back hard and fast, before she has time to respond." Looking at Elena, she added, "We would have died if you didn't help, Elena. Thank you."

Not one for compliments, Elena simply nodded in appreciation. "Let's not waste our chance. We gotta clean this mess up and get out of here as quickly as possible."

13

Chris had been wandering for what felt like hours, but when he checked his phone, he realized it had only been about two. He'd walked away from Marie's property without any direction in mind until his feet took him down Mulholland Drive and into the Valley. He then noticed he wasn't too far from the home of his friend Mel. He hadn't seen her in what felt like forever, but it really had only been about two weeks since Comic-Con. She hadn't even entered his thoughts since then with all the madness that had happened. But at that moment he felt like he could really use a friend. Nick was possibly dead and he'd told Dan to skip town, so Mel was his best option for some peace away from the influence of Marie.

Being a vampire now meant he was no longer under her thrall the way a familiar would have been. Even still, he loved her, and felt closer to her than ever. But what she'd done that night, without consulting him, it hurt more than anything had hurt before. He'd never been cheated on, but he could imagine it felt something akin to this. And so he reached out for a lifeline—his only one in the valley—and soon found himself at the doorstep of aspiring actress Melanie Cooper.

It was late, and according to his phone almost two in the morning. Mel was surely asleep, but he thought she'd come to the door if he sent her a text first. So, he sent the text, then rang the doorbell and knocked. It took a while for lights to come on and even longer for Mel to approach the door. He hoped she had checked her texts or he just might find himself staring down the barrel of a loaded gun. She kept a revolver in her nightstand, a snub-nosed pistol, one of those police specials—as they liked to call them in the movies. She liked that it was easy to clean and didn't jam when she took it to the range.

A lock could be heard turning and the door began to slide open. Chris prepared himself for the worst as the light inside illuminated his presence. "Chris?" a groggy Mel asked. "What are you doing here at two in the morning?"

"I'm sorry to wake you, I just needed somewhere to go for a bit."

Shaking her head, Mel asked, "Is that supposed to make some kind of sense to me? You live in El Segundo." Looking out past him to the street, she then asked, "Where's your car?"

Sighing, Chris said, "I think we have a lot of catching up to do."

"Can it wait till morning?"

"No, I . . . I don't think it can."

Mel sighed in defeat and pulled the door fully open to let Chris inside. "C'mon in, then. I guess I'll brew some coffee."

And so, Mel worked on the coffee as Chris began filling her in on the past two weeks. The new job working for Marie, the attacker who turned out to be a vampire hunter, the cops, the premiere, and of course, Chris' current status as one of the undead. When he was finished, Mel's reaction was pretty understandable.

She laughed.

"It's not a joke, Mel."

"You're right, it's not funny to wake me up in the middle of the night—a weeknight for that matter—and decide to spin some ridiculous yarn about vampires in Hollywood. I mean, peppering in those details about the headhunter around town? That was a nice touch, but you lost me when you said Marie LeBeau is a vampire. And you? No way would *you* be a vampire, let alone in some kind of kinky relationship with the hottest star in Hollywood. It's just too ridiculous."

"I know it sounds stupid, but I can prove it."

"How?" Then Mel shook her head and said, "No, sorry, you know what? I don't care. I'm not entertaining this any longer. You need to go back home, to your own place. I'm sure Dan is worried about you. I should call him, let him know—"

"Just shut up!" Chris found himself belting out. Mel looked positively shook by the outburst, and Chris quickly followed by saying, "I'm sorry, Mel. But this isn't a joke. I wanted your help because I think Marie may have sent some people—other vampires—to kill Nick tonight along with that vampire hunter, Elena."

"And what do you want me to do about it?"

"I don't know. I just had to get out of there. She's . . . she's not the person I thought she was. I thought, I don't know, that maybe she'd talk to me first or something, but it's all about survival for her. It's only *ever* been about survival and somehow I never saw that until now."

Mel looked confused, and maybe a little scared. "I think I'd better call someone, Chris. Like a doctor or the cops or somebody better equipped to help you."

She went to grab her phone, but before she could, Chris screamed, "No!" and leaped out of the kitchen chair he was sitting in, going straight for her set of kitchen knives. Removing the biggest one, he looked at it for a moment, then at Mel, who now seemed more concerned than ever, before he plunged it deep into his heart.

"Chris!" Mel screamed, running to his body, which collapsed on the ground. She cradled her friend in her arms, expecting life to fade from him. Instead, he merely seemed in pain. Chris' hands moved up and yanked out the knife, letting it clatter to the floor. His blood painted the linoleum as it poured out the open wound. Mel gasped, "You're not supposed to remove it!"

"It's okay, Mel. I told you, I'm a vampire now. Only removing my head will kill me."

"Not sunlight?"

Shaking his head, he said, "It's just a myth."

"But you're losing so much blood!"

Looking down, Chris could see that he was in fact, leaking a lot of fluids. He thought as a vampire the wound would just heal up like Wolverine, but he realized now, vampirism had a cost. There was a reason vampires had to drink blood daily. It truly was blood for blood, and that was now clearer than ever. He could see the veins on Mel's neck pulsating, sending blood coursing through her veins. It almost seemed to glow in a way, and it was drawing him closer.

His fangs grew abruptly like an erection, uncontrollable and activated by his base desires. In this case, to feed, to heal himself. To make his body whole again. But Mel was his friend and he didn't want to harm her. Yet in the two seconds it took to decide, he realized he had little control in the matter.

When his teeth sank into the soft flesh of her neck, Mel let out a sort of squeak, like she had been surprised by it. And then he was drinking her blood so greedily and so fast, that she must have gone light-headed. It was as if she was fading into a dream. A dream from which she'd never awaken, unless he stopped. But Chris' hunger had taken over. It could have been one of his parents and he wouldn't have stopped, not until he'd had his fill.

After he felt satisfied, Chris pulled away from Mel's neck and let her soft body fall lifelessly to the floor. He stared it, the blood still leaking from her open wound, but slower now, as her heart had ceased to function. She had a look of shock on her face, and a slack jaw that seemed to ask Chris, "Why?"

Chris wanted to say he didn't know why, but deep down he did. He wasn't the same man he had been before—that Chris wouldn't have hurt a fly unless he'd been attacked first. Now he saw himself as he truly was, standing up and looking at his reflection in the window. His face was bloody, his clothes a mess. He was a killer, just like he'd been callous enough to call Marie. He knew his true monstrous nature now and understood why she was driven like an animal to survive.

<h1 style="text-align:center">14</h1>

After calling Marie and confessing what he'd done, Chris wasn't surprised that she was very calm about the whole thing. She had a few hundred years on him after all, centuries to know how easily the thirst could take control of someone. With all the resources she had available, he also wasn't shocked when a team showed up to clean the area and remove the body of his friend. Part of Chris was still disgusted with himself over what he'd done, but that other part? The part that reveled in the killing, enjoying every last drop of the blood needed to sustain him? That part was perfectly fine with it.

When Marie arrived, she drove Chris home. And her home was now his. Chris' old life died with his friend. He knew there was only one road left open to him and he'd have to walk it with Marie, or face an eternity of loneliness. The alternative was to kill himself, but he wasn't even sure how that was possible. A vampire could only die by decapitation, and decapitating yourself wasn't the easiest thing in the world—plus he was too much of a coward to contemplate suicide.

It was nothing but silence during the drive to Marie's house, but once they were there, she never once grilled him about why he left—or why he killed his friend. She was understanding and caring, a true nurturer. She only wanted him to be comfortable and to love her the way she still loved him. But she must have known he was shaken by the ordeal, so she asked him, as she cradled his head on her bed, "It's hard, especially when it's someone you know. And you *did* know the girl, correct?"

"She was my friend." Chris almost choked up as the words left his throat, but they still came out all the same.

"How long had you known her?"

"Since my last year of college, so about four years."

Marie smiled down at him and said, "That's nothing. A hundred years from now, you'll barely remember her."

"But I do now, and it's still fresh in my mind. I just can't get the image out of my head. Her body lying there, dead, leaking what blood remained in her veins out onto the floor."

Stroking Chris' hair with her fingers, Marie said, "Yes, but it will pass, you'll see. I've been where you are now. There was a man I knew once, who I loved, who I'd have done anything for, but when the thirst took me that first time, he became nothing more than a meal. I was appalled at what I'd done. Tried to throw myself from a cliff, but death didn't take. I landed in the river below, and eventually washed up on the shore, water in my lungs, and I knew then that death does not come easy for us. Life can be hard at times, but we have to make the most of it. We need to feed like any creature that breathes on this planet. We are not mindless, and we *can* control our instincts, with time, and practice. That's why I wished you had stayed here, but I understood why you left in the moment. I hope you also understand now why it's best you stay close."

"What about my other friend? The one with Elena?"

"I don't know. The ones I sent after them haven't reported back, but I'm sure I'll hear from them soon. For now, you should rest. I think you'll feel better in the morning."

"How can you know for sure?"

Smiling at him once more, she said, "Experience has taught

me there's nothing that can't be remedied with a good night's sleep. In our case, that usually is a good day's sleep, but as you woke not too long ago, I think you'll be fine with a few hours. And I'll be waiting for you when you wake."

Looking up at her, seeing the sympathetic look in her eyes, Chris asked, "Will you stay here with me?"

"Of course."

15

Sunrise was drawing near.

The pre-morning light surrounded everything in that not-quite-daylight glow. It was perfect for their needs. As Elena made her way up the hill toward the property, she watched Hector and Liz break off from Nick and her. She prayed for them in her mind, that their feet carried them lightly, and their targets were found swiftly.

Everyone knew the plan, but as Nick was the most inexperienced of the group, it was deemed safest for him to shadow Elena. She didn't like guns, but she would be unwavering in her pursuit of Marie. Nick had never been in a firefight, had never shot anyone before. He was unpredictable and would need constant supervision so he didn't blow the whole operation. Elena wondered before they left if he should have just been left behind, but it was no longer safe for him to stay by himself. The best thing she could do was keep a close eye on him. Even so, they weren't about to leave Nick completely defenseless, so he was given a shotgun and two Glocks—which he'd fired before and knew his way around. The shotgun wasn't something he'd fired before, but she hoped he was smart enough to save it for close range problems. They put a strap on it so he could move around easier.

After taking care of the mess of bodies in Hector's home, the remainder of their night was spent planning. They made a quick detour to Lydia's house and carefully went over the locations of the security detail at Marie's home. It was minimal, and therefore would be easier for them to deal with. There was the possibility of shift changes, but they doubted that would be an issue at first light. What was more of a possibility is whoever had been watching the property all night was on their last legs. Provided they were human, they'd be tired and ready to go home.

Security cameras at the front and back were also an issue. There could be additional ones they missed along the side or inside the house, but regardless, there was nothing they could do about them. Without cutting the power to Marie's entire home and thereby blowing their cover, they would need to move as quickly as possible before they were discovered by anyone watching the security feed.

When the guns were all divided up, Liz took the MAC-10, a shotgun, and two pistols. Hector took his rifle, a shotgun, and two pistols. He had the heaviest load, but he was ready to ditch his rifle as soon as they needed to get in close. He wasn't even sure if they'd make it out of this alive, but if they did, he'd double back to retrieve it. Liz wasn't planning to be so careful with her weapons; she didn't personally own any of them and would drop each as soon as her ammo ran dry.

Thankfully ammo was something they had plenty of. Unfortunately, apart from some tactical vests Hector had also procured, they didn't have a ton of spots on their bodies to store said ammo, so that meant they were still going in fairly limited. It would be a team effort to conserve as much ammo as possible before heading inside, since they still had no idea how many security guards were in there. Liz said she had spotted about five or six when she visited a week back, but that didn't mean their numbers stopped at what she saw—they were only the ones who revealed themselves to her when she entered the house.

Finally, there were the edged weapons—which mostly consisted of machetes and a few large hunting knives that looked like something Rambo would use. Not the best for a quick decapitation, but they weren't useless either. Elena took one knife along with two machetes she kept on her back. She wanted to travel as lightly as possible and only had two hands to wield them. She just hoped neither broke in combat. The rest of them each took a machete, while Hector also grabbed a hunting knife. They weren't about to leave anything behind that they could carry.

Along with Nick, Elena took cover behind some bushes on the eastside of Marie's property. More and more light began to peek out over the horizon. When Hector was in position, he called out quietly over his radio. The headset on Elena's head chirped to life as he said, "I'm in position. Six guards out front, as before. What you got, Liz?"

"Four back here. Let me know when you're ready to take your shots. I can't pick off all these guys at once with my pistol, but I can sneak around to get them. Are there any you can take safely?"

"Yeah, two on the edge by the bushes. I think if I take them, they'll be out of sight . . . until somebody goes looking."

"That's good, that'll hopefully give us some time. Let me know when you take them and I'll see how many I can get here. I've got two on either side of the back, and two closer to the pool. I pick off the houseboys first—nobody will see them unless they're on the bottom floor, which looks empty right now. Nick, you there?"

Elena looked to Nick, who seemed shaken, not expecting to be addressed and clearly in way over his head. She put a calming hand on his shoulder to try and settle his nerves. When he looked to Elena for assurance, he answered back over the headset. "I'm here."

"I'm not going to ask you to coordinate a strike with me. I hope you understand, I can't trust your aim. But if anything goes wrong, I need you ready to at least lay down some covering fire." Elena could see the sweat forming on Nick's brow as he stayed there frozen in place. With how cool mornings in LA tended to be, she knew it wasn't from the weather. He didn't look ready for anything.

Liz seemed to wait patiently for his response, but when it didn't arrive, she once more asked, "Nick?"

Wiping the sweat from his brow, Nick stammered, "I-I'm not sure I can do this. I've never killed anybody before, never even shot someone."

Elena realized he was going to be a problem like she feared. Push came to shove, he'd shoot if he was fired upon, but until he was in fight or flight mode, she'd have to carry him like dead weight.

Keeping her voice as steady and direct as possible, Liz said, "Nick, I need you to stay calm. I'm not going to ask you to do anything you don't feel up to. Elena?"

"Yeah?"

"Keep an eye on him. I'm trusting you to handle everything else."

"I will."

The group had put suppressors on as many guns as they could, but still had a limited supply, only four for the pistols, which meant priority went to one per person, and since Elena had no guns, the fourth went to Liz. Hector had one specially built for his rifle and another for the MAC-10 that Liz was holding. But the aim wasn't the most reliable feature of that gun, so she kept it as a back-up if she needed to spray and pray.

When Hector gave the signal, Liz must have begun moving toward her first target, as it was a moment before she appeared to take down the guard in view. The one at the other end of the house was a good distance away, and Elena grew nervous Liz could hit a target that far, but she managed it beautifully—the headshot laid him out like he was a dummy. Hector confirmed he bagged his targets, but that left four on his end. The two guys by the pool were still facing away from Liz. They were far enough out, she must have known killing them could attract attention from anyone on the second or third floors.

Hector waited until she was ready, and Elena spotted Liz making her way into the bushes to sneak closer. Then she whispered over the radio that she was in position and Hector gave a count to fire. "Taking targets in three . . . two . . . wait!" Elena felt adrenaline shoot through her veins, ready for anything. She was worried Liz might slip and take her shot before Hector, but she clearly had nerves of steel and waited for his response. "The gate's opening."

"Who's coming in? Is it a shift change?" Liz wondered.

"Car doesn't match the others there, so not security, but also not a police cruiser, could be a plainclothes, though. I see a one guy inside, looks pretty stiff, so my money is on a cop. Going to watch him, hopefully he enters the house." Elena waited with Nick, their anticipation growing with their sense of unease about the new arrival. "Okay, I spot a badge on his belt along with his sidearm. He's having a quick word with the two men by the entrance. Now he's moving to the door and knocking. Someone is letting him in. Okay, I think we're clear."

"What'd he look like?" Liz asked.

"Why's it matter?"

"Just tell me, Hector."

"White guy, maybe six feet tall, going gray up top, wearing a tan suit, nothing fancy. Probably wears it to work most days."

"Fuck," Liz spat.

"Who is it?"

"I think it's my captain. He's not human, F-Y-I. Fucker tried to kill me in the hospital, but ended up draining a nurse. We need to watch out for him. Guns aren't going to cut it."

"Well, let's hope guns cut it for the rest of these guys out front. Once we're inside, we'll deal with whatever hand we're dealt. That's what the machetes are for."

"Sure."

"Okay, you ready?"

"Whenever you are. Let's do this. Elena? Get ready to move inside with Nick, I'll follow you two."

Elena drew her two machetes, while Nick tightly gripped the shotgun. She could still see the beads of sweat on his brow and hoped he'd be all right. She'd never have brought him along if they didn't need all the help they could get.

"All right," Hector said, "Three . . . two . . . one . . . take 'em."

Elena watched as Liz carefully took out both guards by the pool and then made her way toward the bottom floor of the house. Rushing up to meet her on the opposite side with Nick, they both scanned the interior, but didn't see any apparent guards on that floor. This made Elena a little nervous in the moment. She hadn't thought about it earlier, but there was no way that floor was completely unguarded; it was likely there was something they missed, but it was too late to turn back. Nobody had shown up to stop them, which meant it was do-or-die time.

"All right, I think they're all down," Hector said. "You in position, Liz?"

"Yeah, waiting on you."

Liz locked eyes with Elena, waiting to give the signal to enter. Hector would be joining them around back any second. When he rounded the side, appearing just behind Liz, he gave a nod and she then nodded to Elena. With two silenced shots in succession,

Liz shattered both of the sliding glass doors. Nick jumped a bit at the sound of the glass breaking, but then Elena led the way inside. Somebody above had to have heard the glass—certainly Marie or Chris if they were awake. Even if they weren't awake, it would have likely woken them. Then there was that cop who'd been turned. He certainly heard the windows shatter. But it wasn't the time for stealth any longer.

It was the time for action.

Footsteps rapidly descended the stairs. Heavy steps, quite a few of them—at least two or three people. As the suits came into view, Elena could tell they were part of the security team. Liz drew up her MAC-10. Elena pulled Nick into cover behind a wall leading down a side hallway. The muffled shots tore into the guards and some of the pictures along the wall near the stairs. She could hear their bodies hit the floor and shattered frames fall off the walls. That's when voices could finally be heard shouting from above.

"We know you're down there! You've gotten lucky so far, but you're not making it up the stairs. Those guys were just testing your firepower. We've got more where that came from, and some of us you'll need more than a few bullets to stop."

Elena couldn't place the voice, but Liz sure recognized it, as she asked, "That you, Ford?"

"Gutiérrez, I admire your persistence! I suppose that drive got you to where you are—or *were*, I should say—within the force. But your time is up now. This is where your story ends. Now it can end with a bang, or perhaps a whimper if you come quietly. What's it going to be?"

"Come down the stairs and find out."

"I'd love to, but I'm afraid we've got a few more appetizers to send your way before we get to the main course."

Elena heard the clank of something metal bouncing down the

stairs. A few somethings, in fact. As they reached the bottom and rolled into view, she thought they were grenades and wondered why Marie would be okay with that kind of structural damage to her home. But Elena didn't know grenades too well and as they hissed to life, she got her first taste of tear gas.

"Cover your face!" Liz cried as she and Hector made a mad dash for the stairs. Clearly, they hoped that charging up was their best chance to clear the gas and get a jump on those upstairs. But Elena didn't have the time and she knew Nick wouldn't make it, so instead she charged out the shattered window in the back and pulled him along with her. When they were clear of the gas outside, Nick coughed a bit and wiped his eyes.

"Jesus," he gasped, "That shit is no joke." Gunfire erupted from the floor above and they could hear Liz and Hector shouting inaudibly. Nick looked to Elena for guidance. "What do we do? Run?"

She didn't have all the answers, but knew their best plan of attack was to move around front and surprise them from there. "Follow me."

Nick did as he was told and Elena crept along the west side of the house toward the front. They stayed low, avoiding the windows, and when they reached the front doors, she pointed to the center between the doors right around where the locks were located and said, "Use the shotgun and aim there."

Moving back a few feet, she let Nick move in closer. He pulled up the shotgun and fired at the doors. Wood exploded around the locks like deadly confetti. He almost toppled over from the recoil, but Elena caught him. She couldn't tell at first if one shot had done the trick, but kicking hard at the doors, she heard a *snap* and they both swung inward. Moving inside, two guards appeared, while others were apparently locked in a gunfight. The guards moved their pistols to shoot and Nick instinctively racked the shotgun and fired back before Elena dove toward the stairs on the left and pulled him with her.

His single blast didn't hit the guards, but instead exploded a statue near them. The stairs that led up to the top floor helped to protect them from gunfire until the guards got a little closer. Elena nodded at Nick, hoping he understood she wanted him to cover her and quietly ascended the stairs. When the guards came into view, she leaped the railing and came down hard on one with a machete. The other guard attempted to shoot her, but before he could, he was knocked to the floor by a shotgun blast. His body lay there lifeless, a bloody mess. Turning her gaze to Nick, Elena saw him holding the smoking gun. He looked both amazed and horrified by his first kill.

Elena worried for a moment he might turn into a useless blubbering mess, but she wouldn't allow time for his adrenaline to lower and rational thought to take hold. Speaking loud enough to snap him out of any potential state of shock, Elena said "Nick! C'mon, they need us."

Looking at Elena, demonstrating he still had his wits about him, Nick nodded. Drawing her second machete, Elena charged forward. Nick followed behind as she rounded the hallway and found two dead guards on the ground, plus another four engaged in a shootout with Hector and Liz—who somehow were still alive and taking cover behind a couch riddled with bullet holes. It was a wonder they weren't dead. Two of the guards were using a wall for cover, but as they hadn't noticed Elena and Nick, they were easy pickings.

Nick fired at one with the shotgun and somehow missed despite the guy being close enough for a blind man to hit. Elena wasted no time skewering the guard with her machete and slicing open the throat of the other with her second machete. A crimson spray erupted out of the wound and painted the wall. The man's scream turned into a gurgle before Elena finished him off with another chop.

The whole event seemed to pull the attention away from Liz and Hector, which gave them the opportunity to finish off the other two guards. Liz then approached Elena, not with relief or gratitude, but confusion. "Where's Ford? You get him?"

Elena knew she had to be talking about the captain mentioned earlier and said, "I don't think so."

"Shit! Look out!" Liz cried and shoved Elena to the side. Caught unaware, the hunter hit the floor hard and looked up to see a fanged face lunge at Liz, sinking its teeth deep into her neck. Nick was in shock, but Hector moved fast, pulling his machete and chopping at the cop's neck. Unfortunately, it didn't go clean through and Ford dropped Liz, hissing and then lunging for Hector. His hand caught him around the throat and squeezed.

Elena looked up from the ground, knowing that Ford wouldn't have the strength to crush Hector's neck in daylight. However, he could still strangle him if given the chance. Springing to her feet, Elena prepared to attack, but Nick beat her to the punch. And Nick being in a state of shock meant he wasn't thinking quite clearly. He drew up the shotgun and fired into Ford's back, also hitting Hector and knocking them both to the floor. Running up fast, Elena pulled the machete that was still stuck in the back of Ford's neck and chopped down once more, this time severing his head from his body.

It seemed the tactical vest had protected Hector's side from the buckshot, but he was bleeding profusely from his thigh. Looking down at the wound he cried, "Puta madre!"

"I'm sorry," Nick squealed as he sprinted over. He dropped the shotgun on the ground, not wanting to deal with it again.

Elena turned her attention to Liz, not knowing how bad the bite was. She could see Liz cradling her neck, which was bleeding, but not profusely. It seemed Hector had stopped the vampire before he did too much damage. Tearing off the bottom part of her shirt, Elena moved to Liz and wrapped it tightly around her neck. "You can pad that more if you want, but the pressure should be enough. Looks like you got lucky."

"I don't feel lucky," Liz groaned. Elena helped the cop to her feet and she turned to Hector, who was still bleeding on the ground.

"I think he needs a doctor," Nick said, as tears cascaded down his cheeks.

"I've been hurt worse, kid." Hector laughed. Still, even to Elena, the wound didn't look good. It had struck most of his side.

"Stay with him," Liz ordered Nick. She waited until he nodded to turn her attention back to Elena. "Let's move. Still one more floor to clear." Elena nodded and the two began to move back toward the stairs that led to the top floor. Liz asked, "You think she's actually up there?"

"She was waiting for us. No way she'd run at this point. We might have caught her off guard with the timing, but I guarantee she's up there. Chris too."

"What about the familiar?" The words hit Elena like a brick to the head. She couldn't believe she'd forgotten about the old guy, the trusty Thomas who was once a vampire hunter himself. No sooner had Liz asked this than a figure had dropped on Elena from above, and knocked her down to the floor.

"I'll kill you!" the seemingly feeble old Englishman shouted. He pressed Elena's face to the floor and the strength he displayed made it feel like her skull would be crushed in a matter of seconds. But then she heard several muffled gunshots and the man toppled off her. Liz's gun was dry and apparently so was any spare ammo, so she tossed it to the floor before drawing her remaining pistol. Seemed this was her last available weapon.

As Elena pushed herself up, Liz approached cautiously keeping her gun aimed at the man who appeared to be dead a few feet away. "Did I get him?" she asked.

Elena had lost both her machetes in the scuffle, but still had the hunting knife and unsheathed it as she got to her feet. "He's human, but I've dealt with a few familiars before and they are no picnic." The two women walked slowly toward Thomas' body and Liz kept her sights aimed at him. Elena then moved up her knife, preparing to stab it into his heart. She plunged it down and mere inches before it struck his chest, Thomas' hand caught the blade. It was cutting deeply into his skin, but he couldn't have cared less.

As his eyes popped open, Thomas cried out, "You'll die, you—" Before he could finish though, Liz fired a single round into his forehead, knocking his skull back against the marble floor.

"That's enough out of you," Liz said.

His hand lost its death grip, allowing the hunting knife to continue its journey into his heart. Elena left it there.

"Was that necessary?" Liz asked.

"Just wanted to be sure," Elena replied.

"Two more to go?"

"God, I hope so."

With that, the two women prepared themselves for the final battle ahead.

16

Chris had fallen asleep with Marie cradling his head. His conscience had not been cleansed by the satisfaction his stomach had attained, but with her by his side, at least he was able to rest. Unfortunately, that rest was cut short.

Marie was first to wake, causing Chris to follow when she dispassionately threw his body off her in a rush to the window. Whatever she saw had disturbed her enough to contact the guards just outside her bedroom door. "We have some uninvited guests, Marco. Give them a proper welcome and make sure everyone is prepared."

The guards hurried past Thomas, who had been approaching from down the hall. "Mistress, you've heard the glass?" he asked.

"Yes, I woke when it happened. Is the police captain here?"

"He just arrived and is downstairs now. Shall I have him call for backup?"

Marie shook her head. "They won't arrive soon enough. The guards out back are already dead. Check the front."

"Of course, Mistress."

Marie closed and locked the door before turning to Chris. "Sorry you didn't get more sleep. But this may be the end of things."

Gunfire erupted from the floors below. "For us?" he asked.

"No . . . for them." Marie grinned and Chris hoped in that

moment she had some kind of plan. Hurrying into her walk-in closet, she moved to the far back where there was a safe.

"What are you doing?" Chris asked.

Marie didn't bother to answer. She quickly worked the combination lock and turned the handle to open the safe. Inside was a number of passports, weapons, and cash. Stacks of cash. But that wasn't what drew Chris' attention. It was the small device that Marie removed.

"What is that?"

"Insurance."

"Am I supposed to know what that means?"

"It's a small explosive device. Just big enough to level the house. If my men fail, I think my time in LA has come to an end . . . and I don't like to leave a trail. So, I'm going to set this bad boy, and you and I will hightail it out of the city. Sound like a plan?"

"What? No, of course not!"

"Well, you're welcome to stay here and die, but that's your call."

"We're vampires. Can't we take them?"

"That's the sun rising over there." She pointed out the window to the east. "That means we're rendered weaker than at night. I've been around long enough that I don't lose as much power as newborns like you, but I'm not about to put you in further danger than need be at this point."

"So what happens next?"

Moving across the room, Marie found a satisfactory location for the explosive to go. "I place this little guy, then we wait for Thomas. If he gives me the all-clear in a few minutes, we're good. If not . . . well, then I activate the explosive and we leave before it goes off."

"Aren't we cornered in here?"

Marie laughed at this, "You really think I'd live in a place like this without an exit strategy?" Moving past Chris, Marie approached the wall and pressed inward on a section to expose a hidden door. This opened into a space between the walls. "We can take this into the garage. With one of my cars, we'll be out of here before they have a chance to harm us."

"Are you sure? What—"

A hard knock was heard from the other side of the bedroom door where Thomas yelled, "Mistress, the guards out front are dead! The others are doing their best, but I am quite nervous for your safety."

Marie moved to the door and said, "You've been a good servant, Thomas. I've enjoyed our time together. Keep me safe for a few more minutes."

"I will, Mistress. They shan't get past me."

Entering the walk-in closet, Marie grabbed a bag and gathered up the passports, cash, and weapons. She put a small pistol into the waistband of her pants and then rushed to the explosive, setting the timer on it for three minutes. "Looks like this is our cue to leave. Follow me."

Part of Chris wanted to follow her, but then there was the part of him that wanted to apologize to Nick, to tell his friend that he was sorry, and hope that somehow what they had could be preserved. If only Nick could let things be and understand that he was different now. But whatever the case, Marie didn't have the patience to continue waiting for Chris to ruminate on the topic.

Grabbing him by the wrist, Marie pulled Chris onward. "Come on!" she commanded. Once she had him in her grasp, he knew he was powerless to resist, and willingly followed her into the space between the walls. Inside, things were dark and dusty, but Marie knew where she was going and as they hit some stairs, she said, "Watch your step." He did as instructed and then they came to another door hidden in the wall. When she opened it, Chris found the garage just beyond with her expensive cars looking as clean as could be, sparkling and untouched.

Marie moved to her BMW, climbed in, and threw her bag into the back. Chris joined her as she hit the button to open the garage door and started up the car. Looking at Marie, he was tempted to tell her that maybe they didn't need to run. But Chris knew it was too late; the explosive charge had been set and he was in the car. She could drive anywhere and he'd be at her mercy.

However, it wasn't as though Marie was unaware how lost in thought he was, and so she reluctantly asked, "What's wrong?"

Chris wanted to spill everything, all the feelings that had been driving him mad since he killed Mel the previous night. Nick was now apparently there to finish him off, and he wanted to say that maybe there was a way to reason with him, to talk and stop the violence for just a moment. But before he could say any of that, he saw two women enter the garage from the house. It was Elena and Liz. As Liz drew up her pistol, Chris shouted, "Drive!"

Marie slammed on the gas and several gunshots pinged off the apparently bulletproof car. Unfortunately, that couldn't protect the tires. One of the back ones blew and Marie lost control. The car veered off the driveway into the garden area. She tried to stop the car, or turn it, but instead, it went straight into the wall surrounding her property.

When the airbags deployed, things got fuzzy for Chris. He looked into the side mirror and saw two figures approaching from behind. Then he noticed another gun Marie had stuffed into the duffel bag. Pulling it out, he hoped it was loaded and ready to go. Marie was just coming to as Chris stepped out of the car. She screamed, "Chris, no!" But he was already out in the open, beginning to fire on Liz and Elena.

Chris didn't want it to come to this, but he wasn't going to let them murder Marie without fighting back. He didn't see Nick, which made him wonder if his best friend was dead. This only fueled his rage. The two women had pulled his friend into this mess, a mess that should never have been created in the first place. If they'd all just left it alone, left *him* alone to enjoy life with the woman he loved, everything would have been fine.

When the clip ran dry, Chris was still pulling the trigger, unaware that he was out of bullets. Not a single one had found its mark. Liz then stepped out from behind the tree she'd used for cover and fired a single shot. It tore through Chris' leg like a hot knife and he dropped to the dirt.

Liz approached cautiously with her gun raised as Elena stepped out from cover. "I got him," she assured the hunter. But when Chris looked back to the car, he didn't see Marie and was relieved at least they didn't get her.

That's when several more shots were fired from an unknown location. The bullets hit Liz's midsection. She collapsed almost instantly and Elena screamed, "Liz!"

"Try your luck with that blade, hunter!" Marie shouted. "See if you can get me before I take you down like your friend there." She stepped out from behind the car and kept her gun aimed at Elena. Chris tried to pull himself up, using a nearby tree for support.

When he was on his feet, he could see the standoff was still happening. Marie hadn't fired yet, and Elena hadn't moved an inch, but her grip was still tight on the machete in her hand. "Take your shot, Marie. How often you even use that thing?"

"Oh, you'd be surprised."

"Then what are you waiting for?"

Without looking at Chris, Marie asked, "You okay, baby?"

"Not walking so great, but I'll manage."

Marie fired the gun once, the bullet tearing into Elena's leg and sending her to the ground. She screamed in pain and stared at Marie with fury in her eyes. "An eye for an eye," Marie said, approaching Elena. The hunter tried to swing up with the machete, but failed to hit her target and landed on the ground again. Stepping on the arm holding the machete, Marie kept it in place and said, "Ah-ah-ah, you really shouldn't bother with those things. You're liable to cut yourself." She used her other foot to press on Elena's wounded leg and the hunter winced. "That'll keep you from trying anything else." Looking back to Chris, Marie said, "Baby? Why don't you join us over here? We need to get that leg of yours healed."

And so, Chris once more did as he was told, limping over to Marie and Elena. The scent of blood filled his nostrils as the hunger began to take hold. The closer he got, the stronger the urge became to drain Elena.

"You just couldn't leave us alone, could you?" Marie said. "What did I ever do to you?"

"You killed my father, you bitch."

"I merely ordered him killed. I didn't bother to do it myself."

"Is there a difference?"

"I suppose not, but it was still an act of self-preservation. He was quite persistent, you know. Meddling in my affairs, killing my brood. I did what I had to for survival."

"What about all the other countless lives you've snuffed out over the years? You kill to live, that's what vampires do. You're nothing but murderers."

"And what are you, missy? Are you not a killer too? And I don't just mean vampires. How many humans did you kill today? All just to get to moi. You know who the last person I killed was? Killed *myself*, I mean? God, I'm not sure I even remember it's been so long. Yes, at one time, I killed to survive, the thirst makes it hard to stop, but there are ways of not draining people completely too. After all, you don't kill a cow after you've gotten its milk, right?"

"So we *are* just cattle to you, then?"

Chris finally made his way over to them, the thirst at its peak. He was ready to tear into Elena the second she was within reach. When he was close enough to touch her, Marie turned to him and said, "Drink deep, my love." So he moved his fanged mouth down toward the terrified hunter.

"Chris!" a familiar voice shouted from back near the house. Before he could bite into Elena's soft flesh, Chris looked up to see his friend Nick running toward him, covered in blood. "Chris, don't do it!" He was apparently unarmed, and as hungry as Chris was, he couldn't bring himself to feed, not in front of his best friend.

"What are you waiting for?" Marie asked. "Shall I shoot him so you can drink in peace?"

"No!" Chris screamed. For the first time, he saw shock in Marie's eyes. She clearly did not expect him to object so strongly. That surprise only lasted a moment, though, as she decided it was too dangerous to let Nick get any closer, whether he was armed or not. Marie drew up her gun to fire, but Chris knocked her arm away and the shot went wide, hitting a tree in the distance.

Then the house exploded.

Wood, glass, metal and stone went flying in all directions. Marie and Chris were knocked flat instantly, landing forcefully in the dirt. Some of the debris hit the trees above them and rained down on their bodies. Thankfully nothing did much damage. When Chris looked up, Nick and Elena were gone. Suddenly, he felt afraid.

Marie pushed Chris off of her and looked furious, "I thought I could trust you! Guess I'll have to do this myself." Getting to her feet, she scanned the area with her pistol. Chris winced as he tried to stand upright to join her, the pain from the bullet wound radiating through his leg. Looking around, he could see no sign of his friend or the hunter. But he wouldn't have to wait long to find out where they'd gone.

A machete chopped down from behind a tree and nailed Marie in the forearm. She cried in agony, something he'd never heard her do before. That part of her arm severed, landing uselessly in the dirt along with the gun. Marie dropped to her knees, holding up the bloody stump and staring at it.

"I hope that hurt, bitch. This is for my father." Elena took a fast swing down at Marie's neck, but still managed to miss. Marie had fallen backwards, the blade cleanly avoiding her and nailing the tree.

"Marie!" Chris shouted as he limped toward her. He was defenseless, but wasn't about to stand there and do nothing. She needed him now more than ever. But before he could make it there, he was tackled to the dirt.

"Stop, Chris!" Nick pinned his friend to the ground and held him there as he pleaded, "Please."

"I can't let her kill Marie!"

"We can get you help, Chris. But we have to get you away from her."

"No! I love her! Get off of me!" Summoning all his might, Chris shoved Nick off of him and launched himself to his feet, struggling through the pain as he tried to get to Marie before Elena.

The hunter had retrieved her machete from the tree, but Marie had also managed to get back on her feet. She seemed dazed, dizzy even—probably from the loss of blood. Even vampires were affected by injury; without sufficient feeding they could grow quite weak. But Marie had a veritable feast right in front of her, and lunged at the hunter before she could take another swing.

The blow knocked the wind out of Elena and the machete went flying several feet away. It seemed she was now defenseless. Marie wasted no time diving into her neck and having her fill. Elena gasped as her life force was quickly drained from her body.

Chris arrived there with no desire to stop Marie anymore, only wishing to join in. He was thirstier than ever and she had started the meal without him. Pulling up one of Elena's arms, he began to drink from her wrist. He was so preoccupied by the act of feeding, that he had forgotten all about Nick.

The machete could be heard slicing cleanly through flesh and bone. When Chris looked up, he could hardly believe what he was seeing.

Marie's head had been separated from her body.

That body collapsed onto Elena and the head rolled away. Chris found a cry escape from the deepest region of his being as he screamed, "Nooooooooo!"

Nick was standing over him with a bloody machete. "I'm sorry, Chris," he said as tears rolled down his cheeks. "I had to."

Chris couldn't even find anger within himself in that moment, only pure and absolute grief for the loss of the woman he loved. He crawled over to her fallen head and cradled it in his arms, the same way she'd cradled his head the night before. He closed his eyes and wished to escape into that memory forever.

Footsteps approached and Chris could tell from the sound alone it was Nick, still holding the bloody machete in his hand. "Just do it, Nick. Make it quick and clean. I don't want to feel it." Chris waited patiently for his suffering to end, but as the seconds passed, he began to wonder what was taking Nick so long. "What are you waiting for?" he asked. Opening his eyes, Chris stared back at his friend, who was still shaken by what he'd done. It was clear in that moment he didn't have it within himself to kill his best friend.

"I can't kill you, Chris. There *has* to be a way to help you. A way to reverse this, to make you human again."

Shaking his head, Chris felt tears continue to baste his cheeks. "There's no reversing this, Nick. I knew what I was signing up for. But I can't face eternity without her. If somebody has to do it . . . it might as well be you."

"Please, don't ask me to do this."

"You've seen what the thirst can do. Look at Elena there. Is that what you want me to do to you before you act? Because I will. Goddammit, don't force me to show you what I really am!"

Chris bared his fangs for his friend, and waited. Nick gripped the machete in both hands. They were still trembling, but together seemed more stable. Chris wanted to make it easy on him, so he leaned forward, gripping Marie's head tighter than ever. "I'll be with you soon," he whispered.

And then he waited for the killing blow.

17

Nick had tried to fight it as much as he could, but in those final moments, the one thing he felt for Chris more than anything else was pity. He felt sorry for his friend and all he'd endured. Part of him had wondered if the path Elena had set him on was even the right one. He'd seen what damage vampires could do. They were killers. But now so was he. Was he in any position to judge a creature that killed for survival when humans often killed for far less? All he could do was try and honor his friend's final request for a quick end.

When the machete struck Chris' neck, Nick was thankful it was a clean cut that went all the way through. But he still had to turn away after. Nick wanted to remember Chris as he was, not as he had ended up. The act was horrible enough in his mind that he didn't need to see the reality.

Walking over to Elena, he checked her pulse, but she was long gone. Life had left her body and that bloodlust for vengeance had gone along with it. Marie's house was a smoldering ruin and Nick could hear the ambulances and police closing in on the location. He knew he wasn't going to escape. There was no walking away from this. And it seemed he was now alone. Hector had died in his arms. The blood loss was too great and he couldn't do much for the man. He'd never be able to forgive himself for the sloppy shooting, but at least Hector was able to forgive him before the end. He died doing what he loved. The guy was a true warrior, and death in combat for an honorable cause seemed to be all he wanted out of life.

As Nick navigated the rubble that littered the ground, he heard coughing nearby and realized it was Liz. She was on the ground, still alive despite taking a few bullets to the chest. Thankfully, the Kevlar in her vest had taken most of the damage. "Are you okay?" Nick asked, holding out his hand to help her up.

"Yeah, just hurts like a son of a bitch." Taking his hand, she pulled herself to her feet and let some of the debris fall off. Liz was still caked in dust from the blast. "What happened?"

"They're all dead. Marie, Chris, Elena."

"Hector?"

Nick nodded. "That leg wound was worse than I thought. I couldn't stop the bleeding. I'm such an idiot. Never should have used that damn shotgun."

He could feel the tears running down his face, but Liz put a hand on his shoulder to assure him, "It's okay. Shit like this can happen. I've seen trained police officers make dumb mistakes like that, but you did the best you could. Hector knew the risks full well when he came with us. Hell, so did I—and I have my kid to look after. But this was bigger than any one of us. Considering your lack of training, I'd say you did pretty well."

"Yeah?" Nick asked, wiping the tears from his eyes.

"Yeah," she said with a smile of approval. "Can't say I expected you to be the last man standing, though."

"My dad always said I was scrappy."

This got Liz to laugh through her apparent pain as she gripped her chest. Sirens could be heard getting very close and she sighed. "Looks like we don't have much time to get away. Guess we'll have to see how the hell I can explain this mess."

"You think we have a chance of staying out of jail? I'm not sure I'm fit for jail."

Liz laughed again and winced. "I'll see what I can do, but please stop making jokes."

"It wasn't a joke ..." Nick said, trying to hide his embarrassment.

<h1 style="text-align:center">18</h1>

A year after the events that took place at the home of Marie LeBeau, Liz Gutiérrez and her son were living comfortably in Las Vegas near her supportive sister. She hadn't realized how much she had missed her only remaining family until she'd been cleared of the charges against her. And that process hadn't been so easy.

Liz and Nick had everything stacked against them. At Marie's home they had racked up a number of charges including multiple murders and breaking and entering. But there was also the murder of Philip Dalton and Liz escaping police custody to consider. The problem was despite all the evidence against the two, there were far too many unanswered questions. Even worse, Ford and the others in the house had been badly damaged in the explosion, so it was hard for anybody to tell what really happened. The one thing that was clear to the police was that Marie and Chris had killed Elena Dillinger, with her blood being found in their mouths and stomachs. Fangs could clearly be seen in their mouths as well. As much as the cops wanted Liz and Nick to cave and confess to something more sensible than what was presented to them, they had no other explanation for the events that transpired.

Worse than all this uncertainty about the truth, the cops were under enormous pressure to resolve the case. The press was dying to get their hands on a scoop and loved to print anything that could be used to further tarnish the department. So eventually, there reached a time where the police had to do something to bring the case to a close. Thankfully, Liz was able to spin a story that they not only liked, but felt comfortable delivering to the press. It wouldn't have been the first time the LAPD stretched the truth, and Liz knew this for a fact. She was counting on their moral flexibility to close the case quietly, rather than drag things out in a court where they could easily become the laughingstock of the country. The evidence would expose the existence of vampires and corruption within the department. Not really something they wanted out in the open.

When the story finally came to light, the version everyone was told included a great conspiracy between Marie LeBeau, Milton Humphreys, Philip Dalton, and Captain Patrick Ford. The three had been involved in drug trafficking operations that went sour and the cartel had sent an assassin after them, who was identified as Elena Dillinger. Detectives Liz Gutiérrez and Chuck Lawson stumbled onto the truth and were framed for the murder of Philip Dalton. Liz managed to get away and attempted to expose the conspirators, but this escalated into a massive shootout at the LeBeau residence. The actress tried to cover her tracks with an explosive device and was successful, but at the cost of the lives of numerous private security guards and Captain Ford. The headhunter then killed Marie and Chris—and that's when Liz had stopped her.

There was no mention of Nick, and he was very appreciative of that.

After she was released, Liz knew nobody in the department would ever trust her again, so she decided to put in for a transfer. Vegas seemed like a nice option to keep her remaining family close. Whatever her reasons were for being in LA, they had pretty much dried up at that point. Nothing remained there but bad memories she was more than happy to run from. All she cared about was her son, and making sure he had a happy life free from any of the trouble that might have followed her around Los Angeles. She wasn't sure if any vampires there still had it out for her, and wasn't about to take any chances with Freddy.

Meanwhile, Nick went back to his day job. Without his friends, though, he seemed pretty down. Liz offered her support if he ever needed anything, but he was still young—she was sure he'd find new friends and new experiences. Hopefully, he'd one day put this behind him. She knew he'd carry the weight of what happened the rest of his life, but hoped he'd use her as a lifeline if things ever got to be too much.

Even a year later, Liz questioned at times if she might one day run into vampires again. It was something she'd likely wonder the rest of her life, but at the end of the day, she knew it would only bring more pain. Violence begat more violence, and she'd seen the cycle firsthand with Elena. She didn't want that for her life—or her family's. There would always be evil out there, whether supernatural or the garden-variety human type, but as a police officer, she'd deal with things as they came. There was no fighting the tide, so she'd remain focused on raising her son and avoid getting swept out to sea.

ABOUT THE AUTHOR

Conor Metz is a horror writer out of Bellevue, Washington. He has loved monsters since the zombies from Michael Jackson's Thriller gave him his first reoccurring nightmare at 4 years old. Most of his life has been spent in the Seattle area, with about a decade in Los Angeles writing screenplays.

When Conor isn't writing novels, he's hard at work seeking out obscure horror films and trash cinema. He also may be found scaling random structures without thought of how he'll get down or poorly practicing martial arts. Eventually, he plans to use this experience to become the notorious Seattle Ninja.

Find all of Conor's books or connect with him at:
linktr.ee/conorwmetz